A Holly Martin Mystery

TWILIGHT IS NOT GOOD FOR MAIDENS

LOU ALLIN

DUNDURN
TORONTO

Editor: Jennifer McKnight
Design: Jesse Hooper
Printer: Webcom

Library and Archives Canada Cataloguing in Publication

Allin, Lou, 1945-
    Twilight is not good for maidens / by Lou Allin.

(A Holly Martin mystery)
Issued also in electronic formats.
ISBN 978-1-4597-0601-9

    I. Title. II. Series: Allin, Lou, 1945- . Holly Martin mystery.

PS8551.L5564T85 2013   C813'.6   C2012-904645-0

1   2   3   4   5   17   16   15   14   13

We acknowledge the support of the **Canada Council for the Arts** and the **Ontario Arts Council** for our publishing program. We also acknowledge the financial support of the **Government of Canada** through the **Canada Book Fund** and **Livres Canada Books**, and the **Government of Ontario** through the **Ontario Book Publishing Tax Credit** and the **Ontario Media Development Corporation**.

Care has been taken to trace the ownership of copyright material used in this book. The author and the publisher welcome any information enabling them to rectify any references or credits in subsequent editions.

J. Kirk Howard, President

Printed and bound in Canada.

VISIT US AT
Dundurn.com | *Definingcanada.ca* | *@dundurnpress* | *Facebook.com/dundurnpress*

Dundurn	Gazelle Book Services Limited	Dundurn
3 Church Street, Suite 500	White Cross Mills	2250 Military Road
Toronto, Ontario, Canada	High Town, Lancaster, England	Tonawanda, NY
M5E 1M2	L41 4XS	U.S.A. 14150

To Shogun,
the man of the family
and the best bear protection in British Columbia.
Much missed by the women in his pack.

From *Goblin Market*

Lizzie met her at the gate
Full of wise upbraidings:
"Dear, you should not stay so late,
Twilight is not good for maidens;
Should not loiter in the glen
In the haunts of goblin men.
Do you not remember Jeanie,
How she met them in the moonlight,
Took their gifts both choice and many,
Ate their fruits and wore their flowers
Plucked from bowers
Where summer ripens at all hours?
But ever in the noonlight
She pined and pined away;
Sought them by night and day,
Found them no more, but dwindled and grew grey;
Then fell with the first snow,
Where to this day no grass will grow....

— *Christina Rossetti*

CHAPTER ONE

HOW DID *GOBLIN MARKET*, a Victorian children's poem, become a "ribald classic" in *Playboy*? By the stark white beam of her headlamp in the small tent, Maddie Mattoon read the 1862 original. Her lit prof knew how to galvanize a bored class when he showed them what Hugh Hefner's flagship magazine had done with the story in the seventies. It was hard not to snicker as the well-worn pages passed around the room, illustrated with colourful, provocative drawings. Erotica was in the eye of the beholder.

The poem featured Laura and Lizzie. The little petticoated sisters had been strolling in the quiet English countryside when goblin men hopped from the bushes to offer "bloom-down-cheeked peaches ... figs to fill your mouth, dripping with sweet juices." Wise Laura cautioned: "Their offers should not charm us, / Their evil gifts would harm us." Unable to resist, foolish Lizzie paid with a ringlet of her golden hair, fatal currency. "Honey to the throat / But poison in the blood" led her to pine away, willing to die for more. Toppling watchtowers, lightning-struck masts, and wind-uprooted trees telegraphed the surrender.

Christina Rossetti had lived as a sheltered virgin even in the circle of her celebrated brother, painter Dante Gabriel, known for his Pre-Raphaelite auburn-tressed voluptuaries. The shy lady poet, wedded only to God and famous for her devotional poetry, would have swooned at *Playboy*'s innuendos about the "pellucid grapes without one seed." The professor had circulated a platter of tempting fruit to add to the effect of the symbolic rape scene. "Remember," he had told them, squeezing the rich, seedy jam from a fig, "that many nursery rhymes had their origins in history, including the succession to the throne and even the plague."

Reading about ripe peaches and succulent pears, Maddie regretted packing so sparely for the weekend camp-out. All she had in the car was cereal, which would make her thirsty, and a softening banana. She thumbed through the volume to something more sleep-inducing, like Arnold's dreary *Empedocles on Etna*. Within ten minutes, she felt drowsy from the pontificating and shut her eyes for a moment.

English or history for a major? Next year she needed to decide. Mom said that both choices were hobbies, not professions; that in this recession where people with Ph.D.s were flipping burgers, she'd do better in something practical like accounting or computing. As an overworked nurse, it was no wonder that Mom recommended a less exhausting job. Maddie's dad was a millwright, proud of his only daughter. He had bought her a small used car for graduation, loading the trunk with a set of chains for crossing the Rockies. "It's only July," she'd said, still warmed by his concern. Once away from the Cambrian-Shield spine of Lake Superior, she'd found the Prairies tiresome, but she perked up as the Rockies roared into sight. When she boarded the ferry headed for magical Vancouver Island, her long-time dream, she felt a continent away from the family.

Maddie pushed the glow feature on her watch. Ten o'clock and dark on this early October night. In the pitch blackness,

stars winked through the lacy tree canopies. By day here at sce-
nic French Beach, city strollers picnicked in the mild weather.
In a few months, locals would come to storm-watch here, a
poor man's Tofino without the hours of travel. Maddie's digi-
tal camera sat in its case in the corner, bearing photos of the
temperate rainforest and three varieties of giant slugs: black,
khaki, and leopard. Home in Timmins, snowflakes would be
in the air, and Skidoos would be getting a tuneup. She missed
her friends, but not the climate. If she wanted winter sports,
Maddie'd go to the snow, up-island to Mt. Washington or to
Whistler on the mainland.

When she returned to the residence tomorrow she'd email
the pictures home. Who could imagine that people surfed along
the Strait of Juan de Fuca? Shelved at each end by black basalt
boulders loaded with clumps of mussels, French had a nice,
long, sandy stretch punctuated by pebbles crisping with white
foam as the waves surged and retreated. She'd watched the sun
go down while eating Hawaiian-style gorp with dried pineapple
and papayas, leaning against a driftwood giant, a bleached and
barkless mighty Douglas fir like those cousins that towered over
the campground. It was romantic out here, making her feel
more alone than normal. Maybe Mom was right, that someone
would see the person inside her instead of stopping at her face.
That was another reason to leave Timmins. Finding a brave new
world with people who wouldn't shield her.

An early-to-bed girl, Maddie yawned, appreciating the
quiet after living with a roommate who bumbled in at two
a.m. and started snoring in minutes. Only a few sites were
occupied in the off-season. Spacious and generously land-
scaped with bushes, the spots had privacy amid a protective
forest. But signs remained of a huge typhoon, a century storm
that roared through in "Ought Six," a grizzled beachcomber
in clogs had told her. Massive stumps had left tons of debris
that took bulldozers and frontend loaders to remove. "I found
orange starfish in the trees," the old man had said, his rheumy
eyes sparkling in wonder. The thought both thrilled and

terrified her. Blizzards she knew. But a typhoon? The west-coast term conjured a storm of biblical proportions.

The triangular tent was barely large enough for her to sit up. Without a breath of wind rustling the bushes, any sound carried in the silence. Cocking her head like her Jack Russell, Finny, she had wondered at first whether the light inside was making a shadow play for passers-by. A hundred feet along the road, a VW van from Washington State had set up camp, and two guys had waved when she pulled in. Steaks had been broiling on the grill when she passed later, and as she nosed the succulence, she thought mournfully of the barely warm canned ravioli she'd had that night along with a chocolate bar. Joining a party of men didn't seem like a good idea, even if they'd invited her. That might have been asking for trouble.

On the beach, grandparents had helped their little grandson make a miniature inuksuk on one of the driftwood logs. The tide was out, and the smooth and glassy sea looked like you could skate across to the U.S. Suddenly homesick, Maddie remembered how her dad had taken her partridge hunting, teaching her to be patient and quiet in the woods, leading the bird with her sights to take off the head and leave the tender breasts shot-free. Could she go home to visit at Christmas if she saved enough from her part-time job? *Snap out of it, you baby. If you're such a scaredy cat, you should have stayed home and gone to Northern College.*

The night was getting chill, so she wore her fleece hoodie and nestled it around her head. Tomorrow if the weather was bright, she could take more photos at the little bridge where the creek came in, and the logs from spring floods were jammed like pick-up sticks. Luminous mosses draped with old man's beard forming their own biospheres covered the big-leafs. Fall was the one disappointment so far. The dinner-plate maple leaves were a scrofulous yellow, without the dazzling oranges, burgundies, and reds of the sugar varieties. Gramps had an erabliere where she watched the kettles boil and pulled luscious maple toffee. She'd traded the crisp nip of fall for something gentle and benign. Maybe that was why Vancouver Island was called Canada's Caribbean.

Her ears pricked. Twigs breaking? A bird or squirrel? What about a black bear! The information board at the entrance had said to pack away food, so the banana and cereal sat in the trunk of her old beater in a sealed cooler. At home she'd had a hundred encounters, and in every case the bear had fled from her clapping and singing, not to mention Finny's barking. She missed his fat little body nestled by her side. Bear bait, they called him.

Then the noise stopped. She took a final slurp from her water bottle, then clicked off the feeble electric lantern and snuggled into the bag perched on top of an air mattress. Call her a wimp, but she didn't fancy sleeping on the bare ground with rocks poking her. She said a few quick prayers, using her folded coat for a pillow as lines from Rossetti's poem circulated in her head. "Twilight is not good for maidens." Sounded like those vampire books set over in Forks. That guy in the movie was a hunk even if he was on the pale side.

She'd pack up and leave tomorrow by noon. They were having their first English exam on Monday. Closed book. Twenty verses to identify from five-hundred pages. The very idea made her sweat.

She rolled over and tried to relax. Last night with all the hiking, she'd drifted right off. Now the mattress was too firm. She fumbled with the nozzle and let some air out, then readjusted her position. What was that? Not waves. The night was still. Now she was creeping herself out. Her roomie Bree hadn't believed that Maddie was camping alone. "Are you nuts? At least take a dog or something. There was a cougar seen on the Galloping Goose in Sooke. They're not going to run like your stupid black bears at home. They mean business, lady."

"Where am I going to borrow a dog?" Maddie had asked with an annoyed frown. "It's a regular park. You can hear the highway. Water taps, bathrooms, campfire rings, the whole deal. You're talking to a girl from Northern Ontario, not Toronto like you. From what you told me, I'm safer at the beach than on Yonge Street."

"And cells don't work past Sooke. You *do* know that." Bree had gone into lecture mode and was wagging her French-tipped finger.

"So what? I'm headed for peace and quiet, not socializing. I don't tweet 24-7 like some people." Bree's fuchsia Blackberry was her lifeline to the world. If Maddie heard that ringtone of "Bad Romance" one more time....

"You wish," Bree had said brushing her long black hair and sticking out her studded tongue. A recent pink-rose tattoo made her scratch her upper arm. "Don't say I didn't warn you if something happens."

"I'll be fine, Mommy." People from the big city thought they knew everything. Let's see Bree muscle a snowmobile out of the slush.

Now more awake than ever, silence was pushing at her ears, and she was poised for the slightest sound. Perversely, she almost missed the sirens and muted noises of the city around the university, the burbling of Bree across the room. Minutes passed. She tried a trick her mother had taught her as a child. *Pretend you're in a snug cabin in a snowstorm. The woodstove's warm. You have plenty of food. Think about making bacon and eggs for breakfast.* Bad idea. Not only was she hungrier, but she remembered that blizzards meant being sent up to shovel the plow line in the dark while her father blew out the drive. Another five minutes passed. She had to stop looking at her watch like a dumbass.

Then, to top it off, her bladder sent her a message. That extra Coke after the salty dinner. Cola had tons of caffeine. And the chocolate in the candy bar. Damn it. Now she'd have to get up and fumble her way to the toilets. Where was that little flashlight? She'd have to avoid shining it near the other campsites.

Shivering at leaving her warm bed, she arched her back to ease into her scrub pants, then stuffed her feet into camp mocs. At the ocean, it was at least five degrees colder than in the city. Slowly, she unzipped the tent flap, wincing at the noise. No need for the mesh screen. She hadn't seen more than one mosquito since she hit salt air in Vancouver.

Maddie ducked out of the tent and blinked in the dark to orient herself. In seconds, her eyes adjusted. She had taken a site far from the bathrooms to avoid the noise, not to mention the smell. A devil in her brain said, "Why not just squat outside the tent? Nobody can see you anyway." She was too good a citizen, and she had no paper. Sometimes guys had the advantage. She giggled to herself as a bluff of reassurance.

The far-off moan of a foghorn made her jump. The fog had been lingering across the strait like a line of whipped cream. Suddenly she felt galvanized, the hairs on her neck rising. Step by step she advanced as the asphalt on the road guided her. The campground roads looped around in all directions. Take the right fork, she remembered. Dark shapes loomed a hundred feet lit by the feeble beams of a moon sliver. Lines from "Sir Patrick Spence" came to her. "Last night I saw the old moon with the new moon in her arms." *Come on, come on. Where's that gravel path marking the cubicles?*

She wouldn't — would NOT — use the flashlight until she got to the bathroom. Her teeth were clamped so tightly that they ached. How much farther? Another hundred feet? Her nose caught the whiff of disinfectant and she moved faster. Suddenly the moon ducked behind the clouds like a shy girl. Pitch black. She tripped over a root and fell, her hands roughed by the ground. Without a light she might end up in a ditch with a broken ankle. Bree was going to pee her pants laughing when she heard this story. A giggle escaped her lips.

She fumbled fingers for the plastic switch nub when something clapped over her mouth. A leg shoved between hers. "Hey, what...." She felt herself dragged from behind by someone taller and a hell of a lot stronger. Toned from jogging and lifting weights on her brother's home gym, Maddie was proud of her 18 percent body fat. Something snaked around her throat and pulled. The pain brought tears to her eyes and she kicked her feet, lifted in the air. "Stop it," the man's voice growled. Her lungs were twin bombs of pain and her fingers tried to get a purchase under what felt like a burning wire. Anything to stop the pressure.

She was pulled along, gasping. Then she found herself pushed through a door, stumbling at the threshold. Not the bathroom. There was no smell. Hands roamed from behind at her elastic waistband. She screamed, but realized to her horror that she was making no noise. Her temples were throbbing with blood. Then an old self-defence move her brother had taught her made her stomp down on the man's instep. He yelped and released her. She lost her balance and reeled, windmilling her arms, gulping huge droughts of air.

"Hey, what's going on over there? Don't you know there are quiet hours in this park?" A dog barked in the distance. Then a blow clipped her chin and she fell senseless.

CHAPTER TWO

IN THE MIDDLE OF a three-foghorn Wagnerian chorus, a discordant ringing drilled Holly Martin's dream of a sun-drenched Kauai beach. "What the…." She sat up and rubbed her gritty eyes as she groped for the bedside lamp. The phone was several feet away, and the clock read 11:59 p.m. Through the picture windows in her tower room, the dark and palpable Strait of Juan de Fuca hung suspended between dusk and dawn. Pillows of grey had swallowed up a highway of cargo-ship lights on the Pacific trade route.

Damn wrong numbers. She grunted a hello, prepared to read the hapless caller the riot act, then smash down the receiver.

"It's Sooke detachment, corporal. Two people on our night shift are out sick with flu, and we've had an emergency call from a Seaside Road resident near French Beach Provincial Park. Can you get down there and secure the scene? We've radioed for the ambulance, but they're tied up at an accident with the night paving crew. West Shore says they'll send someone, but it's going to take an hour and a half with all the traffic snarls." With the burgeoning population in the Western Communities, the only artery along the ocean had become an impossible bottleneck.

"No problem. Is it an accident? Please don't tell me it's a heart attack. And did it happen at French Beach or on Seaside?" This was a first. Her Fossil Bay detachment was a three-officer outlier, operating regular hours dawn to dinner Monday to Friday. The fifteen-officer Sooke post nearer to Victoria handled 24-7 emergencies.

Sitting at her desk still in her bare feet, she came awake faster as the facts emerged. A young woman in the campground had been assaulted nearly an hour ago. Except for a very sore neck and a chin bump, the girl seemed okay. No park rangers were on duty in the off-season, but someone from an adjoining residential street who took late walks had heard the scuffle and come to the rescue.

Hitting the ensuite bathroom to splash her face, Holly heard muffled barks from the room across the hall where her father Norman slept with their rescue border collie Shogun. Trying to be quiet, she dressed in her uniform. Finally she added the Kevlar vest and duty belt with her Glock, and went into the second-floor rotunda. Light from her room spilled into the hall.

"Those damn cats fighting out back again? Somebody ought to get that old tom snipped," her sixty-plus father said, at his door in a paisley robe. His sleek grey-blond hair was mussed into a bed head. Beside him stood Shogun, shaking himself awake and bowing in a nervous stretch, plumed white tail waving as if he knew he was gorgeous.

She spread her hands in apology. "There's been an assault at French Beach. Sooke's shorthanded. I have to go."

"In the middle of the night? A constabulary's work is never done." He yawned and turned sleepily. "Take the mutt with you for company." Shogun was half Karelian bear dog, Norman claimed. That accounted for his unusual gay tail, longer nose, and forty-four pounds.

"Oh, really, Dad. I'm on duty, for God's sake. Next thing, you'll be coming, too."

"No arguments. This is a first, your being out on the job at night. Make your old man feel better. Your mother would have…." He paused and cleared his throat. "And give him a walk later, can you? I'm meeting a colleague for lunch to discuss my next sabbatical." Norman was a professor of popular culture at the University of Victoria. In his ivory tower, a standard work week meant nine or ten hours of classes. The rest of the time was for research, preparation, or marking what some people would call Trivial Pursuit. He wouldn't retire until they wrenched the chalk from his cold hands.

"You win. I'm in too much of a hurry to argue." She gave him a mock salute and dodged Shogun as the dog barrelled down the circular stairs.

Putting on her short boots from the downstairs hall closet, she exited, Stetson in hand. After Shogun decorated the rhodo bush, she boosted him into the back seat of her '85 Prelude and fastened the doggie seat belt Norman had installed in both their vehicles. Headquarters frowned on ferrying a dog in a cruiser, but the sole detachment car lived in Fossil Bay.

Otter Point Place, high on a hill overlooking the Olympic Mountains of Washington State fifteen kilometres across the strait, was deadly quiet. From the copse of trees in the vacant side lot, a barred owl called to its mate, then swooped to the grassy ditch to select a fast-food snack. In the driveway lights that blinked on, a garter snake writhed in its talons, a rare and privileged sight for her, not the serpent. She backed onto the street as the dashboard clock ticked 12:10. With no traffic, fifteen minutes to the beach.

Passing properties with acreage sliced from former farms, overseen by a curious llama with its head over the fence, she turned right onto West Coast Road, skirting Gordon's Beach, a toenail of land bearing run-down shacks from the fifties next to Hobbity half-million dollar homes on postage-stamp lots.

It was a bad place to be without coffee. Urban conveniences hadn't found this part of Vancouver Island. Fifty minutes to the east was the corner that enveloped Victoria, the provincial capital of 335,000 people. Not all the armies in the world could stop retirees from selling their snow blowers and converging on Canada's Caribbean, despite the sky-high real estate prices and costly ferries.

She drove past Tugwell Creek, then Muir, each one with a Protect-our-Resource sign, flagging the tributaries of salmon spawning which, along with timber, anchored the economy. A dark and ugly area of clearcuts flashed by, devastation visible only from the air. Even in this recession, the Chinese dragon had a huge appetite for wood. Enya's *In Memory of Trees* was playing "Pax Deorum." The drumbeats and chorus made her feel like marching into battle instead of enjoying the Peace of the Gods. Slowly her sleepiness turned to energy.

Ten minutes later she arrived at French Beach, easing down a gradual hill into the empty day-parking lot. Campground reservations operated on the honour system, using envelopes and a slotted metal kiosk. Off season, maintenance was sporadic. A heavy gate barred entry into the campground after hours. So whatever happened, no one had driven into the discrete camping area.

After freeing Shogun from the belt so that he could lie down, she left the car, notebook in her pocket and a hefty Maglite in hand. In the pitch darkness, someone waving a beam was hailing her. Paul Reid, a strange old codger who had reported the incident, met her at the main gate. They shook hands.

"I wanted to take another walk around just in case. The girl's at my house. Through the campground, then five more minutes to the end of Seaside Drive."

Holly gave a quick scan. It was still dark as the inside of a closet. Not a creature was stirring, except those nocturnal. "Thanks for taking her in. You might have stopped something very bad from happening."

Paul straightened up, basking in the official attention. He wore a dark knit toque and a heavy woollen shirt smelling vaguely of mothballs. "She's safe now. Do you want to talk to her first or see the site where she was … I mean, where the guy pushed her into a yurt?"

"A yurt?" She was familiar with botanical and zoological terms from university. This brought a mental head scratch.

"A round prefab structure. People who don't want to rough it prefer them. And let's face it, sometimes it rains." He gave a trollish bray that seemed to go on and on. He was probably nervous at being the centre of attention. People living out here didn't have much excitement in their lives, and they liked it that way.

"Right," Holly answered to be companionable. Everyone reacted differently to stress. She'd seen parents turn into robots on hearing of their child's injuries. Others had meltdowns over a lost wallet.

In all their time in the velvet darkness, they had heard nothing. As she suspected, few were camping here tonight. "You've already made the rounds, you —"

"Nothing there to see now. No sir. The joker who did this is long gone, ask me." His long arms were swinging at his side, and he had a rolling gait like an old sailor.

"There's no sense flashing our lights and panicking campers. I need to talk to the girl first. Her name?" She agreed about the assailant being gone. You'd need a massive ego or a perverted sense of satisfaction to hang around, even though arsonists liked to return to observe their handiwork.

"Maddie Mattoon. Short for Madeleine, I guess, but I didn't ask." He shook his head. "A girl going camping alone … I mean I don't have a sister, but if I had…." His voice trailed off.

They walked around the gate on the asphalt road and started through the complex campground. "How many sites?" Holly asked. When she had left the area nearly fifteen years ago to go to university, the parks were a dream under construction.

"About seventy. Full up in summer. Hardly anyone's out this time of year, though. Now's when we locals reclaim the territory."

"How so?"

"Once the place is closed to camping, I get out my wheel-barrow and chainsaw. The parks people let me cart off the down-and-dead firewood. Saves them the trouble and I get free fuel. I'm usually first of my neighbours on the sand at dawn. See the sun come up with a cup of coffee. Watch the seals waddle up on the rocks. Imagine what a private beach like this is worth." His tone was reverent.

Holly agreed about the perks of living by a beautiful shoreline. People who appreciated that proximity didn't care if they lived half an hour from a place to buy coffee cream. The ambience was compensation enough. "We're all lucky to be islanders. Have you lived here long?"

"All my life on the south island, but right here for ten years. Prices weren't nothing back then. I got the place cheap from an old logger whose granddaddy built it at the turn of the century. That's 1900 I'm talking. Just a cowpath from Victoria. Telegraph to Port Renfew was all. So many shipwrecks. The old strait put a lotta bones in Davey Jones's locker."

Until a few decades ago, farm and bush, it probably hadn't changed much since the Gold Rush that exploded Victoria as a jumping off spot for the Fraser River and the mainland interior.

Past the last site, they flicked on their lights, crossed a small creek bridge, and came to a dark little path. It occurred to Holly that someone could have parked on Seaside and entered the campsite on foot. "How's Maddie doing? Was anyone there to stay with her? Your wife?" Holly asked.

"My wife? What do you mean?" His words stumbled from his mouth, and he turned to look at her, his mouth agape.

"Sorry. Just an assumption. No offence." Strike one. He was a loner after all.

"None taken then. I'm on my own. She's holding up well, poor kid. Seems the serious type, not one of your foolish ones. Otherwise, she'd be out drinking, dancing, or taking drugs. Maybe all three at once. Young people today. I don't know." He gave his head a mournful shake.

She nosed a hint of woodsmoke, which they followed like cartoon characters drifting horizontally. After another few hundred feet in the quiet rainforest, passing under dark, banyonlike cedars on the springy peat path, they came to Paul's simple log cabin. A pile of split wood and a block and maul sat by a wooden lean-to covering his supply. The annual drought was coming to an end, and the weather that made it a rainforest would soon be serving up a winter of solid water.

The street was barren of cars. No other houses were visible. Long driveways took care of that.

They climbed the steps to the porch. It looked cheery inside; a beacon of refuge in the night. Around them, tree frogs, sensing a false dawn, put up a mating chorus. Colder temperatures would silence them, but in this climate the geese didn't leave and hummingbirds buzzed for sweet red nectar even at Christmastime.

"I kept the fire going for her. Make her feel at home," Paul said, thumping the back of an old hound who padded up. "That's Bucky," he said. "A big suck fleabag. He's my bud, ain'tcha, boy?"

The furniture was minimal on the bare, varnished plywood floors. An older television. Table and chairs. A woodstove with a glowing fire and a kindling box. On a windowsill Paul had a collection of white and brown ceramic resistors from the old telegraph poles. Privacy curtains made of sheets were crudely basted at the top. Luckily for the girl, the room was like an oven. A galley kitchen with a hand pump showed through the doorway of one back room, the other probably a bedroom. No doubt he had a class five sanitary system, a.k.a. an outhouse. City water and sewer had not made it out here yet; a blessing and a curse.

On an overstuffed but threadbare sofa, wrapped in blankets, was a girl about nineteen. A mop of strawberry-blond hair exaggerated her innocence, along with soft brown eyes inflamed with weeping. Her pale complexion was scarred with the aftermath of teenaged acne. Holly walked over and gave her a reassuring look and a handshake. Any tears were dry now. "I'm glad you're all right, Miss Mattoon. Sorry it took so long for me to get here."

"I feel stupid. Like it was my fault. My roomie told me not to come out alone." She gave a small cough and massaged her neck. The angry line of a ligature showed up. At least the skin wasn't broken.

"May I see? Don't worry. I won't touch." Holding her breath, Holly took a closer look as Maddie lowered the neck of her T-shirt. Too smooth for a rope. That would leave an abrasive appearance, like a burn. No cutting, like piano, guitar wire, or even fishing line. Another minute and she might have been unconscious. "That looks very sore. It's going to take a while to fade. How's your swallowing?" The girl cradled a chipped mug of what looked like tea.

Maddie shrugged and pulled the blanket closer. Were fresh tears welling in her eyes? "I just never expected ... I mean it's so beautiful out here and I...." Her voice had an overlaid hoarseness — small wonder under the circumstances.

"You have every right to be safe in one of our parks. Don't beat yourself up. I was born and raised in the area. This has to be a first. Drunken teenagers acting up are usually our worst scenario."

There was a wicked bruise on her chin, too. Holly glanced at Paul, rocking ten feet away in a shabby recliner and staring at the girl. In the light, he appeared to be per- haps sixty or a hard-living fifty with a short military haircut greying at the sides. Worrying themselves like puppies on his lap, his hands and nails showed a history of rough work. He was rake thin, probably from minimal bachelor meals and plenty of outdoor activity. What was his history, the old hermit? He wore paint-stained workpants, along with a pair of construction boots. Kind though he'd been to offer his house, his hovering presence was disturbing Holly. She arched one eyebrow, and cut her gaze to the kitchen, which brought him to his feet.

"Pardon my bad manners. Momma taught me better than this. How about some coffee, officer, miss? I can make a fresh pot." He blinked an apology, and his fuzzy eyebrows reminded her of a horned owl.

"You must be a mind reader. That would be super. Just a bit of milk. And please call me Holly. If you could give us a few minutes, too, I'd appreciate it. I'm sure you understand." She flashed her best women-need-to-be-alone smile at him as he left. Was it unfair to pigeonhole him as an eccentric? What else would you call it? This was probably the biggest crowd he'd ever had in the room. Except for a pharmacy calendar, it was devoid of pictures. Impersonal. Generic. A nearby bookcase held a selection of battered Western paperbacks. Louis L'Amour. Maddie was sipping her drink, wincing at each swallow. An aroma of cloves and cinnamon met Holly's nose. A nozzled plastic bear of honey sat on the side table along with a spoon.

"Can you talk to me now about what happened, or do you need a few more minutes? That tea should help your throat."

"At first I could hardly talk. I'm ready now. The sooner I can get out of here, the better." She gave an apologetic smile and glanced at the kitchen. "Sorry, nothing personal."

"Understandable. I'd like to get you on your way, too, but we have to do things by the book. This is just a preliminary questioning to set the groundwork. You've been assaulted. The inspector arriving from our West Shore detachment along with the EMTs will be more thorough. Take it slow. There are no wrong answers."

"All right." Her sinking tone implied that she didn't have much choice.

Holly took a seat at the table nearby and took out her notebook and pen, moving aside a jar of peanut butter and an untouched plate of toast. She was surprised to see a well-thumbed Bible open to the *Song of Solomon*, chapter 1. "Let him kiss me with the kisses of his mouth" was underlined in shaky red ink. Holly knew little of mainstream religious studies, other than the twenty-third psalm, which came in handy in her line of work. She remembered that her mother had called Solomon's songs very erotic. For a moment, she felt as if she were intruding on Paul's secret life. But it was just the Bible.

"Go for it, then. I'll take notes, and read it back to you for accuracy."

"He just grabbed me, and ..."

Holly held up a hand. "Whoa. Start at the very beginning."

CHAPTER THREE

"**FIRST LET ME ASK** if you have any reason to believe that someone is stalking you. An old boyfriend? In other words, someone who knew you would be here alone? Or maybe someone you met here who gave you the wrong feeling?"

"Who would … I mean I haven't got time for that. School just started. I have a part-time job in the café in addition to my studies. Only guy I've dated was over for the weekend from Simon Fraser. My roommate fixed me up. Let's just say that we didn't make a good match." Maddie touched a hand to her pitted cheek. A dot of colour appeared.

"Okay. Let's begin from when you arrived. Give special attention to anyone you saw or talked to." That should narrow things. Hardly anyone was there. More would have been around in the daytime.

Speaking slowly but gathering confidence as she preceded, Maddie made a capable and intelligent witness. She'd arrived Friday around four o'clock and made camp. The paths she'd walked in the woods, her beachcombing, all the pictures she'd taken were described. The park wasn't large, only a strip along the ocean bracketed by private land.

"You're doing well," Holly said, earning a smile.

"I was on the debate team in high school. We had to be really logical and lay out our arguments point by point."

When she finished, Holly shuffled back over the notes. "So as for the attack itself, you say that it was dark, and you saw nothing of this man." Peace and quiet were why city people visited. Putting sodium lights all over the place would give the appearance of camping at Wal-Mart.

Maddie ran a shaky hand through her curls. "I kept my flashlight off at first. No one likes to be wakened in the night. It was nearly eleven, but you know how people go to bed early when they camp. No TV or Internet."

Experience made Holly nod. "I always hated making my way to the bathroom in the dark. It's an easy way to get spooked." A primitive sixth sense made the hairs on the neck stand up. Twenty centuries of evolution hadn't changed some instincts.

"I couldn't sleep, and then I had to pee. Typical. But it was creepy. My roommate told me not to come out here alone." Her full lips, along with her hair one of her best features, compressed into a tight line of self-criticism.

"It's understandable that you didn't see him. Let's try for other senses. You look fairly tall. Would you say he was taller?"

"For sure. I'm five nine. He was coming down over my shoulder from behind. It reminded me of a vampire." She stood and moved her arms to demonstrate.

"Which might make him six feet at a minimum. Strong?"

"I'll say. With one hand he was choking me with some kind of wire. With the other he shoved me towards that hut. He was touching me everywhere. Maybe it just seemed like that. I tried to cry out. He was very powerful. In another minute, he ..." She stopped and pulled a sofa pillow toward her like a teddy bear.

Holly gave her a short breather and leafed back a few pages, clicking her pen twice in an unconscious effort to think. The sound couldn't be heard over the snap and crackle of the stove. "This might be hard, but please try. I'm interested in the wire or whatever it was that he used to choke you. Did it go over your head, or come around from the side?" She doubted that they'd find the weapon, but you never knew.

"I can't tell you that. But suddenly it tightened. So fast I couldn't even scream. Out of reflex, I guess, I grabbed at my throat to try to loosen it. But forget that." She looked at her hands with a scowl and sucked on the end of one finger. "Damn. I chipped three nails, one to the quick, and I keep them short."

"The urge for self-preservation is built into us. Fight or flight. Anything else about the wire, if we can call it that for now?"

She thought for a minute. "It wasn't sharp, like thin metal. Maybe it was covered in plastic. Like those old laundry lines. My mom still puts her wash out to dry. I miss those sheets. They smelled so nice and fresh from the air." The sentimental thought hit home, and she brushed at her eyes.

"Since you were in close contact, they'll want your clothes for analysis. I'm presuming you brought a change. And the techies will take scrapes from your fingernails." Everyone knew that drill.

"But there's not blood or anything. I honestly don't think I scratched or hit him. I just wanted to breathe. I stamped down on his foot." Her small voice hesitated as she gave more details.

"From the fact that he let go, you hurt him. Luck played a part, but you bought yourself a bit of time, before Paul came along." Clearly Maddie had been a fighter.

"My brother taught me that move. He's into karate and taekwondo."

"You did very well, Maddie. I'm proud of you. In an attack like this, you don't have much time. Every shot has to count. In one second, things can go either way. You kept your head and didn't panic." Holly remembered her RCMP self-defence instructor saying that you had to work *against* your so-called civilized urges. A palm driven up against the nose could come close to killing. Jabbing someone in the eye was effective, but few could stomach the idea. Politeness didn't cut it if you were battling for your life. Officers had different rules, unless they wanted to be accused of police brutality.

The girl gulped and rubbed her nose. Holly was amazed at her composure. As in wartime, people often held together under the worst pressure, only to fall apart when the struggle was over. So far she was making Holly's job as easy as possible. "And he took my bracelet, too," she said, looking at her wrist with a wounded frown. "It was real silver. My gran gave it to me when I graduated from high school. It has a little trumpet. I used to play first in the band."

Girl trumpet players had to be tough to make it among the boys. And being the lead was impressive. Maybe that fact had helped Maddie fight back. Holly asked, "Do you think that your attacker knew that you were alone? Could he have been observing you during the day?"

"My tent's way too small for two. But I'll tell you something." She gave a sigh of self-criticism. "Next time I pee nearby. Gross or not."

"Don't blame yourself." Smiling herself at that familiar image, she laid a hand on Maddie's shoulder. "Now getting back to your intruder, and we're supposing a male, is it possible that he wasn't alone?"

"I only heard one voice, and he didn't say much. Just 'Stop it!' Like that." She rubbed at her chin. "Like he was trying to disguise it, making it real deep and growly."

Mindful of the time, Holly took a few more notes, closed her pad, and then stood. "They'll bring a paper bag for your clothes. I'm guessing that by the time they're here, it will be nearly daylight. They'll take you back to the scene. I'm going to take a look at it now with Paul. Are you all right with being alone for a few minutes?"

Maddie's hand was shaking slightly as she finished the tea and put down the mug. "Sure." She tucked her feet under her and closed her eyes. In the heat, she had taken off her hoodie.

Holly noticed her muscular arms. Clearly she was in very good shape. If she'd had the chance to run, she might have avoided the attack. But running blind in the dark was a risk.

Holly called to the kitchen. "I want to go back to the scene now, Paul. The others should be arriving shortly." Where were those reinforcements? The girl needed to return to normal life as soon as possible.

"Bucky will keep you company. You got no worries with him around. Likes his belly scratched," he continued without emerging. Clinks and clanks sounded. A spoon perhaps.

Maddie glanced at the oversized hound drooling on his dog bed. "I'll … be okay."

"They'll take you to the General for precautions. Then to West Shore to sign a statement. That's the closest branch for Major Crimes."

"*Major* Crimes, but I'm fine. Why do I —"

Holly levelled eyes at her, softening the effect as much as she could. "That's just terminology to distinguish it from traffic offences and other minor charges. On the outside chance that this guy is going to try this again, we want to make sure we have all the information to stop him. Besides, it's one of our most important jobs to be sure that you're checked out by experts. We are responsible, even though you may feel okay. And it should be considered a sexual assault."

Paul finally returned to present Holly with the coffee, hardly warm, but she had appreciated his leaving them alone. She took a few grateful gulps, raising her mug to him. "That was perfect." She put it onto the table for later. Cold coffee was a way of life for an officer. Had he been listening to their conversation? What had taken him so long?

"It was lucky you heard her," Holly said as they made their way back down the path. She still had an unbidden image of him skulking around the campground. He seemed almost too friendly. But he'd been around for years, hadn't he? Her colleague Ann might know. She'd worked at the detachment before Holly arrived.

Paul yawned, revealing a few gaps in his front teeth. The breath that emerged was no pansy patch. "Couldn't sleep myself last night. My old mom's not well, and she lives in Edmonton. Ninety this year. I've taken to calling her nearly every night just to make sure. Then I take a walk to calm down. I like routines. When I was a lad, I was in the navy for a stretch."

"Sorry to hear about your mom," Holly said. Aging parents were a heavy responsibility. Still, she wished her mother had seen her three score and ten. Bonnie Martin would be forever in her late-forties, frozen in her prime.

"Sound carries in weird ways," he said. "I go around the inner loop road. Sort of make the rounds. That's when I heard the struggle."

"The timing was a miracle," Holly said. "You just might have stopped a rape. Or worse."

A few minutes later they reached the campsites as a dim light began breaking at the Victoria end of the strait. The east was beyond several hills and blocked by trees. She wanted to talk to him alone to get his impressions.

"Officer, ma'am," he said. "I have a funny question."

"What is it, Paul?" She had no idea what was coming.

"Do you think the person who did this is still here now? Thinking on it hard as I can, I didn't hear any car or truck leave the campground. And we're miles from anything." He covered his nose with his palm and then gave an earth-shaking sneeze. "Sorry. Can't figure it at all."

"They are only a few choices. By foot, car, bike, motorcycle. Let's just say that this is not the usual venue for an assault in the dark."

"Venue?" He puzzled. "Oh, cop talk."

Securing the scene with one person or even five was a joke. Anyone could beat it through the surrounding woods. What were they supposed to do, put up roadblocks and stop traffic? People in the boonies "knew" the road and drove like the proverbial bat. Erecting something unexpected was asking for an accident, especially with all the curves and hills. She could imagine one of the hundred timber trucks that passed weekly losing its load and crushing cars.

Maddie had said that she had arrived alone and seen very few people. "But it didn't bother me," she had insisted. "Being from the North, this isn't what I would call wilderness."

Holly agreed. She'd been posted as a rookie constable to some remote places and missed the wide open spaces, but it was good to touch base with her father again, if only for a few years. Moving around was a fact of life for the RCMP. Less so recently, though, because it was hard to get officers to make that commitment when they could be on staff in a city police department and put down roots.

Finally they reached the yurt. The small round enclosure with a ten-foot radius was empty except for two rough wood bunks for sleeping bags. The usage fee bought a roof over the head and a floor. "I found her lying just inside. The door was open," Paul said.

"Did you see anyone else? Or hear anything?" Holly asked. The light-coloured yurt would have been more visible.

Paul gave a negative grunt. "Some footsteps in the brush, crunching leaves or twigs. My beam was in her eyes, and she looked like a scared animal. Whimpering and rubbing her throat. Bucky barked, the dumb old mutt, but I made him shut up. Had him on a long rope in case he had a mind to go after a bunny. All I could think of was to get her help. My night vision's not what it used to be. Geez, Louise, if I could have chased him, don't you think that ..."

"I understand. The point is that you came just in time. We don't want anyone becoming a hero by endangering their lives. He might have had a weapon." Holly didn't want to continue probing. The man felt bad enough as it was. In addition to thick bushes, there were massive trees every twenty feet. Easy enough to duck behind one, then escape in the confusion. Trained though she was, her priority, like Paul's, would have been to assure that the girl was breathing if not conscious. A question of triage.

Holly nestled the light between her neck and shoulder and made another note. The headlamp by her bed at home for power outages would have been perfect. Then again, when would she be called out again like this?

Paul was standing at the yurt door, flashing his beam into every corner. "Maybe there's something he dropped." He made as if to step forward.

Holly took his arm firmly. "No, don't go in. I'd like everything to stay the same."

He gave a light laugh, took off his cap and scratched his elfin ear. "Jesus, there's probably a gazillion prints on the yurt. Everyone who's stayed there throughout the whole summer. And last year and the year before that. They don't exactly have maid service. I pick up some of the big chunks with a whisk broom. That's all she wrote. Big problem is to leave no food around for these mother-sized Norway rats."

Holly gave it an appraisal. The yurt looked cold and unattractive, plastic and impersonal. "Who would want to stay in one of these?"

The geodesic domes could be rented for twenty dollars a night. People brought their own linen, sleeping bags, and pads. "Old folk. Or younger ones who want more privacy, if you get my drift. Maybe they drove for hours to get here, and then it rains. They don't want to head right back. To me it's sort of pretend camping, but I'm old-fashioned."

Holly looked at him. "Was anyone staying in the yurts last night?"

"Not that I saw. I was around earlier on afternoon rounds. Folks on my street feel protective about our park," Paul said. "Sure, sometimes a few teenagers sneak in. We don't keep them locked. Young lovers and all that, but it's a dumb way to save a few bucks. You can get banned from the whole system if you don't have your reservation slip on the post."

Holly wondered if the dawn would ever come. There was no way that in the dark anything was going to come to fruition. They'd been gone a bit long. Maddie might be feeling uncomfortable, even with the dog. A stiff wind was rising off the ocean, though they were sheltered by a greenbelt. Temperate rainforest. Hardly any snow in winter except on the ridges, but cool summers rarely over twenty-five degrees Celsius.

When she had been in her teens, solitary camping had suited Holly. Head out up one of the logging roads on her bike with her German shepherd and stay for the weekend. Her Coastal Salish mother had approved. Her father had worried himself sick until she returned for Sunday dinner.

By the time they re-entered the cabin, from the distance came the familiar Doppler sounds of the ambulance. "About friggin' time," Holly muttered to herself.

As Paul let them in, Bucky gave an obligatory woof. Maddie opened her eyes and sat up. Holly said, "Sorry about all these delays. It shouldn't be long now."

Maddie shook her curls. "I'm fine, really. This is silly to get so many people involved when they're needed someplace else."

Holly folded her arms to reinforce the protocol. "They'd have my badge if I didn't take the precaution. They might want x-rays on your sore throat. You told me that you blacked out for a minute. That could be a sign of a mild concussion."

Maddie moved her jaw back and forth and felt a couple of teeth. "Nothing's loose. And I'd know if I'd hit my head."

Holly used Paul's phone to call the Sooke detachment to give them the update. Bucky had ambled over to Maddie on the sofa and was nosing her leg, his big bleary eyes sympathetic. The girl stroked his broad head. He almost grinned, demonstrating the loss of one canine tooth. Holly doubted if Paul had the income for dental care for himself or the dog. "He's a good old boy," the girl said, with a bit more cheer. "I miss my pup Finny in Timmins."

"You are a long way from home," Holly remarked. "I know what that can be like, having been in The Pas on my first assignment. Similar weather to Northern Ontario. I bet you snowmobiled."

"I had my own little red Bravo," Maddie said. "It rode like the wind."

Holly went out with Paul to direct the ambulance, pulling up in front of the green reflective metal house address. Every rural property had to have a standardized sign with glowing letters. Many people had such artistic, custom-carved signs that they were hard for fire and emergency personnel to see.

"I've taken a statement, and arranged for her clothes to be collected," she said to the two men who pulled up and got out with their kit. A minute of description of the assault clued them in. "I've told her that she'll have to get checked here and at the hospital, too. Right now she's coherent and calm, considering what she's been through. Her throat's pretty sore, though." Taking their stretcher, they made their way to the cabin.

An unmarked car pulled up behind the ambulance and one of the West Shore inspectors got out. Holly had met Russell Crew at a mandatory seminar on stun guns. She filled him in on what she had done and learned. He wore a leather bomber jacket over slacks and a sweater. Holly imagined that he wasn't thrilled to be pulled out of bed this early.

Crew lit up a cigarette and blew three concentric rings, admiring them. "We're no strangers to sexual assaults in town. But here? Go figure. Guy must be a real nut."

She nodded. "Likes the fresh air. Let's hope it's the one and only. Crime should stay in the city where it belongs."

"Hey, why should life in La La Land be any different for you lucky dogs?" He stubbed out the cigarette, flipped it into the wet ditch, and headed for the cabin. "Stick around. We may need you. I've only got one man. It didn't seem like much of a priority until I got the details from Sooke. I'll introduce myself, have a look-see, and catch up with our vic at the hospital after they check her over here."

CHAPTER FOUR

DAWN WAS ARRIVING ON cue, though it seemed like an eternity. Holly sat in the park's picnic area, which overlooked the ocean. Scarcely two years ago, after the typhoon, hundreds of volunteers had helped the park system heal. Stumps and sawdust were the only traces, along with new picnic tables to replace those crushed by a monster Sitka spruce.

In the distance she saw a familiar butt of driftwood. "Ganesh," shaped more like an elephant seal than an elephant. Her Sikh constable Chipper (Chirakumar) Knox Singh had shown her pictures of the colourful Indian gods and goddesses. Pantheist though she was, it seemed a much more romantic and imaginative religion than gory crucifixions and thorny crowns. "Law enforcement could use Kali's six arms," he had joked, along with the fearful goddess's "take no prisoners" attitude.

A normal morning at the Fossil Bay detachment meant monitoring traffic along the fifty kilometres to the tiny fishing village and timber depository of Port Renfrew. Beyond that, petty theft from hikers' cars led the list, followed by an occasional domestic assault and house breaking. Of the several hundred residences in the areas, some were only summer cottages. Drunk driving came next, along with the occasional pot farm bust back in the hills. Recently meth labs had joined the party. With few places to gather, teenagers without cars rarely got up to mischief.

Holly had taken her first command post in Fossil Bay only a few months ago. Seven years had passed since her training at the Depot in Winnipeg. Then came The Pas in Manitoba and a short time as a replacement in Port McNeil at the north end of Vancouver Island. E Division in British Columbia made up one-third of the nation's RCMP total, over 9,500 employees. In the Island District, which included a mainland chunk north of the Sunshine Coast, were about twenty detachments, the number in flux because of an effort to eliminate the old-style one-person posts.

Equal opportunity had come a long way since the first woman graduated over thirty years ago, receiving a pillbox hat, a skirt, and a purse. But with the bad international publicity following the stun-gun death of a man at the Vancouver Airport and more than a few brutality reports during arrests and custody, the escutcheon of the fabled red-serge force was tarnishing. Many citizens were calling for a return to the British Columbia Provincial Police, phased out in the fifties. Large provinces like Ontario and Quebec had their own forces.

Law enforcement had not been Holly's first choice. Even when she was ten, the beaches and forests of the island were her schools and cathedrals. She had enrolled at the University of British Columbia in Vancouver, following her dream of a degree in biology. Her goal was to be a ranger in the wilderness, protecting the land she loved.

Then, before she graduated, her mother Bonnie had disappeared. Full-blooded Coastal Salish, from the Cowichan band north of Victoria, Bonnie had met Norman Martin at the University of Toronto when they were young and idealistic. She had passed the bar exam at Osgoode Hall and begun her career in a small law firm in Victoria. Before long she found a true calling in helping abused First Nations women, especially in isolated communities, find resources to heal and get jobs. Heading out of Campbell River for Gold River and remote Tahsis on the west coast near Nootka Island one fall, she had disappeared. No trace of her elderly Bronco had been found. As frustrated as she was heartbroken, Holly transferred into the school of justice, completed her degree, and joined the RCMP.

Giving her a welcome *roo*, Shogun leaped from the car and was clipped onto a long, retractable leash. Sometimes an unofficial dog helped ease the tensions.

Inspector Crew came walking up, holding a paper bag. "Her clothes. The EMTs gave her an okay to ride back with me to the hospital and free up the ambulance for another call. My constable will take the girl's car. She's packing up now. If you can give her a hand, I'd appreciate it. A woman's touch and all that. We need to get cracking in about ten minutes, so don't waste words. As for your report, send it in tomorrow. We'll use it to flesh out the basics."

At least he knew Maddie's name now. Despite his conde-scending attitude, Holly took her minor assignment in stride. Boots on the ground counted. "Sure. I'll check on her."

"I don't have time to make the rounds, and some people aren't even up yet. That weird little Reid took me over to the yurg, whatever it's called. Nothing smacks me in the eye, not that I expected it at a scene like this. People have been in and out all summer. So you cover the campground and see if any-one saw or heard anything. Shouldn't take that long with so few around." His attitude read: *And I have other things to do.*

"Understood. Thank you, sir." She snapped a brisk salute for the practice. "Just one thing more."

His beaky frown had pushed up the annoyance factor, and he looked pointedly at his watch. "What's that?"

"Should we be contacting the media and making an announcement? Warning women not to camp alone?"

He gave a snort of contempt. "What? You want to start a panic over what could be a prank or an isolated incident?

Are you crazy or just inexperienced? *Women*." After giving
Shogun an odd look, he turned abruptly and left.

When Holly arrived at the site a few hundred feet away,
the tent was already down, the poles and pegs arranged, and
Maddie was rolling up the bundle. Holly helped her stuff
in the ground sheet. Unleashed for the moment, Shogun
roamed the perimeter.

"I always hated this part," Holly said. "The tent comes
out of the bag, but refuses to go back in. It defies the laws
of science."

"Thanks," Maddie said. She wore a sweatshirt, shorts, and
a plastic poncho, likely all she had left to put on.

"The inspector said to give you a hand." She spoke with
as little prejudice as possible. The title deserved respect, even
if the man didn't. "He's … in a bit of a hurry to get back to
the city."

"Me too. If I'd thought this would take so long, I might
not have reported it. My study schedule's going to take a hit."

Holly's mouth made an O. "You can't mean that about
keeping quiet. What about someone else running into this
guy?"

"I guess. It seemed so weird that I can't imagine it happening again. It's really deserted around here."

Holly gestured around the campground. "Just those two
groups? That's all there were? The gate isn't open yet, so no
one has left."

"There were a few more Friday night, but it started to
rain in the morning, so that put people off. It's not that cold,
but who wants to get wet and sit around when you can't make
a fire? It might be different if …"

Healthy colour was returning to the girl's friendly, heart-
shaped face. Once the smile emerged, her flaws faded into the
background. Perhaps small Timmins didn't have a dermabra-
sion clinic or family money was short. Maddie had learned to
live with her condition. Holly gave her credit for resisting the
urge to slather on heavy makeup. "Yes? Go on."

Maddie looked off to sounds of laughter in the distance. Was she thinking about how much cozier it would be to have a partner to share the tent? "If I hadn't ... Oh, nothing. Forget it."

Surely Maddie wasn't imagining that she had incited her own attack. Clearly the girl was no flirt. Her old Ford Focus looked empty except for the gear, a camera, pop cans, and a chip bag. On the picnic table was a Coleman lantern. A half-eaten, overripe banana on the table was the one sign of food. With that sore throat, not much would go down easily.

They started loading the car. "Did anything else come to mind after our talk? Any details, no matter how small?"

"One little kid was riding his bike. Making a racket, but you know kids. I had some stuff to read for my English test Monday." She gave a rueful laugh. "I'll have to hit the books until midnight, maybe even pull an all-nighter ... if I can concentrate."

"You remind me of myself. A real keener, if they still use that word."

Maddie tucked away a couple of textbooks and looked around with an involuntary shiver. "I'm not sure that I want to come back here alone again."

One repercussion of a sexual assault was that the individual grew so timid and wary that life constricted to nothing. That was worse than being too confident and taking chances. Maddie had a tough shell. Or was it merely a façade that masked a shaky self-concept?

"It was so different years ago," Holly said, watching an ant vie for crumbs below the table. "I grew up around here and camped out year-round. September and even October can be the best months. But the island was a different place then. Half the population."

Holly's watch registered that ten minutes had passed. She could imagine the inspector walking toward them with an annoyed look.

Shogun was nosing near the banana, and Holly clipped him back on his leash.

Brushing a lock of hair from her forehead, Maddie asked, "Do you think that you'll catch him? How many cases like this have you had?"

"Frankly, it's my first. This kind of an attack is rare." She wanted to reassure Maddie, but without being unrealistic. "As for catching him, the odds aren't great. I'm being honest with you."

A trace of irony crept into Maddie's young voice. "Unless it happens again. Right?"

Holly felt a weight of truth in ugly percentages descend. "I won't deny that. It's a cruel irony. You've heard the word on television. M.O. *Modus operandi*, or method of operation. And this certainly is one distinctly different method. If I know the inspector, he'll tell you to keep the details to yourself."

The last of the gear disappeared, and the girl shut the trunk, wiping her hands as if to put paid to the whole experience. "Don't worry about me. I know when luck's on my side. I could just as easily been raped or left for dead." She looked out towards the ocean as if wishing to walk clear out of the scene.

"You'll be fine," Holly said, wondering if she should suggest that the girl see a counsellor. Beyond her jurisdiction, probably. At the hospital there would be somebody tactful and sympathetic. But in a time of cutbacks, maybe not.

Maddie tightened her lips and toed the ground with the top of her moccasin. "And what I said earlier, about being … Forget it. I was just feeling sorry for myself. I'm a jerk sometimes."

"No problem." *A stupid cliché, but they came so easily to the lips.* She tried to erase her inanity with a warm smile. Often that helped as much as words.

"Can your dog have this banana? I tried to eat, but …" She fingered her throat. The marks were beginning to fade, even after a few hours.

Holly laughed in spite of herself. "He'll be your friend for life."

Freshman year was tough, especially far from home. If Maddie had had the courage to come all that way alone, she had the guts to stay and graduate. The first semester was always the hardest. For all their bravado, teenagers still needed their moms. You never outgrew that.

For one brief moment, always playing with possibilities, she entertained the far-fetched notion that Maddie might have staged her own assault. It wouldn't be the first time. Men had been lynched on false charges in the old days. But French Beach? Why not on campus? Then again there was lonesome Paul. A bit too quick on the scene? And that Bible underlining. She wished she'd had the time and nerve to page through the other parts. But maybe it was a used copy marked by someone else.

The inspector finally appeared, stopping short of tapping his watch. He clapped his hands together in a let's-get-going gesture. "If I can have your keys, Ms. Mattoon, we'll park your car in the hospital lot." His constable walked behind him several feet in practiced Mandarin deference. The nuances were small but telling in this dance of order and power. She remembered how obnoxious one inspector had been when brought in to investigate a suspicious drowning. With his ego and assumptions, he'd been 100 percent wrong.

When Maddie and Crew had left, Holly got out her notebook and headed for the other two inhabited sites. On occasion she was called out when men hoisted a few too many and got into what Chipper called a pissing contest. Roughing it might be a vacation, but it brought out the worst, even in close families. Tents that wouldn't co-operate. Meals late. Food raw or burned. Damp sleeping bags. Crying kids. Complaining teenagers. Coming back from a three-day hike to find your car window smashed for the loonies in the cup holder or worse yet, a broken CD player.

What were the odds that this person would hang around, making himself useful by giving the wrong information? What a Machiavellian she was becoming. Yet thinking like a criminal had its advantages. That was how the prey survived the predator, how a deer escaped the cougar's sharp talons.

Setting her cap, she headed down the park loop. At the first campsite to the right, an older couple in a VW van with a *Support the Right to Arm Bears* bumper sticker smiled at her. "Something wrong, officer? We heard a siren over by Seaside. Then you were over at that campsite with the girl. I hope you didn't have bad news for her," the man said, arranging a coffee pot on a grill over the fire. Three bowls held instant oatmeal sprinkled with brown sugar. Wearing a salt-and-pepper beard, camo pants and cap, and an Elton John T-shirt, he resembled an old hippie. During the Vietnam War, the island had been a magnet for draft dodgers. Welcomed by the more liberal country and eventually pardoned by Clinton, now they were in their sixties and seventies. The woman was a Joan Baez double, graceful in stature, with lustrous greying hair with a leather clasp. She wore colourful glass beads, an East-Indian print dress, and clunky Birkenstocks.

"I'm afraid that there's no easy way to say it. A young girl was assaulted here late last night."

The woman put a hand to her mouth. "In the park? My Goddess. Was she hurt?"

Holly removed her cap to wipe her forehead. "Not to worry. She fought the assailant and he ran away. It was a very close call." More than that, she didn't want to reveal.

Dave and June Larsen, from Duncan up-island, said that they had turned in around nine, and hadn't heard a thing. "There was a bit of noise with the party down the way." He pointed to a tent site a few hundred feet farther.

Holly saw three young men standing around a small campfire. Dave grinned, forming a dimple on one cheek. "Hell, we all were young once. They piped down before I got up to ask them."

His wife nodded. "They seemed like nice young men. No girls, so maybe it was a case of boys' night out. Their licence said Washington State."

A child about five years old rolled up on a bike with train-ing wheels, making *vroom vroom* sounds as he rode. "Our grandson, Tyler," the woman said, ruffling his short hair. With the bike, he might have been all around the area, at least before dark. This was probably the lad that Maddie mentioned.

"Did you see anyone else around the campground last night?" she asked him, kneeling down to his level. Uniforms were scary for kids. "Other than those guys down there?"

His eyes got wide as pie plates as he smiled broadly, reveal-ing the family dimple. "Just a monster like in the movies," he said, leaving them all laughing.

His grandfather tousled his hair. "Tyler is into action figures." The boy wore a Spiderman sweatshirt and jeans.

"He had a big head and bright green eyes. Lasers maybe," he insisted, making gestures to imitate pop-outs like the cartoons.

Holly gave him a sceptical look, though she tried to con-ceal it. "When was this, son? Can you tell time?" She noticed a huge children's watch on his wrist. Didn't they all learn in kindergarten? Or was that the alphabet?

"It was darrrrrrrrrrrrrrrrrrrrrrrrrrrrrrrrrrk," he said, making more *wooooooo* sounds. "It was eleventy seven o'clock."

"You didn't leave the tent after we went to bed, did you, little monkey? I told you to wake me up if you had to go," the woman asked, eyes narrowed in grandmotherly suspicion. With a smirk, the boy picked up a Hulk figure from the table and ran around with it, making buzzing noises. "We just got him the watch yesterday. Kids. Quite the imagination, God bless them," the woman said. "When do we lose that spontaneity?"

After taking their contact information, Holly moved on. At the other site, a Mazda SUV with a Washington plate sat next to two tents. One young man about twenty in a tank top and board shorts sat on a picnic table with a can of beans, spooning them directly into his mouth. Another male rustled inside the tent, and a third fiddled with the car radio. Not much came in this far west except NPR, which would make them feel at home in the news and weather at least. She doubted if they liked classical music.

"Hi, guys," she said, flashing a friendly smile.

"'Sup? Hey, that's one weird police dog," the man at the table said, putting down the can to squirt in some ketchup. An elaborate Māori-style tattoo ran around the top of his shoulder and down his arm. Holly could feel her stomach churning from so much coffee but no food. As soon as she got home, she was heading for a plate of bacon and eggs.

Shrugging off his question about Shogun, she started her questions, but they looked puzzled. "Geez," said the first, whose name was Barry, "it was deserted around here last night. Except for that chick down the way. We were gonna invite her over for some marshmallows, but she didn't seem that friendly. Wouldn't come over when I waved."

As she took their names, Ryan Warren and Sean Coates joined Barry Raines at the table, glancing from one to the other. Maybe they were in the right demographic for a sexual assault charge, but Holly doubted that they would have the nerve to attack someone on the grounds like a pack of beasts. Still, they didn't seem that relaxed. Their eyes darted to the SUV. Other body language like shifting their stance and folding their arms made her suspicious. Acting casual, she got up and strolled over to the vehicle. There was a case of empty beer bottles in the back, partly covered by a towel.

"Party time?" she asked with a straight face.

Sean looked away into the bush. Ryan rubbed a hand on his weekend stubble. Jumping in first, Barry cleared his throat, but one corner of his mouth rose. "No way. We collected those cans by the roadside. Gonna take them back for recycling."

Odd that they were all Snowqualmie PGA brand in a neat cardboard box. Not available anywhere around here. Holly gave an internal shrug. They didn't seem drunk or even hung over. Whatever they'd consumed was ancient history. Certainly alcohol was enjoyed privately in tents as long as no one reported it and the drinkers stayed discreet. As for soft drugs, even harder to prove except for the tell-tale aroma. Here was another question of knowing when to press the issue and when to back off.

"What's this about, officer? That family over there didn't report us, did they? I mean we were up a bit late, but we weren't exactly having a wild party," Barry added.

Time to cut to the chase. She'd turned a few screws on them as it was. Holly mentioned the attack on Maddie, watching their faces for reactions. All she saw was total surprise. Or they were super actors.

"Poor kid. We weren't even sure she was alone. We should have been keeping an eye on her. Right, guys?" Ryan smacked one ham-size hand into his palm. The others nodded.

When she asked if they had seen anyone else around the park last night, two said no, but Ryan shook his head. "You guys remember that I left to go down to the crapper. Someone was in it, and I couldn't wait, so I went over to the main parking lot where I knew there was another can. I saw a small car drive down through the main parking lot."

"And that was about …" Why would anyone be coming in after dark? Looking for trouble?

He stroked his chin, where two days' worth of beard bristled. "Nine maybe. Car cruised through. It parked. I heard a few clanks, doors closing. When I got finished, I flashed on the licence. Whoever had been in the vehicle had gotten out. I didn't hang around."

"So you didn't see anyone."

"No, but I have a good memory for numbers. Have to be since I'm in accounting." He tapped his temple with a proud grin.

"Show off," Sean said, punching him on the shoulder. "You flunked it last semester."

"Good memory," Holly said. It was amazing to find such a perfect witness. Was he making it up as he went along?

"It was a B.C. plate. Dark little compact car. A Jetta. Corolla. I couldn't say. The number was 549 JXC."

"Nice going, genius. There's hope for you." Sean gave him a high five.

An unexpected lead. Or part of the "too good to be true" department. The boys were visiting from the University of Washington and had come over to surf at Jordan River. A cartop carrier had a couple of fancy boards. Low tides and serene seas had nixed that, so they were camping at French Beach instead, heading home that day. The van had a U of W decal on the back window and a bumper sticker: "Lacrosse Men Do It With Sticks." Holly checked their vehicle registration. Little details made up the major steps of police work.

"There's a bottle depot in Sooke near the cemetery and grade school," she added as she left, tongue in cheek. "It's closed today, but you could leave them off. Unless you want to haul those back across the border." As she left to manly shrugs and one self-conscious grunt, Holly smiled to herself.

At the car with Shogun, she sipped from the water bottle. So much for her final tour. What more could she do? Contracting her brows, she decided to take one last look at the yurt. Ben Rogers, her mentor, had always said that checking twice never hurt. "Like carpentry. Measure twice. Cut once." Then he'd died when a deaf boy shot him with a .22 that they'd thought was a BB gun. Ben was months from retirement, and he died in her arms. That had taught her an ugly lesson, but every time she had doubts about going the extra mile, she knew she owed him.

It was now total daylight, and as the sun began its cycle the guardian trees cast long shadows over the area. As she approached, she kept her eyes on the ground, searching for the incongruity of shape or colour like she did when she hunted for mushrooms or plants in her youth. Except for the indeterminate scuffle of shoes in the dirt outside the open door, nothing indicated that anyone had been there at all. She stepped over the doorsill and knelt down, peering under the empty bunk. Along with desultory pine needles and duff was a tiny white fragment in the corner.

She considered its microscopic nonentity. It might have come from anywhere, now or a week ago. The wind was up, and it might have blown in this morning while the door was open. This wasn't a hotel, and no one vacuumed daily. From her mini-kit she took a pair of tweezers and placed the fragment inside a collection envelope. Whitish paper, very thin with no writing. About a quarter the size of her small fingernail. What in the hell was she going to do with it? The inspector would think she was around the bend. Better to look foolish than to avoid the problem through ignorance.

CHAPTER FIVE

MONDAY, EN ROUTE TO work, Holly turned at West Coast Road and Otter Point. The sign "No Gas for 130 Kilometres" was still up, a timely warning for tourists about what dragons lay ahead in the Grand Circle route through Port Renfrew and east all the way through Clearcutland back to Cowichan.

Only a few hundred lucky souls lived in quiet Fossil Bay with a convenience store/gas station, a grade school dating from 1930, and Nan's restaurant. With land too rugged for the large-scale farming that opened up the eastern island, only loggers and fishermen had lived there. Then their cottages began to be purchased as weekend getaways by urban dwellers. Development on a large scale had not yet arrived, leaving the village in a pleasant time warp. For a year or two, they might be safe from "prosperity."

She pulled up in front of the remodelled white clapboard cottage with a Canadian flag and the RCMP/GRC crest on the door, St. Edward's crown adopted for Her Majesty Queen Elizabeth. The lone Impala cruiser, a seven-year-old castoff from West Shore, was parked beside Ann's new Outback. Behind the building was their ancient four-wheel-drive

Suburban for off-road or snowy routes high in the hills. Few realized that on the tops of the San Juans along the coast, as many as twenty feet of snow fell and stayed all winter.

Opening the squeaky screen door, she removed her cap and jacket and tucked them into the closet. Following her, Shogun made his way to Ann Troy's desk in the reception area for a treat. Everyone was used to him coming to work. The kids and volunteers who stopped by loved him. This was as close as possible to the old-time style of policing where Officer Friendly walked the beat. Ann tended the marigolds, tulips, and zinnias that made the cottage look like a home. Chipper, mindful of his lower status as a constable and duties as a modern male, did the cleaning.

Nearby was his corner and desk. The other rooms served as Holly's office, a lunchroom, and a tiny bathroom. Ann had ten years on Holly, the same one-hundred-thirty-five pounds on a two-inch shorter frame. Her clipped brown hair was curly, and she wore reading glasses, a recent but necessary surrender to early middle age. "Babysitting again, eh?" she asked.

"You know my father," Holly said, pouring herself coffee from the carafe, the last of the Kona that Ann had ordered from Hawaii. "He wanted a dog, but somehow I get the walking duties. Kind of like a kid in reverse."

"Another day in paradise, or so the realtors claim," Ann said. "We don't have a stoplight, so it can't have changed." This was her favourite joke.

Passing Ann the report she had typed up at home Sunday afternoon, Holly told her about the attack at French Beach, earning a raised eyebrow.

"Sounds like she was a lucky girl," Ann said, blowing out a breath. "This is really very bad publicity. Watch it hit the local paper for sure, maybe even the *Times Colonist.*"

Holly turned to her with an ironic smile. "Inspector Crew already bit my head off to suggest that. They'll downplay it for the sake of tourism. Maybe issue a very mild and incon-sequential advisory at the most. Call it an isolated incident."

She drew air quotes. "Nothing will be allowed to tarnish our image. But you must admit that this is unusual."

"Not the beginning of a trend, I hope. We've been blessed with our boring jobs for so long," Ann said. If the alternative was gang wars, they'd settle for traffic duty. "When a strangler enters the picture, you aren't in Kansas anymore."

Island homicide statistics were well under the national average of about 3.2 per hundred thousand. A spousal murder, an errant drug deal, those were expected. A predator on the loose was another matter. Mainland police were still smarting from the national shame of a pig farmer with a subnormal IQ, who had murdered over sixty women. Because most were prostitutes or transients and the mainland jurisdictions overlapped, he had gone unarrested for over a decade. If the police had listened to some of the early warnings, dozens of lives could have been saved.

Holly remembered her mother fuming whenever another First Nations woman disappeared. "When a blonde, middle-class girl is killed, it's on television 24-7," she had complained, punishing the table with her small first for emphasis. "It's a damn shame. Everyone has the same value." Holly had little idea that her mother would become a statistic. She often wondered whether her mother's dangerous job had something to do with it. Without a doubt, she had enemies.

"Let's pray it's a blip on the radar," Holly said. "At least it didn't escalate into a rape. And Maddie seems to be holding up, or as well as anyone could be." She described how the girl's fitness helped her put up a fight and bought extra seconds. "She was shy but tough underneath. We could use someone like her in the force. She's wasting her time as an English major."

Ann sat back in her lumbar-support chair, a sceptical look on her round face, much more of a pessimist than Holly, due either to age or experience. "Too bad she didn't clock him with a Maglite like yours. We don't stand a chance of finding this lurker. We are assuming that he acted alone, right?" Stats supported that idea.

"This doesn't sound like a tag-team crime, but a question of opportunity. Anyway, I have the plate someone saw. I'm running it on CPIC in a minute. I stopped in yesterday afternoon, but the system was down." Holly said. The Canadian Police Information Centre also scanned for pending cases and checked "wants."

"Working on Sunday. This is a change. And you made the rounds of the park. So nice of Crew to allow you to assist his royal highness." Ann popped a jot of sarcasm into her observation. Inspectors were not her favourite people, especially the men. "They don't call it the *Peter* Principle for nothing," she'd say, referencing a bestseller that claimed that people rose to their own levels of incompetence.

Ann finished speed-reading the report while Holly talked. "And this little kid said … oh never mind. You know kids. Imagination and embellishments." Eye-witnesses were known for unreliability. Four people often had five different descriptions, according to their discrepancies in vision or hearing or even their preconceptions. Kids could dream up details from a fantasy world or even have it implanted by an unethical interviewer.

Ann indicated her approval with an arched eyebrow. "You scored there. A licence plate is gold." She pointed out an "affect-effect" error in the report. Then she put down the papers and levelled her hazel eyes at her corporal, adding a long, suspicious *hmmm*.

"This guy who scared off the assailant? Sounds pretty coincidental that he was strolling in the park that late. Creepy. There's a thin line between maintaining a community watch and being a peeper," Ann suggested.

"Paul the Peeper? That's good. Paul Reid lives on Seaside Drive. It's a close-knit little community. The residents consider French Beach access part of their manor privileges. Something else was odd, too." She told Ann about the Bible verse.

"Too bad you didn't get a look at the rest of the book. It's not in our purview to do that, but you'd be surprised at what can turn up. Some teens stole videotapes from a house once in Wawa, and it had kiddie porn on it. They turned it in and we put their principal away."

Pouring herself another cup of coffee, Holly took the report and went into her office to make the corrections, calling over her shoulder, "He seemed like a decent guy to me. A little rough around the edges. Not my kind of date besides the fact that he's several decades older."

Ann's sharp pencil tattooed the desk. "My brain cells are running slow this morning. Still, that name...."

In her small office, cozy or cramped depending on state of mind, Holly looked at her reminder ticker for the week. End of the month reports were due. She couldn't help but think of Maddie. Did the girl make it to her exam? Maddie had her card. Maybe back in a safe and familiar place, some other memory had occurred to the girl. On her desk sat the envelope with the miniscule fragment of thin white paper that she had found in the yurt. Was she being ridiculous or merely cautious? She set it aside in a "wait and see" plan. Even mentioning it to Ann seemed premature.

On the file cabinet was a selection of pamphlets. *Sexual Assault Awareness* caught her attention. Things had changed since 1983, when the Criminal Code replaced rape, attempted rape, and indecent assault with three levels of sexual assault. Use of force without someone's consent, followed by kissing, fondling, or sexual intercourse. The Midnight Choker, or so she thought of him, hadn't gotten that far, thank God. The determining factor became the use of force itself. Contrary to what some thought, sexual assault was not a crime of passion against young, attractive women in dark, isolated places who asked for it by their suggestive dress or lifestyle. It was aggression and power, plain and simple.

Her mother had stressed that fact when Holly was nine and a pregnant woman in far-off Bamfield had been killed by her husband, despite a restraining order. "Murder is the leading cause of death for pregnant women and for babies, too. I don't want you to be scared, but that's a statistic that explains why I do what I do. These women are victimized by their bad choice in men." She had made Holly a special egg-nog with a half-teaspoon of rum, and they sat at the kitchen table in the old house in East Sooke. The towering firs meant that the lights were on all day.

"Mom, are you a fem … feminist?" The term tripped off her inexperienced tongue.

"Where did you learn that word?" Her mother's light brown face wore a look of wonderment as she shifted her thick ebony braid over her shoulder. The first streaks of grey in her hair highlighting the cheekbones were making her more beautiful every year. "Are they teaching you about feminism in grade four? Maybe the system's better than I thought."

Holly tried to remember. "I think I heard it in a movie on TV. It sounded kind of bad."

Her mother gave her a hurt and surprised look. "There is nothing wrong with that word. I don't know how it got distorted in the last twenty years. It merely means equality and liberation for all, men as well."

"But Mom," Holly had said, wondering how her father could be liberated from what seemed like a life of total freedom. "Why did that woman have to die? Can't the police stop this from happening? You said they were our friends."

"Honey, there aren't enough to go around. Many units up-island have one officer for every four hundred square miles. How can they be everywhere? It takes a community and a strong protective wall of women. Men have their good points, I won't deny it. Your father is a gentle soul, his silly profession aside. But women have different priorities. Wars and power trips are not important to them. Housing, food, warm clothing, love, and safety. Those are their motivations. We're hard-wired that way."

"Hard-wired?" Holly gave her temple a rap, which made Bonnie reach over for a hug.

Now these one-man detachments were being phased out, meaning fewer officers for even more square miles. Shaking herself back to the present, Holly tapped into the database and got a name and a description which matched what the young men said. A dark blue 2005 Jetta. "Yesssss," she said, with an air punch. The car was licensed to a Victor Grobbo on Coppermine Road in East Sooke. She made a quick call. Nobody home. No answering machine. That in itself was strange. How many times in science was the key phrase not "eureka" but "that's funny"? But she needed backup.

CHAPTER SIX

CHIPPER ARRIVED AT TEN, music from his car echoing long before he came through the door. The young Sikh corporal was due to stay until seven on their overlapping schedules until November brought an end to the major tourist wave. Everyone at the detachment preferred the busier months, although the winter meant time for extra training and updating of their skills.

At six-foot-three, with his café-au-lait skin, short goatee, and light-blue turban, Chipper was probably in more holiday shots than any other Mountie barring those protecting the Houses of Parliament. Even though he didn't wear the dress-uniform red serge, visitors, Americans especially, loved to take pictures of Canada's multiculturalism at work. The uniform privilege had been a hard-fought case all the way to the Supreme Court, which ruled over twenty years ago that Sikh RCMP officers were entitled to wear the five K symbols of their religion, including the kirpan and the signature turban. The Sikhs had a proud history of fighting for the British Empire in the First and Second World Wars. To the shame of Canadians, Holly felt, nearly two hundred thousand people had signed a petition against the idea.

"Hey, Guv. Yo, Ann," he said, tossing a gleaming white grin as he saluted. On the table he deposited a dozen assorted muffins from the Tim Hortons in Langford. "Low-fat carrot and pineapple for you two."

"Chief, boss, or your highness will be fine," she said, though secretly she enjoyed his little joke. People gave you nicknames if they liked you. Nice nicknames, that is. "And you might avoid the chocolate one yourself. Don't they have 550 calories? I thought I saw some love handles. The Big 3-0 is looking over your shoulder." To his amusement, she gave his tall figure a challenging onceover, even poking his slim waist. How much easier it was to interact with a modern man instead of the mastodons from her training years. Most were at the "she's gotta be able to take it, so let's lay it on" stage. Change came slowly in the established military machine. It would take another generation to catch up, but progress was being made.

"No way. You are looking at the king of crunches. I picked up a Bowflex on Used Victoria. Mr. Universe, here I come. Maybe I'll even get in one of those calendars like the firefighters. Can you imagine what a date magnet that would be?" He pounded his flat stomach with a modified gorilla growl, then went to his desk and picked up a bulletin, which he brought to Holly. "This came last week. Roadway deaths have gone up by nearly 8 percent this year. Fifty-one on the island. The Integrated Road Safety Unit is coming to Victoria for a seminar next month. I'd like to go."

She gave him a folded-arm response. "Sure you just don't want to get out of traffic duty?"

His expressive mouth tossed back the challenge, then he dropped to one knee as if proposing. "Losing me, even for a day, will be tough. Be generous. Think of the lives you might save."

Ann was clearing her throat, her hand levitating over the muffin box. They both knew that she was watching her calories. Then with a small groan, she opened a paper lunch bag and took out a celery stick, popping it into her mouth and chewing with little satisfaction.

Holly gave the bulletin a once-over. Recently B.C. had enacted the toughest drinking and driving law in the country. Blowing even .05 instead of the standard .08 could mean a three-day suspension and a fine of $450 plus towing and impound costs. "Speed and alcohol lead the lists, followed by driver inattention. Someday every car will have a breathalyser." The worst living nightmare was being on-call in a traffic fatality, especially when children were involved. Or animals. Nobody ever spoke about poor little Schatze heading like a furry missile through the windshield. Her father was right to be cautious about Shogun.

Chipper folded his hands on the desk and looked up, his boyish face a roadmap of innocence. Her extra four years in the field made the difference. He had yet to draw his gun on a person, a milestone few wanted to reach and a good reason why holsters had snap covers. Once he'd had to use his side-arm to dispatch a deer because the cruiser shotgun was being cleaned. "Those dark, beautiful doe eyes. I'll see them in my nightmares," he'd told her, then not spoken the rest of the day.

"Islanders don't know how to drive in winter, that's for sure," Holly said.

"Spare me, you two." Ann had entered the force in her mid-thirties, having raised her son on her own into his teens before pursuing a law enforcement career. She never spoke about those early struggles, nor the father. For all Holly knew, the contribution came from a sperm bank, except that young single girls didn't usually have that option. "I spent two years in the Wawa area, remember? The *Edmund Fitzgerald* didn't go down for nothing in Lake Superior. Every week-end brought another lake-effect blizzard. One snowflake falls here, and it's a three-ring circus. You'll be sorry you bought that Mustang with no weight in the back, Chipper."

"Come on, Ann. No comparison," Holly said. "There are what, twelve people living in Northern Ontario? Once a winter there's a bloodbath here on the Malahat. That bus driver who avoided a beer truck saved the lives of everyone on board last week."

The Island Highway traversed tortuous territory on its way through Goldstream Park up to Nanaimo. Rockcuts on one side and forested cliffs with jumbo Douglas firs on the other. Year-round tourists gawked at the postcard views across to Vancouver and the white-capped mountains beyond. Few invested in snow tires despite the warning signs.

Just before she left, Holly told Chipper about the incident Saturday night. "No kidding," he said, his tilde brows rising over eyes of velvet brown. "Wish I could have been there."

"I know you mean that in the right way. You're not suggesting that a big strong man was needed, are you?"

He tipped back his chin with a slight narrowing of the eyes. Was that a blush she saw?

"Never. A woman's touch comes in handy dealing with other females. But you say you have a lead? That's a bit of luck."

"Good police work makes its own luck." Another nugget from her mentor, Ben.

Chipper thought for a moment. Then he said, "Get this, then. Does this sound like a coincidence or what? Milt Carroll from West Shore stopped in at Dad's store last week and told me about someone they're having trouble with in Langford. He rushes out of nowhere to assault women walking alone after dark. Then just plain vanishes. Do you think it's the same person?"

This was a perfect example of why communication between detachments was critical. She pooched out a lower lip in thought. "Langford's twenty kilometres away. But this guy sounds pretty bold if he's struck several times. What are the women like?"

Chipper ticked off points on his long, slender fingers. "The ages range from twelve to seventeen, all on the short side. Five two or less."

Holly headed for the Mr. Coffee for a fresh cup. "Maddie Mattoon was taller than I am and very athletic. This M.O. is different, too. Middle of the city versus a quiet campground. Our guy has only hit once, but in my mind he's much more dangerous. What kind of assault are we talking about in Langford? How far has it gone?"

"All he's done so far is grab a quick feel, then run. He isn't hanging around to strangle them."

"Sound like a different animal to me. For one thing, he'd need a vehicle out at French Beach," Holly said. "But keep track of this for us. We want to keep the avenues of information open."

Ann said, "It's not impossible for a clever felon to change his M.O. just to throw things off. They know how much we depend on force of habit. Look what happened with that Beltway Shooter. Two African-Americans. Totally out of profile for snipers."

"True. When the criminal goes upstream against all the educated guesses ..." Holly gave a disgusted shrug. "I love our park system. But it's tough for us to spread out along sixty kilometres of beaches. Some spots don't even have car access. They're hike-in only. No opportunity to stake out the place or set up a decoy. And the Park-Watch people from the summer are gone now." Sitting all day handing out brochures about avoiding car theft wasn't Holly's idea of a good time, but it appealed to a pensioner looking for a few seasonal bucks.

Chipper crossed his long legs. His shirts and pants bore razor creases thanks to Mom's faithful ironing. "It could be a one-off. Or at least, let's hope so."

"The whole thing happening in the dark makes me nervous. I wonder if anything will turn up on the clothes she submitted. I haven't gotten word back on that. Not that I even will unless I make a request. It's their case." She shivered. "But that wire. Talk about nightmares."

Ann spoke up. "Don't count on hearing anything soon. A friend of mine in Major Crimes says forensics are backed up to the Stone Age in anything less than a homicide."

"Botched job or not, the premeditation bothers me. Who walks around like an all-purpose handyman carrying wire for strangling? He may be practising for something much worse."

"So not a trace of him? No tire tracks?" Ann put in, arching her back in a routine stretch. Tuned to *CSI*, the public expected a crack unit in white and sometimes even black suits and booties combing every site with the latest in diagnostic tools.

"In a public park with wind, dust, and leaves blowing around? The inner grounds were locked to traffic. If he had a car, bicycle, or motorcycle back at the road, how would we know? It's not like we have CC cameras operating like in some parts of big cities. I surveyed the campers. Unless three university lacrosse players are in league, forget it." She paused and tugged on an earlobe. A slight flicker of her eyelids signalled hesitation.

"Yes?" In unison.

"When I went back after the inspector had left, I found something in the yurt."

"The what?" Ann asked.

Holly drew a hut shape with her hands, adding after the description, "A tiny piece of what looked like tissue paper. I'm not sure what to do with it. Nobody wants to look like an idiot, but with nothing else …"

Ann and Chipper exchanged amused glances. "Let's see this piece of evidence," Ann said. "And don't apologize for going the extra distance. No one can make you feel inferior without your permission."

"That's a great quote. I may use it someday. Oprah?"

"My grandmother, channelling Eleanor Roosevelt, one of her heroines."

"Okay. But no laughing." Holly went to her desk and collected the envelope. She removed the scrap with tweezers, and Ann applied her large magnifying glass as Chipper came over to peer over their shoulders.

"That *is* small all right. Paper, but it's pretty degraded, whatever it was. It's probably been wet and dry several times over," Chipper said. Holly wondered if he was suppressing a smile, but his deadpan look was hard to read. "Not much to go on. It could have floated in from anywhere. It's a micro-sample."

"I asked HQ if I should send it to Vancouver and got laughed off the phone. We don't have the resources, they told me in a nutshell."

Ann asked, "What about that wire? I'm surprised that she wasn't cut."

"Maddie was too concerned with simply breathing. I would have been, too. Pitch black, and it all happened in seconds. Otherwise she might have passed out … or worse."

"Seconds count when your air's off. Lucky she didn't end up brain damaged," Chipper said with a dark look.

Holly went on. "Indulge me, gang. Let's go back to what exactly he could have used to choke her."

Ann adjusted her seat and stood to do a few back stretches. The others were accustomed to this once every hour. "Rope, for one. Polypropylene or old clothes line. Even something heavier. We live in a fishing village."

Holly shook her head. "I saw her neck. Whatever was used was smooth. There were no abrasions, no discernible fibres." She struggled to remember exactly how Maddie's bruises looked. Pinching her fingers together, she added, "Thinner than this. Thicker than that."

"Say the size of a coat hanger but supple," Chipper added, running a finger around his collar in discomfort. "Lucky it wasn't piano wire or that stuff to hang pictures. Poor kid."

Holly gave a slow nod. "Very true. It would have cut into her skin. She was red and bruised from sticking her hands under it to try to breathe. Her fingers were marked but not cut. Her nails were short, so forget getting anything from beneath them, even if she'd had time to scratch the guy." She demonstrated what she thought had happened.

Chipper raised a hand. "Hey, lawn trimmer line. That's everywhere." He made a pencil drawing about the same thinness. "I have to keep the weeds down around the back of the store where there's a small lot. It's very tough stuff. You can't break it with your hands. Hard to cut, too. You need secateurs or tin snips. A perfect weapon. Well done, ladies. Now we're thinking like a crim."

"A crim. Don't let us hear you talking about skels, or Holly's Dad will give you one of his pop culture tests." Ann chuckled to herself. "Anyway, getting inside a felon's head is our job, Sonny Boy."

"Everyone I know has a trimmer. Even I do," Holly said. "Keeping blackberries at bay is a west-coast pastime."

"Gas powered or those wimpy electric ones? You could be dangerous." Chipper spread his hands to ward off a mock punch from Holly. "But in the meantime, what can we do? Put out the word?"

A line of exasperation creased Holly's forehead. "The inspector deliberately told me to sit on this unless something else happens. I don't feel right keeping silent."

"We can't put up signs in all the parks. What about a newspaper story?" Chipper asked.

Ann held up a warning finger. "It's a very fine line between heightening awareness and starting a panic."

"Panic, that's what *he* said. It's a sad day when a reliance on tourism covers up the truth and endangers people. If there were a cougar in the area, no problem. That's part of our mystique." She thought of the famous Jane Doe case in Toronto where a woman sued the police because they hadn't notified the community that a rapist was operating in the area and that women needed to be on their guard.

She picked up the phone and dialled Pirjo at the *Sooke News Mirror*. "I have a leak for you. Write it up discreetly. And you have no idea where it came from." In a few politic words, she put out an advisory. It was vague, but it would do the job. If she were strung up by her thumbs at the Evergreen

Mall, Pirjo Raits would never give up her source. She was a nationally award-winning journalist who used her small-town stage for provincial improvement and dared her critics to try to stop her.

"Let's get onto that licence-plate lead." She tapped Chipper on the shoulder. "I'll sign for your seminar. You've earned it. Let Shogun out for a whiz if I'm not back in a few hours, Ann. And, constable, come along for back up."

"I'll drive," Chipper said.

Minutes later, Chipper sped off down the road. That left the detachment shorthanded, but they wouldn't be far away. It was embarrassing and awkward to have only one official car like some backwoods boonie when they were next door to the provincial capital. They didn't even have their own FB decal on the back trunk for aerial surveillance, not that they had ever been part of any. As for office furniture and electronics, they got castoffs if they were lucky.

Holly scanned Bailey Bridge near where a homeless man had died late that summer, pleased to see that the rains had ended the problematical free camping. Cold was one thing. Wet was another. In combination, they were not only uncomfortable but deadly.

Ten minutes later they entered the village of Sooke. A stable population of a few thousand in the fifties had mushroomed when a huge housing development spelled the end of the quiet fishing enclave. As prices in Victoria skyrocketed, developers bought up the picture-postcard harbourfront for condos, townhouses, and even a splashy hotel with a conference centre and wine bar. Driving an extra half an hour could save a homeowner one hundred thousand dollars. They passed the first traffic light near two small stripmalls. Fast-food incursions had been limited to McDonalds and A&W. Not even the ubiquitous Tims had made it to Sooke, the locals preferring their Serious Coffee and The Stick in the Mud. The tipping point was approaching. To update Victor Hugo's saying, "Nothing, not all the armies in the world, can stop development."

The car crossed Sooke River on the old bridge, the serene harbour on one side and the emerald chain of hills on the left. A pair of swans swam below. Leaving the forested hills of Saseenos, Chipper made the first right turn at Gillespie, then onto East Sooke Road. Thanks to no commercial development except for Bill's Food and Feed, time was standing still for the moment. Houses had more acreage, which gave privacy but raised security concerns.

Gradually rising into the hills, she made another turn at the fire station onto Coppermine. Hidden by the bigleaf maple and alder foliage amid the evergreens, few homes were visible from the road. Late fall mums and asters in glass jars and fresh eggs in coolers sat for $3.50 on the honour system at makeshift stalls. This wasn't strolling territory. Anyone who would steal eggs or chrysanthemums didn't deserve to live in paradise.

House 1233 was at the end of Coppermine, down a long winding private road with a Beware of Dog sign. The west-coast-style Craftsman house trimmed with cedar was only a few years old. A large cream and brown Afghan hound with a long-nosed head turned limpid eyes toward her and loped over in an innocent fashion. A man in his thirties came down a temporary ramp from the deck, a puzzled look on his smooth, round face. His raven hair was razor cut, and he carried a can of soda. Holly and Chipper got out.

"Officers, hello. What can I do for you? Is there a problem?" He wore chinos, low cut boots, and a denim workshirt with an Orca embroidered on the pocket. Around his waist was a tool belt with a hammer and screwdrivers. At one corner of the yard, a shed was in progress. The dog came closer and nosed her knee with its muzzle.

"Cloudy, go now. The lady does not care for your drool." He tossed a stone, and the animal trotted off in pursuit. "Ten months only. A baby. Good for prowlers who judge only by size."

Jetta with the license plate in question was parked in a carport. Holly took a deep breath and scanned the yard. This was getting all too easy. In age and height, the man fit the suspect's profile.

Holly introduced herself and Chipper to Victor Grobbo, who stood with broad shoulders, the neck of a bull, and arms folded in a less-than-happy pose. Then she explained what had happened at French Beach, watching his face for a reaction and resting her palms on her hips, slightly grazing the top of her holster. Victor brushed his hand down one sleeve, releasing a scatter of sawdust. "My God. That's the same age as my little sister. Was the girl all right? You're not saying that ... and why come out here?"

"She's doing well," Holly said, then pointed to the vehicle. "But someone reported seeing your car at French Beach Saturday night. Would you mind telling me where you were from dusk to around eleven?" Knowing that the longer time frame might worry him further, she gave him a neutral stare, watching for body language. Words lied easily, and so did vocal tones. Posture, movement, and general tension were something else. Few people wanted uninvited police arrive at their home, even if no neighbours could witness the arrival.

"Saturday? Why, my wife Karen and I ..." Then as his sharp, emerald eyes crinkled in mirth, he laughed loudly. Turning, he beckoned to her to come to the house. "There's someone I want you to meet."

"Perhaps they had better come outside." Holly looked at Chipper, and he notched up his posture one crank while he scanned the yard.

Holly's defences tweaked, but a glance at a nearby clothesline changed her mind. Underwear and T-shirts, ladies' panties, a bra, shorts, and jeans. So he didn't live alone. She trusted her instincts, pulling along Chipper with a nod. His eyes narrowed a fraction.

The side door opened into a spacious gourmet kitchen with cherry cabinets and dark granite counters. Behind was a great room. A couple at retirement age sat on the sofa with mugs of coffee at their side. He was reading the paper. She was knitting a long and elaborate scarf. A wheelchair was parked nearby. It was hard to tell whose.

"My parents," Victor said, motioning for them to stay seated. "They are visiting from Comox. Took the train down." He put a hand on his mother's shoulder, and she looked up at him adoringly. "I think you might want to talk to them."

"The police? What's the matter, Victor?" the mother asked in mild alarm. Her silver hair was pinned in an elegant chignon and she had taken the trouble to dress in an attractive peach pantsuit good enough for church. "Is it a neighbour-hood break-in or a bear on the loose?"

"The officer tells me that someone saw the car at the beach Saturday night. I wondered where you two lovebirds had been," He shook his finger in good natured fun and earned a blush from his mother.

The couple, introduced as Elsa and Frederick, looked one to the other. "We were down there admiring the moon like we used to do when we lived here," Frederick said. "We had a place on Invermuir Road. An old friend next door invited us to dinner. Later we went to the beach. Why are you asking about this? What happened?"

The old woman finished a stitch and jabbed the needles into the ball of wool. "What's all the fuss about? It was such a beautiful night. When we were young … and more daring … we used to build driftwood structures and camp on the sand. You could do that before the park went in. We like to watch the freighters go by at night. Then there are the little fishing boats, too. A few were still out. We had a boat ourselves for halibut and salmon."

Holly explained what had happened at the park. Shaking heads and *tsks* were their response. But neither had seen anything. "It was pitch dark," Frederick said. "But there's an easy graded asphalt path from the lot to the beach area. Easy access is very important for us now."

His wife gave him a bittersweet look. "You almost had a heart attack pushing me back up."

"Sorry that you made a trip for nothing," Victor said to the officers.

Though she felt chagrined, Holly shook hands before they left, thanking them. "Don't believe what you see on television. We might come to a hundred dead ends before an arrest. Hopefully there will be a final turn that takes us where we need to go."

"I was a car salesman," the old man confessed. "The last answer before yes is always no."

Chipper offered her the wheel in fair turnabout, but she declined. "Too good to be true after all," she said, watching the elegant Afghan caper like a ballerina. A nightmare of grooming. "And forget any cracks about making my own luck."

"No way, Guv!" But a ghost of a smile played around the corners of his mouth before he turned the key and hit The Ocean 98.5, a soft rock radio station. K-os was singing about crabs in a bucket.

Driving back to Fossil Bay, Chipper braked for a buck that jumped across the road. Savvy residents had a habit of scanning the perimeters. This time the animal got away, and they sighed with relief.

They couldn't do the same for the case. The odds of solving this assault were slim to none. Endless beaches surrounded by wilderness was big territory for three people and a communication system on a par with smoke signals. Unless, as Maddie had suggested in an unfortunate truth, he struck again.

CHAPTER SEVEN

AROUND FOUR O'CLOCK THAT day, Holly faxed in her report on Maddie's attack. The young girl had seemed in good spirits when Holly made a follow-up call. "This isn't going to stop me," she told Holly from her cell phone. "My roomie, her brother, and I are going up to Cathedral Grove."

"That's a holy place. You'll love it. I'm going to get out to Avatar Grove in Port Renfew, too," Holly had told her, glad that the girl had not lost heart about the wilderness even though it was doubtful that she would tent alone again.

In her old camping days, Holly had always had a German shepherd by her side, the best deterrent short of an Uzi. Norman's protests were overturned by Bonnie: "We know where she's going, and we know when she'll be back, Norman. The bush is her friend. In my culture, boys younger than Holly went on vision quests. Our daughter deserves an equal opportunity to learn about herself. And not just because of her Salish blood."

On one such weekend so many years ago when her mother had revealed Holly's deer totem, they'd been camping with the Bronco at remote Hadikin Lake in Carmanah-Walbran.

During this female bonding ceremony, they ate what nature provided — trout, berries, miner's lettuce — but cheated with sweet bannock from Great Aunt Stella's recipe.

Chipper was overdue from his routine traffic check. Neither he nor Holly enjoyed that duty, which consisted of holing up with the cumbersome radar gun and reading bulletins when the road was quiet. In addition to erratic tourists, craning their necks for ocean views, and locals who hit 110 kph on the straightaways, West Coast Road was jammed with logging trucks from the increased cutting. That summer a truck had dumped its load in a giant pick-up-sticks accident at a wicked curve by the Seventeen Mile Pub. A century ago, horses had pulled eight-foot-thick giants past that 1895 Tudor-style watering hole. Now a busy liquor store takeout and Adrenalin Lines Adventure swelled the number of turnoffs. It was pure luck that nobody had been hurt or killed. The infrastructure was being pushed to its maximum.

Chipper's father Gopal had been raised in a Scottish orphanage in the Punjab. Along with his wife Ishar, he had emigrated with a single suitcase and a single purpose: to build a new life in a land with more opportunities. Two decades of menial jobs had finally bought them a convenience store and ethnic grocery in nearby Colwood with a second-floor flat as their living quarters. Chipper complained about having no privacy, but with the high rents on the island, he was sacrificing his personal life for his savings account.

Four years younger than Holly, Chipper sometimes flexed his masculine muscles to assume the role of an older brother. Being the only man at a post with two females of superior rank demanded the patience of Gandhi, though when cornered by both, he turned his eyes upward, placed his hands together in prayer, and whispered, "Women." He had the neatest desk and the most meticulous handwriting, making up in precision what he lacked in experience.

At last he came through the door, looking subdued. "Your turn tomorrow. Can't be soon enough for me," he said, sitting at his desk. He glanced at the last paper from the inbox, signed it, and moved it over to Ann's desk.

"What's the matter?" Holly asked.

"I hate giving tickets to women. The older ones remind me of my mother and my grandmother. The younger ones, brutal."

"Softie. You can't let everybody off with a warning if they smile at you, pretty girls or not. We've all had our turn, so suck it up. This post hasn't had one complaint yet, and I intend to keep it that way," Holly said with a mild tease. As if anyone could find anything wrong with Mr. Perfect. As an officer, he was a dream walking. Holly had no doubt that he planned to go up the seniority ladder as fast as he could. A B.A. in sociology with a 4.0 grade-point average testified to his academics.

His answer was to crack his knuckles loudly. "Huh." Then he stuck out his lower lip, as close to pouting as he'd ever come.

"Poor baby. Tell Mom all about it. Auntie Ann can get you a hankie." Holly gave him a light push on the shoulder.

He loosened his protective vest as he sipped cold jasmine tea left from the morning. His small nose flared slightly and he drummed his fingers on the desk. Usually his mild face was an open book. While she and Ann had their crabby days, Holly couldn't imagine him losing his temper. He'd once confessed that he came close to decking a guy outside of Saskatoon who had split his pregnant wife's lip with a bullwhip when she objected to his spending his pay check on rye and lottery tickets. "Then she bailed him out of jail, crying 'My man. My man.' Go figure," he had said, baffled and frustrated.

His sleek eyebrows warred with each other, and he picked up his citation book. "Maybe I'll feel better telling you guys. I was on a roll. Got a timber truck with an unsafe load. Caught another guy for using his engine brakes on the Shirley hill. Two speeding tickets. No one was drunk, but it was only eleven in the morning...."

"Every hour is happy hour for some," Holly said.

Checking out another page, his expression grew stormy, and he slapped the book on the desk. "Then came the last one. I was more than ready to go off-duty when I saw her. My ears are still burning. What a garbage mouth. If looks and words could kill, I'd be a dead man. This girl was just plain nuts."

Reminded of many a distasteful traffic stop, Holly grew intrigued. If Chipper nearly lost it, she must have been a pistol, in her father's historical vocabulary. "A girl? A teenager? Are you serious?"

"She was hell on wheels. I pulled her over down at the Pike Road mailboxes. Where the salal goes way up the hill."

Ann had amusement on her face. She and Holly exchanged womanly glances. They'd all hidden in that corridor. It was a perfect spot.

"Don't stop now, man. This is getting juicy. Did she threaten to hit you with her purse?" In Holly's experience, women were the deadlier of the species. Over the last fifty thousand years of walking upright, they developed wily tactics in place of brute strength. No wonder men couldn't figure them out. Some fought dirty and had no scruples about using tears as a weapon.

"They don't call it trash talking for nothing." He stabbed a finger on the form. "Not only was she twenty clicks over the limit, but driving without an adult in the car. She had an L sticker. Seventeen according to her licence." The province's graduated system was one of the strictest in the nation. Learners were mandated to have one qualified chaperone. The large green letter on the back of each car caught the attention of the law.

Holly leaned forward and folded her arms. "So what did you do? Make her leave the car where it was?" Once up island, she let a teenager drive home because there was no alternative. But he hadn't been drinking, and she followed him the ten kilometres on the bush roads. A good officer knew when to be flexible and when to toe the line to the exact millimetre.

He flicked a piece of lint from his shoulder. "I let her call her father on her cell phone. Luckily we were far enough east that she got a signal. I didn't need any more complications. I wanted her out of my life fast. If Mom ever heard me talk like that, I'd get my mouth washed out with soap."

"Was she a local?" With so few people in Fossil Bay, Holly was on her way to knowing all their names, including the family dog and cat.

Chipper gave a snort. "Negative. I know every teenager in town. The dad had to take a taxi all the way from Victoria so that he could drive the car back. We had to sit there for an hour and a half. One dude went by with his truck fender flapping, and I had to let him pass."

"A four-hour round trip. Ouch. And I suppose he had to leave his job. That must have been one mad father." Her own dad she could have talked into anything. Luckily her mother held the line.

"But that's the protocol. You're not saying I should have let her drive back to the city, are you?"

"Of course not. That traffic's harsh. What was she driving anyway? An old beater?" Cars lasted forever in the island's mild climate and unsalted roads. Classic '57 Chevys, Elvis Caddies, even Rolls and Bentley owners had their own clubs and Sunday parades.

"A gold Toyota Solara. Two seater. Creamy leather from top to bottom with a sound system to blow your ear canals. The plate read 'SAMMIE.' There's forty grand."

Ann groaned. "Ouch. All my son Nick had when he went to university was a three-speed bike."

"With the double fine, that's an expensive lesson." Holly gave him a thumbs-up. "Hey, you scored. She should have known better. Now she'll have to re-qualify. With the backlogs, she'll be off the streets for one heck of a long time."

Chipper sharpened a pencil but said nothing. Two tiny lines were forming on the bridge of his nose. For him, that was serious.

"You're whining about that? You'll never make corporal with that kind of sensitivity, laddie. You need to buck up." Ann was on her way to the closet to get her coat. A spattery rain had begun to pock the windows.

Holly saw that something was very wrong with Chipper. "Go on. Tell us the rest."

"To be honest, I never saw it coming. First she was kind of flirty, trying to talk me out of it. Then when she found out I was for real, she turned nasty big time. Like she was used to getting her way, and I'm not talking about her brains."

"With her looks, you mean?"

"Push-up bra with plenty on display. Eyelashes out to here. All the bells and whistles. For some, maybe, but she's not my type. Personality counts, too. This one was a biotch, as they say on the Net." He passed a glance at the women. "No offence, ladies. Just a psychological observation."

"What does 'turned nasty' mean? Physically, or ..." Holly's eyes narrowed at this departure from the norm. "Did she make racial comments? Is that where you're going?"

Canada had very strict hate-language laws. An effort had been made to take back the Order of Canada from a man who had issued anti-Semitic slurs. In another case, an American arch-conservative pundit had been warned to curb her language while speaking at the University of Ottawa. It was no secret that Chipper had been called a Paki, a general-ized and ignorant slur for all East Indians. The taunts had started young, and tempered the steel in his backbone. At twelve in middle school, he'd been teased for carrying a curry lunch, he'd said. But his height even then and his leader-ship qualities brought others to his side. Holly and Ann knew the drill. They'd had their own shares of good-old-boy club jokes, tampons taped on lockers, and water-filled condoms. Women had come a long way and were finally entering upper management ranks.

He dismissed that idea with a wave. "Are you kidding? She was more subtle. 'Too many of *you* in this country. Go back where you came from.' That could be interpreted a couple of ways."

Ann blew out a contemptuous breath. Holly had a feeling that Chipper was almost like a son to the older woman. She suspected that Chipper opened his heart to Ann more than he did to her, his contemporary.

"Weasel words. I hate that. So Daddy came and collected the little witch? I wouldn't have a problem smacking her on the bum. It worked for Nick through high school," Ann observed.

"Daddy's little girl. Isn't that always the case? Some people should be licensed to have children, so my parents used to say," Holly added. "Did he make her apologize on the spot?" That would have been the first step in her household.

"You won't believe it, but he tried to get me to admit that I had scared her and chased her down. Big bad man. Entrapment. Legal terms were flying. Never mind that she had been poking me in the chest with six-inch nails that looked like she had taped Chiclets to her fingers. Kevlar saved the day." Chipper's voice had been rising. Sitting back, he snapped a pencil in two.

"This is making ugly sense," Ann said. "Legal terms, eh? So he was a lawyer, or, worse yet, a politician?"

"Administrator at UVic. VP, he said. Sure has some opinion of himself."

Holly's spine felt a tremble of liquid mercury, like a thermometer rising. Even if he'd been a mere professor, trouble had walked in the door. Who would have thought that a quiet little post would attract this kind of negative attention? If this escalated, fraud though it was, the public attitude would be "Not them again. What do you expect?" Every time she read about another RCMP blunder she felt personally guilty, as if the force needed to take back its reputation one step at a time. Then again, if the parent had blown off some steam, they might not hear about it again.

"What's his name?" Now and then her father mentioned a few people, but usually only in his area. As far as she knew, there were several VPs.

Chipper didn't have to look at the form. "Leo Buckstaff. Think your Dad knows him?"

"Rings no bells with me. UVic's a pretty big place, and people come and go. Biggest problem in the last few years has been the bunnies." One Easter, someone left a few pets on the campus green, and they made themselves at home on the tasty turf. Over four hundred rabbits dug burrows and polluted the grass with their pellets. To neuter or not. To cull or not? To be fricasseed for the homeless? With no foxes on the island, they all ended up trucked to a Texas ranch. Such were the usual problems in Canada's Caribbean.

Ann was never one to waste time. "What's the address? Assuming she's living at home at seventeen. That might tell us more about the family."

Chipper pursed his lips as he read. "2202 Saanich Road."

Ann Google-mapped it in seconds, then whistled. "Jesus Lord. They have four acres on the Georgia Strait with a view clear to Mount Garibaldi. We are talking huge money. Their taxes must run close to fifteen thousand a year."

"And the girl's name?" Holly asked.

"Samantha. No surprise that she put on a crying show when the father arrived and not one second before. Cocky as hell and then boo hoo. You'd think she'd been beaten. A regular drama queen."

The women exchanged understanding glances. "Typical girl tactics. Right, Ann?" asked Holly.

Ann gave a sardonic smile. "Major criminals aside, I'd rather deal with a male. Guys come right out and tell you what they think. Girls can be sneaky." She checked the regulator clock on the wall as its hands tipped to five. "You handled it like we would have, Chipper. She was way out of line. Stop worrying. I doubt you'll hear any more about it." She'd told Holly that her own efforts with her teenager Nick had once led her to threaten to leave him at the Children's Aid. Now the reconditioned son was a teacher near Prince George.

Chipper seemed to relax, though a certain storminess in his face worried Holly. "I'm not so sure of that. He asked for my name, rank, badge number, superiors, you name it. All the way to HQ in Vancouver. Sounded like a federal case. Like I'd used the stun gun on her, and I don't even carry one. But it would have given me great satisfaction."

"You said she touched you?" An attack like that could be grounds for serious matters. Then again it might be he-said, she-said.

"She was pounding the hell out of the steering wheel. I made her get out of the car and do the usual walk to make sure she hadn't been drinking, not that I smelled it or anything. That's when she shoved me, not that it knocked me off balance or anything. I saw a pack of cigarettes on the dash and checked it for doobies." A typical toker trick, but it gave him grounds for a further inspection.

Ann asked, "Do you think drugs were involved?"

"She wasn't slurring her speech. There was no paraphernalia in the car or in her purse. The old man was really mad about the search. Lord of the manor kind of thing."

Well aware of the occasional bout with people overwhelmed by their own importance, Holly avoided the temptation to sound the alarm. "Academics have a sense of entitlement. Life in the ivory tower makes them little gods. Even my father can be a bit of a snob sometimes. My mother used to bring him down to earth with one sharp look."

"Go home and forget all about it," Ann suggested. "Take yourself out for a large pizza loaded with the kitchen sink. Have a couple of beers at your local. Meet a girl. Whatever happened to that Mindy you were dating? Sounds to me like you need to settle down with a good woman." That finally coaxed a smile from him.

CHAPTER EIGHT

PIRJO'S SHORT ARTICLE IN the *Sooke News Mirror* was to the point but politic, caution without alarm. "A failed attack on a young girl at French Beach at night suggests that women should be aware that a possible predator is in the area. Although the girl escaped without serious injury, women are advised not to camp alone in the park system until an arrest has been made."

Holly put down the paper. The problem was, only locals read this weekly. Anyone coming from outside the area, either Victoria or beyond, wouldn't get the warning. Still, she had done what she could. The number of people who still camped at this time of year was decreasing exponentially.

She yawned in the late afternoon torpor as three o'clock rolled around. It had topped 20°C, nearly a record on the island's Three Bears porridge meter: neither too hot nor too cold. Air conditioner salesmen did little business.

She was looking forward to a run with Shogun, a shower, and her father's Betty-Crocker cookbook corned beef hash. Coleslaw had better appear this time instead of boiled cabbage, no matter how much he claimed that crucifer was a staple of the Depression. She popped a stick of peppermint gum into her mouth to stave off hunger pangs.

Chipper was due back in an hour. Then the phone rang. Since Ann was doing mat exercises in the lunchroom, she took the call herself. Her stomach woes ratcheted to ten as she heard the first few sentences. She snapped to attention, all drowsiness gone.

It was the secretary of the chief superintendent in Nanaimo, district commander of the island. Had they read the news story and connected the dots? Who else would have tipped off the press? Whatever they wanted, it couldn't be good. Tiny out-liers like Fossil Bay never were contacted by HQ any more than a storefront church got a call from the Vatican. Higher than this meant Vancouver and E Division itself. The Deputy Commissioner. Holly waited until the secretary made the con-nections. Microseconds passed like minutes. Suddenly she knew what people drowning meant when they saw their entire life pass before their eyes. She wasn't even aware of her own breathing until she had to suck in air.

Another few sentences and she knew the worst. Her hand shook as she picked up a pen. A cold sheen spread on her fore-head. She willed herself to concentrate as the words "weak in the knees" took a new meaning.

"Excuse me, but can you please slow down and repeat that, ma'am? You got a call from the ... Deputy Commissioner?" Was it about her request for testing that scrap? Why would such an insignificant request trigger an attack from the high-est levels? The voice on the other end kept talking over her until she heard Chirakumar Singh. His real name, one he'd left behind at twelve, sounded unfamiliar, like a stranger.

But if this were a complaint, why start so high? Proper protocol started with the detachment commanding officer, namely her. There was a five-page form online that could be mailed in. "Too damn easy," many officers complained. In a new era of total transparency, it seemed as if the public was *encouraged* to make complaints.

Then the bombshell dropped, and if she thought that she'd suffered a blow, she'd had no idea. Chipper was being charged with assault. And even worse, sexual assault.

She struggled to maintain a professional tone with the proper submissive behaviour, trying not to choke on her words. "My gosh, I mean, not Constable Singh? No way in the world that he could have assaulted a young girl. Entirely impossible. I'll stake my career on it." An out-of-body experience took her to another place. She was listening but not hearing.

In the torrent of forceful words that followed, Holly swallowed back the urge to scream. Details included his touching the girl's breast, an offence so far from his character that it made her nauseous with outrage. Trying to kiss her as he backed her up against the car. Issuing threats like "I'm an officer. No one's taking your word against mine. Cooperate and maybe I'll forget about your tickets." Calling her "slut" and "whore."

"We are not talking about mere brusque language, something open to misinterpretation, or mere hurt feelings. This involves a violation of the Criminal Code. Am I being clear?"

"Yes, I do under … He's been a by-the-book man from day one. I get compliments about him every week. Why …" Now she was babbling.

Hearing a "that's quite enough," she shut up before she got into more trouble. Why make it worse for him? Then there was a pause even more ominous than the stun-gun words.

"I'm not sure I like your attitude, *Corporal Martin*. Remember who you are talking to. It's a *fait accompli*. Charges have been filed. We are wasting no time. Justice will not come slowly here, nor let it be said that we place a curtain over our activities. Complete disclosure and responsibility are our watchwords. We're going to fast-track this."

Holly swallowed as her heart thumped in protest. If she didn't defend her own team, who could? Would Chipper have an appointed lawyer? What kind of decent counsel worked for the RCMP anyway? Some public-defender that couldn't cut it in the outside world? Clearly the force was speeding up the handling of complaints to please an angry public that had accused it of protecting its own. She juggled choices for the right tone in her reply, but her knee was jumping spastically as if she'd escaped a head-on crash. "My apologies, ma'am. We're very close here. I mean my staff. There are only three of us, so we ..." She had no idea whether to say commander, superintendent, or Your Grace.

Holly's superior lowered her voice, and the words came slowly like hot coins dropped into her hand. "I don't need to tell you that the force has had a sh ... a lot of bad publicity the past few years. This we don't need. And with a minority group. Very damaging. Do you see what I am driving at? Or are you being deliberately obtuse?" The force was still in the Middle Ages as far as visible minorities. Only 6 percent across a country where multiculturalism was legion.

Chipper's race has nothing to do with this bullshit. Keeping her temper was getting tougher. "Isn't he innocent until proven guilty?" Suddenly she heard the toilet flush and covered the receiver. Ann returned with a puzzled expression fast turning to concern. She had probably been following the one-sided conversation. Holly motioned her to a chair, and their eyes met. Holly hit the speakerphone.

"Don't read the law to me, officer. This case is very high-profile. Dr. Buckstaff is a close friend of the mayor as well as members of the provincial parliament. He's on a number of influential boards outside the university. We want it expedited. Not one T is to be left uncrossed."

Holly felt like asking why a minority group would need rules any more stringent that the majority's, but she held her tongue. She tried to recall what Chipper had said. He'd been upset, but she trusted him as much as she trusted herself, her father and mother. Chipper was family.

"If you please, superintendent. He told us everything about that encounter as soon as he returned. He said that the girl had been very upset, in fact rude, about the ticket. She even shoved him and made threats. He did everything according to the rules. Naturally she couldn't be allowed to drive home herself in any case. Dr. Buckstaff came and got her and the car. He was very belligerent to our officer."

"Did you ever take a law course? That's pure hearsay. Totally useless. Don't tell me you're not prejudiced in his favour. I wouldn't expect you to say anything else. Things are close in small detachments like yours. It breeds a certain slackness." What did she mean by that? Or was Holly being super-sensitive?

"I …" Blisters of rage crept up the back of her shirt like the Tingler in that fifties horror movie her father loved. Why say more and risk infuriating the chief super? Suppose Holly had been the one with the bogus charge? How would Chipper and Ann handle it? She clamped her jaw and listened for instructions.

"He's to report to the deputy commissioner in Vancouver tomorrow morning first thing. Pending that interview, he'll be placed on administrative leave until …"

"Leave?" A worm of a vein pounded in one temple like some vascular alien. Aside from accusations short of murder, serious assault or theft, she'd never heard of this strong a step.

The voice softened a fraction of a degree. Coming from a woman, it was like being lectured by your mother. At least the chief super wasn't talking down to her. "You didn't hear this, do you understand? Some very high cards are being played. We are not talking about sloppy paperwork or rough language. There will be a hearing, and we'll proceed from there. If disci …"

Despite struggling for control, Holly couldn't help herself. "You mean there's an outside chance of disciplinary action? Why that's just … and according to protocol, as his commanding officer, aren't I supposed to conduct the initial …"

"Corporal Martin. If you please!" A pause and a sigh. "As I have already explained, if you'd been listening, your detachment is far too small and your relationship far too close for *you* to do the investigation. How do you think that would look to the civilian world? Constable Singh's case will be handled initially by an expert squad from West Shore headed by two detectives. We can't afford a single error. It's been suggested that we convene a special tribunal consisting of law enforcement people outside the RCMP. That would be in Vancouver, of course, using their people for impartiality. Then we won't be accused of bias in protecting our …"

"So he'll be on administrative leave here in Fossil Bay?"

"Of course not. Corporal Troy handles your deskwork. He'll be at West Shore, probably reading cold cases, someplace out of the normal channels for his own protection. It's more convenient for the investigation to have him closer to the proceedings. Where is he now? Put him on the line. I've wasted enough time with you."

Somehow she had to stop her voice from quivering. They needed a united front. "He's out … checking on a noise complaint. Not far. I'll radio for him to come in ASAP." She heard a few more words she couldn't decipher, then all was silent. She stared at the receiver as if it were a live and venomous thing. Ann came over and took it out of her hands with one gentle motion, listened, and then hung up.

Holly sat at her desk, astonished beyond words. There was no way that Chipper was guilty of anything more than too much patience under pressure. She'd seen him talk down unruly drunks, break up rowdy groups of teenagers on the beach, and even collect the same cat from the same tree four times, without breaking into a sweat. He knew that he had to work twice as hard as the next person did, just as she and Ann had in their early days. That made the victory against the odds all the sweeter. But now it had come back to bite him. How fragile was the status quo when hard-won gains could evaporate like a frost on the February grass once the sun was up.

"It's bad, then," Ann said, folding her hands in her lap, though the whiteness in her fingers revealed tension. "I just caught the second half."

"They want him over in Vancouver first thing tomorrow morning."

"My God. This *is* serious."

"On disciplinary charges." She gave a sigh that passed all understanding. "Sexual assault. Jesus."

Ann started to her feet, but a wince revealed that she regretted the fast move. Her back didn't take kindly to unplanned movements.

"Take it easy, Ann. I don't want you out, too." After those eternal minutes on the phone, her own face and ears were approaching code red.

"No worries. I'm relaxed now. Boil has dropped to simmer." Ann spread her hands in a placatory gesture. "Now would you please tell me *what* in the hell they are talking about? Chipper would never do anything to jeopardize his career. Not if they applied hot irons to his bare feet."

"You heard him yourself. It's about that girl he stopped. The one with the mouth." She gritted her teeth until the molars shrieked for mercy. Smoking seemed like a good idea. That and a tumbler of scotch. The few facts from the chief super came out fast as Ann frowned. "So I don't know what to think. It wouldn't be the first time a civilian pulled something like this just to make trouble. But why did Chipper have to draw this little viper?"

"Bad luck, that's all. To take it this far, she must be a very disturbed girl. Even if you'd been on duty, something similar might have happened, the sex charges aside. We're talking ego here. These people make their own law. Sociopaths in training. They may seem as slick as silk, but cross them at your own peril. Once I knew a man who ..." She let her voice trail off and waved aside her comments.

"You got that right. She's batshit crazy. A good man's career is in jeopardy." Chipper had just started out. He'd invested his whole life in his job. And for this?

"Now that I think about the situation, the father and all, it's common for young people to invent excuses or fabricate when they're afraid of a parent." Ann rubbed the bridge of her slightly pointed nose where her reading glasses had left a groove. Her intelligent eyes were calm and assertive at the same time.

"Her father's behind this. I'd bet the farm. He must have pulled plenty of strings in the old boys' club to go straight to the top. Naming connections like that. And to get the chief super on board so damn fast." She took another gulp of breath. "I'm going to ask Dad if he knows Buckstaff. That might give us an advantage if there's a way to fight."

"Make haste slowly, as the saying goes. Everything we do has to count for our friend. We can't have anyone getting the idea that he's getting preferential treatment. What a hell of a night he's going to spend worrying. Poor guy."

It warmed her that Ann called him a friend. They weren't merely ships that passed in the day or night, but linked to each other. Their lives might one day depend on it. "How will he tell his parents?"

"No worries there. Like us, they know their boy." She paused to reflect. "But they aren't familiar with the RCMP and its protocols. Do you know that he will have to testify, like in the military? He doesn't have the right to remain silent and all those protections under normal law."

"Where's a union when you need one? That alone should be a violation of the Charter of Rights. What a mockery of justice. And put on leave, too. How long will this investigation take? A few days is one thing. But there could be delays of weeks, even months."

"Despite what the chief super said about fast-tracking, don't get your hopes up about a quick end. They're going to be extra cautious with this baby. Count on it that they will be going over his service record with the finest comb they can find. If there's anything in his past, the other side will pounce. It's probably better that he keeps busy and doesn't stew at home."

Holly felt as if she were riding an elevator and the cables had failed. They hadn't landed yet, but the result was not going to be good. The old saying about a head being bloody but unbowed made sense. "Ann," she said. "Do you remember when he told us about his first posting in Prince Rupert, before he went to Saskatchewan?"

Ann nodded warily. "I see what you're getting at." Chipper had had a run-in with a grizzled old sergeant who bore a serious prejudice against the First Nations and anyone with a darker colour. On two separate occasions First Nations men had been found frozen in the middle of nowhere. Some suspected that he'd picked them up drunk in town and left them to die with no witnesses, but nothing could be proved. He'd given Chipper some of the worst schedules and made him redo reports for the most spurious reasons. Bearing his cross silently, Chipper had never complained. The man had retired not long after but had many cronies still at the detachment. Luckily his kind was disappearing, but old boy connections ran deep. If he were contacted on this matter....

"And our staffing. With only two of us ..." Her leg was bouncing from adrenaline and inaction. If she didn't get out of here and run off some energy ... "What a total idiot I am, worrying about schedules when Chipper is in trouble." Her voice came close to breaking. "Do you think one of us should offer to go with him to the hearings? Moral support and all that?"

"What are you talking about? This isn't a high-school detention. He's a man. We have a detachment to run. What about that attack at French Beach? A united front is important. We need to show confidence in him. Don't act like there's any possibility that this won't be over soon and entirely in his favour."

Holly stood up like a chastened pup and shook herself. "I know. I know. You're right. I'm not showing much faith. It rattled me speaking to the chief super. She's like God almighty."

"Much more powerful. She knows when you've been bad and good, as the saying goes." Ann's voice soothed like warm butterscotch. "Settle down. Let's put on a brave face for him."

"Better men than Chipper have been victimized by con-spiracies. Even cleared from scandal, their lives never resumed in the same way. Like a wound that never heals. A scab that ... "

Ann raised her voice for the first time to Holly. "Would you stop it? He'll read you in ten seconds."

"You're the boss." She tried for a half smile but was unsuccessful. Ann was holding the place together as if she had been born to the job. Holly had taken it from her.

With a matter-of-fact voice on the radio, Ann told Chipper to return. She gave Holly a steely look and slapped a hand on the table for emphasis. "Buck up, baby. It's showtime. Let it be said that this was our finest hour."

It seemed forever before they heard the rasp of pebbles from the car pulling into the parking lot. His favourite rock station clicked off. Chipper's light steps tripped up the wooden steps. The door opened and closed.

He saw them both standing there, looking at each other, then at him. Putting his hands on his hips, he looked puzzled, as if they might be playing a joke on him. "I was supposed to be out until five. What's going on? Did something happen? I didn't hear any sirens. Hey, is this an early birthday party? It's not until next month. What did you get me? Socks again?"

Holly opened her dry mouth, but no words came.

"Listen, constable. We don't have much time," Ann said. Like a professional poker dealer, she laid out the situation slowly and deliberately. As Chipper's face lost colour and his muscles tensed, Holly swallowed back doubts. Ann's tone was so strong and dependable that Holly would have followed her to the ends of hell and back. But how could they fight these outrageous charges?

CHAPTER NINE

"**YOU TWO HAVE TO** be joking," Chipper said when Ann finished. "I can take it, but this really isn't funny." Holly blinked again and shook her head.

"It's true," Ann added. "Damn it all. We're both so sorry, man."

At first he felt like a soldier whose badges and stripes had been ripped from his uniform after a court martial. And a hearing. That wasn't even a trial. Then he began pacing. He could see his fist smashing into the drywall. What good would that do? His speechlessness was probably making him look guilty. *Stop it*, he screamed in his head. Holly and Ann were on his side.

"This is total garbage," Holly said, hand on his shoulder as she looked at his wounded eyes. "That will be obvious to anyone who knows you."

Ann came over in a rare personal gesture. She wasn't the type for group hugs, but thumped him on the back. "One of my colleagues had to go through this in Wawa once. He was alone in the detachment when a bored teenager came in and chatted him up. He was new and wanted the local kids to like him. Luckily her girlfriend stepped forward with the real story. Nothing happened. He had sent her home after only five minutes."

Chipper thought that Ann had told that anecdote before, but with a different ending. Was she lying to give him confidence? Holly stood by with her hands folded, but he could see the muscle tension. She wasn't correcting Ann. A lump formed in his throat as he realized that they were supporting him the only way they could.

Ann made a few notes to herself as she sat straight in her chair. "Remember that we're dealing with a teenager. Chances are that the girl will fold under questioning. She'll see the seriousness of what she's done. Maybe the mother will get into it, too, if she knows her husband's grandstanding. I'll try to pick the brain of one of the lawyers at the old HQ on the mainland. It's better than the old days when you could get canned for nearly anything." Conservative forces said that unionizing would make the RCMP look like a bunch of dockworkers. Even the rank and file were divided on the idea.

"I don't know," Chipper said, as he turned to leave, hand hovering above the doorknob. "Her father will be with her since she's underage. They'll have the best-paid legal advice in Canada. Count on it. She'll be lying to him, and he'll coach her on what to say. They'll probably practise until it's down cold. Maybe even with a lie detector. This doesn't sound good."

"That's stuff from the movies. Listen to Ann. We'll be thinking of you. Call us as soon as you can tomorrow," Holly said.

"I will." He gave them an okay sign. "And thanks, guys."

Though he'd only had it a month, Chipper took no pleasure in driving home in his brand new Atomic Tangerine Mustang. He felt anaesthetised. Tigerstyle was on the CD, its strong drums and wild riffs an invitation to the dance, but he turned it off, trying to concentrate. Tears did not come from the men in his family, though the women did their share. His chest constricted around his heart like a steel band and his breath came in shallow draughts. An overloaded Brick furniture van swept around a corner two feet over the line and he steered onto the berm, sending up a cloud of dust. In a waking coma, he had driven ten kilometres.

At Muir Creek, he pulled off into a parking area and tried deep breathing. He laid his head on the top of the steering wheel. It wasn't as if he couldn't have seen it coming. He'd had teenagers as argumentative as that before, though never with a hair-trigger temper. Maybe he shouldn't have searched the car. On the other hand, Ann might be right that Samantha was afraid of her old man, and given that course, was protecting herself the only way she could even if it meant taking an innocent officer down. He almost felt sorry for her. But he was damned if he was going to give up without a fight. How did life get so complicated? Yesterday he was going to ask Mindy to have dinner at the Canoe Brewpub in Victoria and then go clubbing. Now he had no idea when he might talk to her again. Certainly his dating career was off the rails now.

Walking to the beach, paying out time like a rope, he climbed onto some driftwood and sat, looking out over the grey and choppy strait. Churned up with a cloud bank approaching from the south, it cast a malevolent eye at him, but mirrored his feelings. A group came up from behind him; three children and their parents. He'd seen them in the lot in their van with an Iowa licence. A place not unlike the fields of Saskatchewan. Tons of corn, but warmer. A long way from home, and even on this bleak day, they were awed to silence by the massive power of the strait. He nodded and attempted a smile.

The man came over to him and bent down. "Would you mind if we took a picture of you with our kids, officer? It would mean a lot."

His solid Midwest accent spoke honesty and sincerity. Chipper rallied for a moment. The kids looked up in awe at his blue turban. Probably not too many Sikhs in the cornfields. Maybe he'd be transferred to some remote place with snow seven months a year.

"Sure thing." He posed for several pictures, standing straight as if he heard the national anthem and forcing a smile. Was this his last hurrah as an officer? Would he have to find some other profession? Ever since he'd been ten, when an RCMP corporal came to his fourth grade class, he'd wanted to be a Mountie. The other kids laughed, but the man gave him a card and told him to get in touch when he finished school and turned twenty one. He still carried the piece of ragged cardboard in his wallet. For luck. That was a laugh.

He returned to his car and pumped the gas pedal out of frustration, revving the motor in a silly gesture. In half an hour, he'd be home. He thought about what Ann had said. *Trust that the force will come through for you. You're innocent.* At this he shook his head. She was only a corporal like Holly, but with her age, she would side more with the older, more conservative and perhaps naive members of the RCMP. For the first time in his life, he appreciated the feeling of being an innocent person heading for a trial and perhaps an unwarranted conviction. Would they throw him under the bus to make the force look better, even if the charges were a lie?

At least since he was still on duty, they weren't going to stop his pay … for now. The Mustang was costing him five hundred a month since he'd taken only a three-year loan. His parents depended on his contribution to add a bit of indulgence to their ordinarily frugal life. They'd been able to buy a new car after fifteen years with the old one. They'd brought his grandmother over from Durgapur for a visit. He had saved up two thousand dollars to help them fly back to the old country this winter. That was to be their surprise anniversary present. "Yes, my only child, my most intelligent boy, is an officer in the Royal Canadian Mounted Police," he could hear his father Gopal telling the relatives in an official tone, standing up tall for his five foot six. Chipper got his height from his mother's side. "He will be the commander of his own detachment any day now. You will see."

Chipper barked out a laugh and pulled into traffic. A car came streaking down the hill, right up to his bumper. The guy hit the horn and gave him the finger. Chipper checked his speed. Eighty kph. Right on. Let the asshole pass if he dared. Fortunately the old truck pulled off at Anderson Road. For once in his life, Chipper was mad at the world.

Twenty-five minutes. Life as he knew it was ticking down. This would kill his parents. His mother was a born panicker. He could see her face now. She would dissolve in tears and sit wringing her hands like she had done when a downturn in the economy occurred just as they had expanded their convenience store into speciality Indian groceries. As for Gopal, nothing would faze the little man ... on the outside. But his doctor had told him to slow down, that his heart was sending him signals of a blocked artery. With Gopal's orphan background, there was no help from family history. So far the condition was being handled by medication, but down the line who could tell? His mother could never get the man to a doctor for monitoring. And he seemed to be nodding off earlier than usual lately. Sixteen-hour days were not good for old fellows even though his hair was black as ever. A bit of spring had vanished from his step, and he seemed to tire easily.

Chipper felt nauseous and doubted that he could eat. If he didn't make a showing at dinner, that would send his mother over the top. Tonight she was making honeyed jalabis. But that brought up another subject. Timing. When should he break the news? Before dinner, during, or after? For once in his life, Chipper wished that his parents lived on another planet where this would all be over and done before they had to find out.

After the sweet, the bitter, then. That's when it would be. He suspected that this would be the last meal he'd enjoy for a long long time.

CHAPTER TEN

"**WHEN SHALL WE THREE** meet again?" The ominous words of Macbeth's witches kept running a Mobius strip through Holly's mind despite her coolness to Shakespeare. At her Catholic school, the good sister had made them all memorize Marc Anthony's oration over Caesar's body. When Chipper had walked out the door, slowly, deliberately, the atmosphere had been funereal, much though the women had tried to assume brave faces. Still bowled over from the phone call from Island Division, Holly didn't have much faith in the due process to come. Ann was trying to keep up their spirits with her take-charge attitude. If she had a totem, it would have been a cougar or bear.

In twenty minutes Holly reached home, charging up the hilly drive spewing grit from her tires and tearing up a piece of volunteer grass sprouting among the gravel. As she got out, Shogun started a howl of greeting inside.

Opening the new back door to the foyer and giving the dog a head rub, Holly straightened her drooping shoulders to dispel the gloom of the last two hours. It would feel good to have someone to talk to about this. Otherwise she'd sit and brood, helpless as Chipper made his way to the last ferry later tonight. With her foot, she pushed the door shut, a little too hard. "I'm home."

She hung up her vest and jacket in the closet and shrugged off her hot boots, passing through the TV room. She'd painted the room a pale green and added handsome accordion blinds on the bay window. The forty-two inch plasma and oversize chairs made watching her father's classic films almost like a real theatre.

"Dinner in half an hour," Norman said. "I just popped the cork on some primo pink Zinfandel. But what was with slamming that door? With that stained glass, it cost me nearly $1,400."

"Sorry." Holly leaned against the kitchen doorway.

"Is something wrong? Why that face? Don't tell me that there's been another attack out at Fossil Bay." Having lived with two strong women, he knew better than to suggest that it was the time of the month.

"Tell you later. I have to unwind. And don't worry. It's not about me." But it was about her, and Ann, and the force. If Chipper wasn't exonerated she'd lose faith in the entire organization. Law and justice were not the same animal. She might even quit, and join a city-police team like Victoria's or Vancouver's. But surely it wouldn't come to that. Was there some way to turn the case in Chipper's favour? Using the end to justify the means she might even lie for him, and that frightened her.

A fifteen-minute kiwi-gel hot bath in the impossibly raspberry colour soaker tub didn't soothe the knots in her neck. The builder had been so cheap, constructing the house of flimsy two-by-fours and picking up castoffs like the tub. The Chainsaw House, neighbours called it. Pretty Grecian-villa face, rough-cut plywood underneath. People could be the same.

From her window, the strait was painting one of a thousand pictures, a thin silver band underlining the shore on the other side while the gradations of mountains behind purpled the palette. Little Egypt's pyramid poked between two snow-capped giants in the Olympics. Against the patio door, a crane fly tried to batter its way in. The ephemeral creatures were often found desiccated in house corners, seeking refuge only to die. Nature made up in fecundity what it failed to supply in brute power. She felt a strange kinship with its struggles and felt her throat constrict against a sob.

Dinner brought little appetite. And thinking about her father's latest vat of homemade wine left her less than enthusiastic. His sweeter varietals were so cloying. She changed into yoga pants and a T-shirt, then joined him in the kitchen.

He passed her a full glass. "My new batch," he said, swirling the wine to admire the pale-pink lemonade colour, unique for the worst of reasons. His rotgut Merlot was probably the most drinkable of all his two-buck bottles. "So lay it on your old man. I'm here to listen. That's my job, the best one on the planet."

His gangster slang mixed with a classic television commercial made her smile against her will. She took a sip and tried to sluice it past the tongue. His beer was worse. One batch blew up in the crawlspace. It still smelled of malt fifteen years later.

Jiggs and Maggie night. The thirties. Every semester Norman taught a different era, and he adjusted his clothes, cooking, reading, and entertainment. No television in this decade. Perhaps he'd play a tape of *Amos 'n' Andy*, two white comics who had listeners thinking that they were black. A screwball comedy might help. Grant and Hepburn in *Bringing Up Baby*. That scene where Hepburn ripped her dress and they walked out in tandem always made Holly laugh.

Chipper must be home. Had he told his parents? And tomorrow on the mainland as he saw the full weight of the conspiracy against him, how would that feel? Rewarded for years of hard work against all the odds by a bogus accusation by a spoiled twit. At least she had her father as a sounding board. Not that he had any political pull, but he must know someone at UVic who could help.

Norman returned from the laundry room bin with a smelly bowl of salmon-based dog chow. Shogun had followed him, licking his black velvet lips. As a rescue dog, he'd had two other names in his checkered history: Hogan and Logan. Called to dinner, Shogun would answer to any name. The plumy white tail looping over his back was the "lantern" to see the shepherd home.

Finishing her first glass of wine before her father returned and pouring another for maximum numbness, Holly took a chair at the simple pine table in the kitchen. Like all the front rooms, it overlooked the shimmering strait. In the choppy Prussian-blue waters far across, a freighter labelled *Hanjin* headed for China. From down below in the high-ceilinged solarium, a CD player sent Kate Smith's upbeat "Sioux City Sue" from her early days. Trained as a toddler, Holly had become such a connoisseur that she could tell the thirty-year-old from the seventy-year-old by the tone. The voice grew richer with time.

"I'll rope her and I'll brand her, and I'll use my old lasso. Gonna put my brand on my sweet Sioux City Sue," the song continued. Today purists might say that the lyrics were an attack on women. Sometimes Holly yearned for the innocence of the past her father revered, but how innocent had it been? Modern laws skewed statistics. What was now rape once had been a time-honoured marital prerogative, one step up from being allowed to beat a wife with any stick smaller than a thumb. Better record keeping and a different protocol had also brought more charges and assured that cases went to trial even if the battered woman objected.

"God bless our Kate," Norman said, wedded to Yankee culture. "A big girl with a big voice. An American institution until the day she died. Re-invented herself decades later to sing the anthem at Phillies hockey games. Do you know she had a monopoly on that song? That was one smart business-woman." Norman squeezed a loonie until it yodelled. He picked up the bottle to top his glass and gave an odd double take at the lowered level. "You must really like this batch.

Don't drink it too fast, though, or you won't appreciate the cherry nose and deep tannins."

His deep blue eyes, crinkled with age at the corners, focused on hers, but Holly turned away to swallow another sugar surfeit of wine. Not even eight years on the job and she was folding like a cliché. Her father had skirted depression several times after his wife had vanished. Maybe the same trait was finding its way home to her. She wanted to forget what had happened, but she wanted for it to be tomorrow and tomorrow and tomorrow until Chipper returned to work. The three of them were more than the sum of their parts and less than two-thirds without him. She wanted their lives back.

Norman took salad makings from the fridge and assembled the promised slaw. Holly picked up the paper and read the headline of the *Times Colonist*. "Morale remains high in E Division." What kind of propaganda was that? As if you said something enough, people would believe it. Public relations was smoke and mirrors.

Norman's long nose wrinkled as they heard a sizzle from the stove. "Can you flip the hash? You like it nice and browned."

She replied with a barely audible *mmmmm*. Even after being stuck in the Colwood crawl, Chipper would be sitting down to dinner now. His mother would have ready his favourite curry, steaming parathas, homemade lime pickle, and his hard-working father would be dozing in his chair. Then he'd have to tell them the bad news. She'd bet that he got right to it. Short and straight. Nothing sugar-coated. His mother might dab her eyes. His father would clear his throat. To them he was still a boy. Chipper loved his parents with unshakable devotion, but he would stand or fall on his own. Only children had to be tougher. She was one, too, and Ann. What were the odds of that?

Accustomed to lecturing, Norman was never one to let silence fill the room. "Did I tell you that I had Shogun in for his shots? The new vet had someone working for him that we knew years ago. Barry Metz. Remember when he took care of our shepherds? Never had his own practice. He preferred working all over the island as a locum."

Holly shook herself back to the moment. She remembered Metz. An opinionated loner, but a wizard with animals. "Right. He could clean dog teeth without the expense and risk of putting them under. That was a gift all right."

"Saved us hundreds on the anesthesia. Didn't have the same success with women, though. His wife left him about ten years ago. Since then he's been in Port McNeil, your old detachment. Then Comox, Parksville, the rounds. We ought to have him over for dinner some time. I think the guy's lonely. Still couldn't keep talking about her even after all this time. Broke his heart. Wouldn't hurt to get a free opinion of that dandruff Shogie gets, too."

Holly sipped quietly. Her father loved free professional advice. But Metz was on the obnoxious side. Why, she couldn't say. Female instinct maybe. Norman could have him over for "old times" talk some night that she was away. Their neighbour's diesel Dodge chugged up the drive and stopped the conversation for a minute.

"Helllooo, daughter of mine," Norman said, chucking her under the chin in a gesture that melted her heart. "You're in a trance after only one ... make that two, glasses of wine. It's not that strong, is it? What's on that legal-beagle mind of yours?" He flipped the hash himself and added a dash of paprika.

Holly pulled herself back to attention, banging the heel of her palm on her head. "Sorry. Bad day." What was taking her so long to get to the point about Chipper? Because if she didn't speak, it seemed less real?

"We all have those. Did I ever tell you about the time at the Faculty Club that the chairman went to toast the dear old queen and said the queer old ..."

"Yes, several times. And you said it happened during Victoria's Jubilee." Then back into action with an economy of words, she related what had happened as she heated two plates in the microwave, eased the hash onto them and placed them on the table with ketchup. As an afterthought, she grabbed two paper serviettes from the shelf and sailed them onto the table. Instead of digging in, she parked her fork and stared out the window. Then, almost as if in a haze, she told him about Chipper.

Norman listened with customary patience. "Holly, my dear, I'm sorry to hear about your friend, but you can't take it so personally. You're starting to remind me of your mother. She wasn't moody like I get. When she was passionate about something …"

"It's not as if I can *do* anything about this. I wasn't a witness. This poisonous little snake is going to take Chipper down." She made a pistol of her hand and shot several times.

Norman wiggled his eyebrows, for him a nervous habit. Then he took a few small bites, casting worried glances across the table. "Eat up. I'm not giving yours to Shogun. He was over twenty-two kilos at the vet. You know what a chow-hound he is." The dog was seated at attention, staring at them, a string of drool coming from his mouth. She snapped her fingers and waved him away into the TV room, knowing that his incorrigible appetite wasn't really his fault. Her father was trying to distract her, bless his silly heart.

"But Chipper. He's so young and he has such … this just isn't fair …" Against her will, she felt moisture well at the corners of her eyes and turned away. A third glass of wine appeared at her hand.

Her father gave her the cool assessment that made him the kind of a professor that could quell tempests with a rapier phrase. "Does this young man mean something more to you than you're letting on?" He'd never questioned her on her love life, non-existent though it was. Her privacy was respected. "None of my business," he'd often say about common gossip about departmental marriages and the occasional affair.

Her quick answer surprised even her, and the edge of her mouth rose in a nervous smile. "Don't be ridiculous. He's my colleague. And of course he's my friend. So is Ann."

Was she protesting too much? Norman took her at her word, then blotted his mouth with the serviette. "You're coming to realize that not much is fair in this man-made world. If it were, your mother wouldn't …" His voice weakened and trailed off. His gaze looked up to Bonnie's university graduation picture on the wall, lustrous raven hair falling to her shoulders. Holly was now seven years older than her mother had been when she passed the bar. Life was carrying them on while she lingered behind, forever ageless. When people asked to stay young, they needed to understand that it was not an unmixed blessing.

Injustice had come even earlier to Holly. In second grade, she had been wrongly accused of copying from another student on a spelling test and was made to stand in the corner by the asbestos-covered water pipe poking between floors. Her teacher Miss Henderson, pushing retirement age, had frayed nerves and often shook children, one hand for minor infractions, two hands for serious. The principal resembled Captain Queeg in *The Caine Mutiny* and was no help. When Holly had come home and cried to her mother, Bonnie had said, "I know you did nothing wrong. Miss Henderson will be retiring in June, about forty years too late. Stay out of her way and let her leave with dignity. Always take the high road even though it's not the easiest choice. You'll sleep better. And the view is better from above." Perhaps now she appreciated the loyalty, misguided or not, that the principal had shown the teacher. A leader supported the troops. Problem was, there was nothing she could do but stew.

"After a life in the classroom, I've seen pretty much everything. Professors are rather tame, but every now and then … We've had a few who tippled or crossed the line on dating female students. Complaints come with the territory. Take the eternal carping about grades. A C used to be average." Norman shook his head.

Holly forced a smile, unable to see her father committing any of those crimes. Nor was he an easy marker. He knew students often took popular culture because they thought it was a bird course. Then they found themselves with a fifteen-page essay exam and never-ending term papers with every footnote eyeballed. "You've been to a few grade appeals, I know, but …"

"And never lost one yet. My records are sterling." He paused to brush his hand over his Brylcreemed hair in a mild preening gesture. "Not that professors don't get involved. There's so much temptation from those nubile young girls who idolize you, especially in the humanities. All that poetry, art, and music attracts the dreamers."

"But surely you …" She gave him a fresh assessment. An attractive man, he was still no George Clooney. Imagining one's parents as sex objects had to be the last thing on any normal person's mind. She cast her thoughts back to her own university days. What about that law professor with the curly hair and chocolate brown eyes? His Irish accent could undress any woman without body armour and, acting many roles, he'd spun dramatic courtroom scenes that mesmerized them. Once, in innocence she was sure, he had put his hand on her shoulder as she wrote an exam and said …

Holly looked up.

"I'm the old man to you, but don't be naive. There are a few who are out to make trouble. Think of the odds." He spun out points on his fingers. "Hundreds of students passing each year through your classes. You're going to hit a bad one every now and then. One girl threatened to tell the dean that I propositioned her unless I gave her an A."

Holly stopped short of snorting wine out her nose. The batch was beginning to taste good. "Really? I mean, of course." Her mother, frustrated over the years by her husband and the trivia he worshipped, had finally found a soul mate in a social work instructor at nearby Camosun College. Once Holly got to university, the divorce would have proceeded. This shocking fact she had realized only after returning to the island. Norman claimed that he had had no idea and was the one at fault in any case.

Intrigued, she'd gone to meet the man, surprisingly a decade younger than Bonnie. Ordinary next to her father. But he'd had something Norman didn't. A passion to help others. Planning to hate him on sight, she found that the striking pastel portrait of Bonnie on his office wall nearly brought her to tears. He was an honourable man. Her mother would have had none other. He had a rock-solid alibi for the time Bonnie disappeared. He grieved as much as they did.

"So what did you do? It must have been complicated." Could his advice help Chipper or the detachment?

He swept his hand in a grand gesture, narrowly missing the oil and vinegar carafes. "I told the little baggage to take it to the bank. I had always kept my door wide open, despite the lack of privacy. Male professors know that much. I bluffed her plain and simple like she was bluffing me. Little Miss Evil turned on her wicked heels and dropped the course that afternoon. I asked around and found that she'd tried the same thing on three other men in the last year. They'd capitulated. I went to the chairman post haste and put a letter into her permanent file. Game, set, and match." He crossed his silverware on his empty plate and let his serviette drop in a gesture worthy of Clifton Webb.

"Nice going. I had no idea. But this is different. It happened out in the middle of nowhere. No witnesses. It's going to be a case of 'he said, she said.' The way Chipper described her, I wouldn't put it past her to give herself bruises." She found herself surprised at the hostility she felt towards a girl she had never met.

"What happened to that union you talked about a while ago? Is there no one to speak for you?"

"We have the right to form one, according to a recent court decision, but you know how long it takes for wheels to turn and the organization to be built. According to the RCMP Act, the Commission for Public Complaints Against the RCMP, as cumbersome as a woolly mammoth, should be handling Chipper's situation. Very in-house. That's why the average person thinks that we close ranks to protect ourselves."

She told him what she had learned about the process. The stats weren't that bad, even though the press could sensationalize any event. Among twenty thousand officers across the country, there were fifty to sixty formal disciplinary cases a year. Four constables were asked to resign. They had uttered threats, improperly used a police vehicle, had sex while on duty, or committed sexual assault. That put Chipper in a very rare category. Lesser charges involved loss of pay and simple reprimands followed using bad language or viewing pornography at the office. One officer was suspended for taking small change from the desk of another. Sacrificing a career for seventy bucks?

"I see. And since the protocol's being fast-tracked, you're thinking that Chipper ..."

"May not get a fair hearing. And worse yet, he might have to face civil charges for sexual assault." She forked into the hash, realizing that it was nearly cold. "And even if he's cleared, the suspicions will remain. Everyone jokes about getting sent to Atlin up on the gold-rush trail. Just when I have us all working as a team."

"What about the girl? What kind of connections does she have to carry this so far? Is she related to the Governor General? The prime minister?"

She gave a self-critical bark of a laugh. "That's what I forgot to tell you. Her father is Leo Buckstaff."

"Aha. The thick plottens." He drew his slender fingers along his chin in contemplation. A mischievous gleam came into his eyes. "I know the old bastard. Pardon my language. The word suits him."

A breath caught in her throat. "Tell me everything." Karma was coming up roses for a change.

He started to clear the table. "Leo's been a thorn in my side at the faculty senate for years."

Holly barely noticed the Neapolitan ice cream he brought. The major three flavours in a block. Exotic for the time. The

Toll House cookies redeemed the meal. "How long have you known him?"

He spooned up a mouthful. "He and I came in the same year. Pompous ass. Graduated from Yale like Dubya and thinks he rules the world. I've been on several committees with him. He hogs the floor and crushes any opposition. Hates foreigners, as he calls them, even though he came up from the States himself. He tried to deny tenure to Jerry Chan. The man nearly won a Nobel Prize for his work in chemistry. Almost succeeded until the entire department came down on him."

"So he's a bigot. That could be good or bad for us. It sure does explain his daughter's attitudes."

"He disguises his prejudice in ambiguous words. Scratch his skin, and you'll find a holocaust denier too careful to be caught. We've made jokes about his wife washing his sheets with eyeholes in them. She's another royal pain. Butter wouldn't melt and all that. Heads up some charity but she'd run over a street person with her BMW and ask the victim to wipe off the bumper."

"Surely not the klan in Canada." The mother sounded like as much trouble as the father. Chipper would have the wrath of an entire family.

"He's from South Carolina. His accent gets thicker every year. Calls the Civil War the War of the Northern Oppression. Or Aggression. Whatever." Norman got up to bring cups of decaf.

"So you think he can be taken down?"

Norman gave a cautious whistle at her insinuation. "He's a VP now. Wields plenty of power around the university in his little kingdom. Wants to be president, but that's against protocol. We always fill that position from outside, even out of province if possible. Less cronyism. It's significant that he thinks that he can get away with that breech. 101 percent ego."

Holly felt more cheerful at this inside information. That accent wouldn't help him up here. It might even alienate people. She felt her appetite returning and was sorry that she had seen the rest of her plate go to Shogun, who was now snoring on a sheepskin down in the solarium. "And his daughter?"

"Samantha? She who can do no wrong? Got into the university at sixteen. Thinks she's the queen of every class. Obnoxious little prig. But brains don't equal common sense."

"So in temperament she's like the old man."

"That's the word. But I haven't had any contact with her, thank God. I think she's majoring in psychology. Everyone who needs help does that." He tapped his temple for effect.

She finished her dish of ice cream and called Shogun to lick the bowl. "I have a favour to ask."

"From me? I'd give you the world on a string."

"Wrong period, Dad; 1922." He'd done his best to spoil her despite her mother's influence as the tough cop. "Find out whatever you can about Samantha. She may have used this tactic before. Ask your colleagues but only the discreet ones."

He smiled enigmatically and blotted his mouth demurely. "Discretion is my middle name. Do you have to deputize me?"

CHAPTER ELEVEN

ANN HAD THE CPC website on her screen when Holly arrived, including the four-page online form for making complaints. "This is such crap even if it is an improvement over the last one," Ann said. "Look at the timeline. Complaints as well as the request for materials are acknowledged within a few days, but it can take up to six months for a report to be delivered to the complainant."

"Six months is a lifetime when a career is at stake," Holly added.

With her brain honed sharp as a straight razor, Ann provided an executive summary as she read. The most frequent complaint from the public was member attitude, a highly subjective situation which could include dismissive, rude, non-responsive, or biased behaviour. After that came the quality of criminal investigation. Typically an interim report was sent to the commissioner of the RCMP and the Minister of Public Safety. The commissioner was to prepare a response and then would come a final report. Timeliness was important to maintain the credibility of the force, and efforts were constantly being made to speed the process. When months and years went by, a case was severely compromised.

"I'm not sure this fast-tracking is better," Holly said. "We could have a witch hunt."

"A few years ago, before the latest scandals, this situation might have been dismissed, not that you or I would want that were the accusation true. The worst thing is that there is nothing we can do now to help him," Ann said. "The idea about replacing us all with a provincial force is not an idle threat. One more huge scandal could start the process in earnest. It's looking as if the only factor preventing it is the cost, which could run into the hundreds of millions in an otherwise bleak economic period So much for our proud history." She snapped her fingers in a derisory gesture.

Holly looked at Chipper's neat desk, where three pencils with perfectly sharpened points sat in a "Welcome to SuperNatural B.C." coffee mug along with three pens, red, black, and blue, next to a tattered pocket dictionary. His computer screensaver played a series of scenes, one for each province. The Saskatchewan wheat fields gave way to the majesty of the Rockies. Imagine them someday without the RCMP. It could happen.

"I'm hoping my father will find something, but quietly. We don't want this backfiring." Holly told Ann what he'd said.

Ann pooched out her lower lip and nodded. "That's the first good news we've had. I knew this girl was a psychopath in training. She had to leave a slime trail somewhere."

"Have you heard from Chipper? There's nothing on the answering machine. We asked him to keep us posted."

"He could have called us at home, too, if he wanted to stay off the record."

"It may be a question of his pride. Let's stop brooding and get back to work on the French Beach assault case. He'd want to know that we're tending to business, not despairing about his chances. The show must go on, as they say in the movies. I could use a bit of Ethel Merman's energy right now."

"Your dad sounds like a lot of fun. Mine was in business. Rarely home even on the weekends. And my mother demonstrates the phrase 'only the good die young.'" Ann crossed herself for luck.

With Ann's direction, Holly checked the records back ten years to when the detachment had been opened. Given the burgeoning population, the decision to expand west beyond Sooke had been amazingly proactive for an organization that resisted change.

Hours later, they compared notes. Aside from a few domestics and drunk and disorderly, no women had been assaulted, and certainly not in any of the parks.

"I'm no profiler, but we have a rogue male here. Chances are, under thirty."

Ann chuckled. "That's what the stats say, but keep an open mind for the anomaly."

"That Paul Reid character. If he hadn't come by ..." She kept remembering the Bible. Was she misjudging the man? Condemning him for an innocent act on the level of a repressed Victorian thumbing through the ladies' under-wear pages in the 1897 Sears Catalogue that her father had shown her?

Ann's unplucked eyebrows formed a question arch. "I've been wondering about him. You said he lived alone. Sort of a recluse? You do see where I'm going."

"Around here, there's one on every corner. That's hardly a crime." The area was full of harmless eccentrics. Long before the draft dodgers arrived, artists, conservationists, gadflies of all varieties found homes on the island. If you were content with a mossy trailer, you could live on minimal pensions.

The phone rang with another noise nuisance call. Bread and butter of the small detachment, but Holly disliked it more than traffic duty. People felt that they lived "in the country," where dogs could run free and bark their guts out. No one wanted to put up expensive fences for half an acre. Rover might be fine in the yard, but the next moment he was off chasing cars or deer. Dr. Joe and the crew at the vet hospital made strong suggestions about neutering, but people often ignored them, especially those with pit bulls. The worst "dropped off" their kittens and puppies so that they could have a "happy home" in the wild. More and more roosters were arriving from Victorian "city farmers."

"Ouch," Ann said, moving with obvious care.

"What's wrong?"

"Damn. I reached the wrong way under the sink last night."

"Take care of yourself. We may be short-staffed for a while."

"It's a muscle strain. Not my damn discs. Give me credit for knowing the difference."

"Okay. You're the boss on that subject." Holly spread her hands in surrender mode.

Shortly before Holly came, Ann had tackled a robber on a crime spree and could have retired on a disability from her back injury. Through the force's policy on accommodation, she had been allowed to stay on at a desk job. Holly had been told by Ann's former boss never to call her after dinner when she might be into the sauce and adding a few painkillers. Their first few weeks had been prickly when Holly took the place Ann had earned, but common goals had brought mutual respect.

Remembering what Chipper had said about the sexual assaults in Langford, Holly called West Shore Detachment to check their crime stats. West Shore had over seventy employees with four teams of six investigators and not only a Major Crimes unit, but one for street crimes, fraud, and firearms. The integrated unit downtown was developed to assist small detachments and devote heavy resources to the first few days. They also handled police dog services and a provincial general investigative unit for mid-level crimes like extortion and grand theft as well as gangs, crisis intervention, and child exploitation. Only if they failed to get their man could a lowly corporal become involved in the process re-inspecting a pot on the back burner in her spare time. In those few unsolved cases, Holly liked to think of their detachment as the "Court of Last Resort."

She was routed through to Inspector Lee Skeffington. "With our increased population, our stats are way up in every category," he said.

"Sexual assaults?"

"Unfortunately. Most of them have centred around a few hotspot bars like the Logger. But there was an attack in the park the other night. Right at the Five Points." At this confluence, the Esquimalt and Nanaimo Railway bisected five streets and a park.

Holly's radar perked up. There were plenty of streetlights around, and the detachment was across the street. Quite the nerve. "An arrest?"

"I wish. The guy got away. He was one fast mo-fo. Maybe he ran track. Ripped the blouse off a grandmother coming home from a movie on her bike. Then he grabbed her shoulder bag."

"Then it's not the same M.O. as the other man who's been after young girls. My constable lives in Colwood, and he told me about your mugger."

"I'd say not. This woman was quite hefty, not a little one like the others."

"Do you think he lives in the area? He could have walked, or had a car nearby."

"We sent a cruiser after him. He disappeared into Mill Hill Park. Game over in the dark."

"Maybe he's even camping in there."

"That was our thought. Damn new laws are handcuffing us." The extensive urban park covered over seventy hectares, much of it on steep slopes up a hill with nooks and niches impossible to patrol. It was a haven for wildflowers and homeless. The view from the top was spectacular, if you could overlook Costco.

A recent B.C. high court decision allowed people to camp in public parks as long as they were packed up and out between seven a.m. and nine p.m. Pandora Street downtown now had a regular army of tents, and the waste situation was getting out of control. Still, what were people to do without a bathroom? "Any descriptions we can use? I'm pretty sure we aren't talking about the same person. French Beach is twenty-five clicks from you."

"Just a sec." A minute later she heard a rustle of papers. "Tall guy. Mid twenties. Good condition. Works out, maybe. It was dark, and she was going pretty slow. That's how he was able to pull her off the bike."

"How about his face?"

"Long-billed baseball cap pulled down. Too bad he wasn't stupid enough to have it turned around."

"Was the woman hurt?"

"The fall bruised her legs. Scratched up her bike." He paused. "Luckily a guy walking his dog pack came along through the park and the barking scared off the assailant. The man called us from his cell."

"Did she say anything else? What about voice?" In the dark, that might be another feature.

He paused. "Low and sinister. Kind of disguised. Just yanked her off the bike and pushed her into the bushes. It's funny. Islanders pride themselves on being fit, using cars less, public transportation more, and then look what happens."

"Sounds like he was just after the bag. Send me a copy of that report for our files," she asked, remembering what Maddie had said about the voice of her assailant. "We've only had the one incident. Not enough to see a pattern."

"It could happen again," he said. "Guys like this get off on terrorizing women. That's half the fun, the sick pukes."

When she got back, Ann had a cream-lapping look on her face. "You're not going to guess what I turned up," she said, peering around into Holly's office.

"Don't leave me hanging. I need some good news," said Holly, following Ann back to the foyer and pouring herself a cup of coffee.

"That name Paul Reid rang a bell, so I checked the records. It happened the year before Chipper came. Just

Reg and me." She eased herself down into her chair, took out a bottle of coated aspirin, and swallowed three with a slurp of water.

"What happened?" Reg Wilkinson had been a one-man detachment for a few years. He was the product of high everything but IQ, he joked, and was living in retirement in Chemainus up the east coast. A triple bypass had been the last event levering him from his beloved post. "Doing a run to Rennie to check on a rockslide after one of our deluges, I caught Paul taking a leak down at Jordan River. Around the back of that take-out hamburger joint that closed down."

"If he was exposing himself, there's a connection," Holly said.

"Like serial killers practising on animals. Or peeping Toms graduating to rape."

"Tell me more. I'm guessing he was charged with public indecency."

Ann shook her head and a frown crept over her wide brow. "Out here? No way. His back was turned to the road. No one was around when I drove by. I was pissed. Pardon the pun. I took his name, made the report, and went back to HQ. Reg laughed me out of the office. I nearly clocked him. The big, soft-hearted jerk."

Holly gave it some thought, recalling how harmless Paul had seemed. "It could have happened that way. Guys are casual and careless about their plumbing. The rest of us end up peeing on our shoes."

"So should we follow up? I'm thinking yes."

"Why don't you give Reg a call and refresh your memory? Maybe something else will occur to him."

Holly set out to check on the dog complaint, grabbing a copy of the Capital Regional District bylaws. The statutes were fairly liberal about barking as long as it wasn't between key hours. If only they could regulate noisy geese. When she returned, Ann was still on the phone. She held up two fingers, and Holly went to her office.

On the wall were pictures of her German shepherds. One fading Polaroid showed her mother and father in their early twenties, long locks for her father and braids for Mom, tie-dyed shirt and a soft deerskin dress. Fate was a strange animal. If they hadn't met in university, would her mother be around today? She herself wouldn't be, but that would hardly matter. Holly tried to relax her shoulders, where a knot was forming. Thinking like that was plain nuts. But she didn't believe that everything happened for a purpose.

She should have started her search for her mother when she had been posted up north near Port McNeil, but a full-time job left little time off. She thought over the facts, something she did like a mental tune-up.

That last weekend, Bonnie had called from a motel in Campbell River, then headed into the interior. It was wild country, pierced with twisting fjords and tiny enclaves on the uninhabited west coast. Why had she taken that old Bronco into the bush in the fall when the weather was so unpredictable? Because she had promised the small community that she would come. "Promises are to be kept, little Freckle Pelt," she'd told her daughter, referencing a common lichen whose name amused them both.

Recently, Great Aunt Stella Rice had given Holly a lead from Bonnie's shoebox of work records left at her farm in Youbou up in Cowichan. The trail wasn't only cold after ten years, it was icy. If only she had the time and resources. Was she taking one step back with each two forward or the reverse?

A receipt from Otter Aviation. Cryptic notes on a pad. This information had caused her to try to contact her second cousin in nearby Sidney. Any day he'd be back from a fishing trip in the remote part of Yukon. What could he tell her about that mysterious flight to Williams Lake on the mainland that Bonnie had booked but never taken?

It was all as frustrating as this case at French Beach. She looked glumly at the envelope on the desk. A scrap of paper. Sometimes the smallest of clues led to an arrest. Police had caught the Son of Sam killer decades ago because he had received a parking ticket on the street where the murder went down.

"Stop playing detective," Inspector Crew at West Shore had told her when she called on a follow-up. "We put our resources where they do the most good. This was a sexual assault, not a rape. The clothes turned up nothing. If you're trying to make a name for yourself, little lady, you're going about it the wrong way. Know how many corporals there are? Over 3,600. Don't overstep your authority or you'll still be at that rank when you're old and grey." She snorted in disgust at the memory.

A car with no muffler blasted by, rattling the single-paned windows. No sense even bothering. They couldn't continue to do the same work with one less man. Luckily they weren't as busy now as in the middle of the summer.

Ann called, "No luck with Reg. His machine says he's moose hunting on the mainland. That usually takes him at least a week."

Then Ann's phone rang. A minute later, she appeared in the doorway of her office as Holly turned from the files. "Good news, or maybe bad. We should have anticipated this. They're sending someone out to fill in for Chipper." She glanced up at the clock. "In fact, she should be here now ... or he should."

CHAPTER TWELVE

"**SHE OR HE? THEY** didn't give you a name? Just constable?"

Ann looked at the note she had made. "It's another case of *The Young and the Restless*. Ashley Packke. That's with an E at the end of the last name. Two K's. I'm thinking female, but you never know."

"That soap's still on, but they turfed Ashley a few years ago. I remember a bunch of Crystals from *Dallas* just behind me in school. My dad would point to the many Shirleys in their seventies now. And the Marilyns in their fifties. But Ashley was a man in *Gone with the Wind*."

Ann held up her hands. "Creative spelling makes me crazy. Sean, Shawn, Shawon. Nick knew a girl called Six once. Maybe her mother needed to number them."

"My girlfriend Suzy Tune looked and acted just like her name. Perky and cute. Ashley was smart and gorgeous. It's a hard name to live up to."

The noise rose to a climax, then stopped. A lawnmower? A local senior had ridden his John Deere all the way to Steak Night at the Sooke Legion. Normally Chipper would be out like a shot. Holly gritted her teeth and stayed put.

"Whatever that noise is, they're here. Maybe they need help. Go on out and ..." She turned as the fax began printing.

"This may free me from some traffic duty, but I really don't want to have to adjust to someone new for what could be a few weeks." Holly folded her arms and leaned against the wall, predisposed to dislike the intruder on the spot.

"Did I hear you use the word *adjust*? Ten demerit points. You're in the army, after all." She gathered up the pages from the fax machine and began to read. "This might tell us more about Constable Packke."

Footsteps sounded steps outside. A muscular woman six feet tall designed for the word *Amazon* pushed open the door with her hip, banging it against the closet. She wore a set of black leathers and carried a full-face flame-decaled motorcycle helmet under one arm. She dropped a duffle on the floor.

Her hair was curly and strawberry blond, sticking with sweat to her forehead. The prominent nose had a distinctive point. She booted the door shut the door behind her with a tiny *oomph*, then put the helmet on a table of brochures and stepped forward with her hands on her hips, looking the room up and down.

"How do you stand it out here? Any farther and Honolulu, hello. There isn't even a Starbucks or a Serious Coffee in half an hour."

Holly stepped forward from the lunchroom. "Excuse me. Can we help you with something?"

"I'm Ashley Packke. You should be expecting me."

"Tact isn't your middle name," Ann observed, her mouth tight as her observant eyes. Like an observant hawk, she was sizing up the competition.

The woman shot her an irreverent glance. "Since you're sitting out here playing secretary, you can't be the boss. So where is he? Alls they told me was that this was a shack in the boonies where the living is easy."

"You're looking at her," Holly said, keeping her voice even. So far the tension in the room had escalated to a level even Valium wouldn't crack. She wanted to shake this woman's hand about as much as she wanted to put her arm into a cobra cage. And they'd thought things couldn't get worse? Still, she made the politic gesture. "I'm Holly Martin."

Ashley gave her the roughest shake she'd ever felt. It went on for at least thirty seconds, though who was counting? Holly refused to back down by being the first to pull away. Did the woman squeeze exercise balls hours each morning? If she pulled that on Ann, with the woman's occasional tendonitis, there was going to be bloodshed.

Ann folded her hands on the desk in an assessing gesture. She'd taken off her reading glasses and fixed the woman with a piercing stare. "I find it strange that you weren't briefed on our detachment when you got the assignment. HQ isn't usually that sloppy."

"Whatever. I'm a fast learner. Where's my office? Then I want to get changed. And never mind the orientation. I can tell that dick all happens here except for nap time," Ashley said. "Well, ladies? Don't tell me that *this* is it. You gotta be kidding."

Things had happened so fast that Holly hadn't thought about clearing Chipper's things. "What you see is what you get." She pulled a small box from the closet and started to collect his personal belongings. The silver Ganesh paperweight gave her heart a pull. Then came his Vancouver Olympics glass. Small tokens of a soul. The other drawers simply held stationery. The framed picture of his mom and dad standing proudly in front of their new store she plucked from the wall. For safekeeping she took the box to a shelf in her office closet, forcing herself to take her time. It felt like he had died.

"So this is your desk." Holly said with a quick exhale when she returned. "Why are you still in civilian clothes? Or are you fresh from an undercover assignment?"

"Very funny. I brought my uniform. Where's a place I can change?"

Ann pointed with a thumb. "We have a bathroom with a sink. No hot tub or sauna, despite what you imagined. You can change in our lunchroom." Her frozen expression said *shove us and we shove back.*

With a "huh," Ashley took the cue to disappear.

Holly gave Ann a quizzical look. "What do you think?"

"She's a big girl. In good shape, too. Did you see those biceps? No one's giving her a tough time on traffic patrol or breaking up a bar fight, not that we have any bars. But a charmer this one ain't. Then again, neither are we."

"Speak for yourself, Ann," Holly said, patting her chest. "I am known for my cooperative personality and generous spirit."

Ashley returned in a few minutes, rolling her substantial linebacker shoulders. In the uniform, she looked even more formidable. Neither Ann nor Holly was a fragile lily, but Ashley looked as if she could wrestle each one with one hand and win. Had she been a professional bodybuilder? With her abrupt personality, perhaps she was on steroids. Holly felt her neck hairs prickle. "Loose cannon" had been invented for this gal. On the other hand, perhaps, thrown into a strange and obviously different situation, she was overdoing the bravado. Some people chose law enforcement to exercise their aptitude for being a bully. Most of them didn't last long.

Ashley chuckled, a nasty sound that conjured memories of revolving heads. "They said Corporals Martin and Troy." She sat in Chipper's chair and crossed one leg grasshopper style, taking a tissue from a box on the desk and giving her boots a buff. Holly noticed that her shirt could have stood a pressing. "So why are there two corporals in a three-man post? Somebody lose a coin toss? You look to be the older one by ten years. 'Sup?" She shot a glance at Ann.

"Now wait a minute," Holly said. "Who do you ..."

Ann held up a hand as her pupils turned to pinpoints. "Let that be a mystery for you. It will make life more interesting." She inspected her short nails as if they told a story. "Corporal Martin is head of the detachment, as she already told you. Your short-term memory needs a booster shot."

"No need to hit me over the head. I can see I'm push-ing the wrong buttons. Don't be so sensitive. Time of the month or what? So where's the guy I'm replacing? I heard some funny rumours." ·

Although she had a symmetrical face and expressive lips, her combative attitude was making her uglier by the minute. Holly's clenched jaw was making her molars ache. Where would things go from here?

"On a need-to-know basis, here's the answer. Constable Singh's case is in the bullshit machine, and you know how long that process takes. Without revealing any details about this false accusation, we're confident that he'll be back here very soon." Holly looked at Ann, who gave a confident nod. "So don't get too comfortable, *officer.*"

Ashley's nostrils flared as she tipped back in the chair and put her boots on the desk, pushing aside a pencil holder. "So what do you do for fun around here when dead whales aren't floating in on the beach?"

Whale watching was big business. Every tourist wanted to ride in those Zodiacs. But recently due to a krill shortage a right whale had starved. When people were photographed hacking pieces from its rotting carcass, to respect its spirit the local Coastal Salish tribe had towed it away for a decent burial.

Ann bristled as a wave of red was beginning to build at her neck. "No shoes on the desk, honey lamb. We're casual on the island, not sloppy. Didn't your mother teach you any manners?"

Ashley complied with a shrug, moving her lips silently in mimicry. "Jesus H. You got more mysteries around here. Leave me to think the worst if you want. Sounds like you're protecting him, though. Are we talking denial? You're both nervous. I can tell. Psychology was one of my best subjects."

Holly and Ann made visceral eye contact, for once in total agreement. It felt good to be on the same side, but they were stuck with this idiot until Chipper returned. Instead of look-ing forward to coming to work, she'd want to head the other way. "If you came here to do a job you're paid for, get to it.

Our constable's personal belongings are cleared out. There's a closet for gear."

"You must get lots of sleep around here. Don't pretend anything much happens in Lalaland. Myself, I'd prefer the big city. I'm a woman of action." She mimed a sparring bout, ending with an uppercut and a "Pow!"

The tendons in Ann's neck tightened as Holly said, "Come into my office, constable, and I'll give you a brief orientation. We're not as busy here as in the summer, but we got a sexual assault last week."

From a small leather backpack, Ashley pulled a giant-sized energy drink in a neon can and swilled it in seconds. "An assault, eh? That sounds interesting. Maybe things aren't as dull as I thought."

In Holly's office, Ashley took a chair, pulling the back in front of her and straddling it cowboy style. She cocked one plucked eyebrow. "So what's the story on the crip out there?" To her credit, she had lowered her voice.

Holly felt her blood heading for a quick boil. She got up to shut the door, before biting off the words. "Corporal Troy is a hero. She tackled a gunman on a crime spree a few years ago and sustained a serious back injury. She saved a clerk's life. Instead of taking a disability, she decided to pitch in where she could."

"Sure." Ashley's bone structure would serve her until seventy, but without a smile, what did it matter? "Tell me another one. She's too out of shape for anything but answering the phone and filing. Standing in the way of the younger generation, ask me. The force isn't a nursing home."

"Nobody asked you. You have one giant Douglas fir tree on your shoulder or maybe in some darker place. Were you sent here to fill for some kind of punishment? We can ask questions, too, and you might not like to have to answer them." Confrontation wasn't Holly's strong point, but Ashley was asking for it.

Ashley blew out a breath, taking her time. "I'm waiting for something to come up on the mainland. They're cool with promoting women faster now, and I'm heading straight for the top. So get to it. Or are we going to stand here all day chatting like second graders?"

That's the last time I rise to your bait, Holly thought. She and Ann were going to have to discuss tactics for this live one. "Fine. I assume you've had experience with traffic duty. We have a radar gun, and usually spend two hours a day on patrol in one of four hot spots." The gun was ancient. Was she going to have to apologize for every sub-standard part of the detachment? Fossil Bay was like the Sargasso Sea. Old and used equipment floated in on the tide.

"Does that junker cruiser even run? Or do the wheels fall off at fifty kph?" Ashley inspected her fire-engine-red fingernails.

"You're not getting into high speed chases here. Not unless you want to go home in a body bag. The roads aren't made for it. They're narrow and winding. Not to mention wet. Our monsoons are overdue. Tactics trump speed." She added, "There's an older Suburban for our work in the bush. We use it more in winter when there's snow up ..."

"You mean you operate in winter? I figured you closed up and went to Phoenix."

Let her spout off for now. It was obviously a defence mechanism. For what, though? Holly spent half an hour explaining the routines and making sure that Ashley knew where all the forms were kept. Then she went to the foyer closet for her coat as Ashley followed, scribbling notes on a pad. "If there's nothing else, I'm nearly due for patrol. One more thing about our communications. Our radios are better than they used to be, but they're not totally reliable. In other words, expect to be out of contact from time to time, especially west of here."

"Why am I not surprised?" Ashley rolled her eyes, heavy with mascara and perhaps a little too bright. "God, am I thirsty. Road dust." She opened another can from her duffle and finished half.

How many of those energy bombs did she inhale every day? Enough to give her a permanent caffeine jag. Now that Holly could focus on Ashley's face, she noticed an application of foundation on the windburn, and her eyes were enlarged with mascara and eye shadow. An impervious light coral outlined her mouth. Neither Holly nor Ann had the time nor inclination for more than a touch of powder and the odd kiss of lipstick. Holly's nostrils flared at a musky perfume that might have been deodorant or even a men's cologne. Heavy scents were becoming an anomaly noticed only in close places like an elevator or small office.

"Ann can answer your questions. She'll also show you where the stationery is and set you up with supplies if you need something that's not on Chipper's desk," Holly said.

"I get you." Ashley flopped back onto her chair and did an easy twirl. Then she reached into her duffle for a bag of chips.

"And by the way, this is a public place, and times have changed. Whatever that perfume is, save it for date nights."

"Sheesh." Ashley crunched, her mouth working. "When do you break for lunch?"

Back in her office, Holly tried to relax by taking a few deep breaths and thinking of the Queen, whose picture in her riding uniform, circa 1960, looked down from the wall. This was going to be brutal if it lasted long. Circles of hell opened before her. That big mouth. One of the most important characteristics of a good officer was tact, especially speaking with the public. This woman had all the sensitivity of a raging bull like the one on the cans. There was no question they needed a third person, but at what price? And what she'd said about Chipper. Was she really a bigot or just careless with her language? Her own Coastal Salish background made her even more sensitive about loaded words.

With a raised eyebrow, Ann brought Holly the fax that had arrived a few moments before Ashley. The woman was twenty-eight, same as Chipper, same point in her career. She'd been born in Kirkland Lake, a down-and-dead Ontario mining town, and taken a law and security diploma at the local college. Instead of getting a degree, she'd worked for a year in Sudbury as a night guard at Costco, then passed the RCMP exam with high marks, being posted to Moose Jaw. It made sense to leave Ontario, since the OPP ran the show only outside of city police departments and a few remote postings.

Holly paused and tallied up the evidence. So the girl wasn't stupid. She read on, interested in how that combative personality had informed her work. After a year outside Regina, she had been moved to Golden, B.C., on the other side of the mountains from Banff. Then, after six months, which struck Holly as odd, she had been sent to the island, filling in for a woman on maternity leave up in Cowichan, where many of Holly's relatives lived. That post had ten officers.

Now here she was down on the coast. Four detachments in as many years. Something smelled very bad, and it wasn't what had rolled in at high tide. Holly consulted her set of provincial maps. Each of the posts had been on the border of a reserve. Curious. If there had been serious trouble, how she had managed to stay in the force? Was someone protecting her?

So much for Day One. What about the next few weeks? If Holly couldn't rope her in, she'd face a rebuke about her own leadership role even though it was more than possible that other posts were passing on the problems by transferring Ashley. What might Great Aunt Stella Rice in Cowichan know? The tribal leader had a finger on the community pulse. Holly sat back. For now, she'd let the obnoxious newbie prove herself. Or hang herself. Odds were equal.

CHAPTER THIRTEEN

AGAINST HER BETTER JUDGEMENT, a few days later Holly sent Ashley on her first assignment, patrol duty east of French Beach, where speeders loved to flex their muscles. A dense thicket of blackberry bushes and a convenient curve camouflaged the car. Ashley was still laughing about the antique radar gun, brandishing it like an Uzi, yelling, "Chucka chucka chucka" and jumping from the "recoil."

Holly frowned at the woman's Yamaha 125 motorscooter outside. It barely did eighty kph, which made it marginally legal. Going that fast was tantamount to sitting on a skateboard and rolling down the Malahat. It wasn't inconceivable that a fatal accident would remove her from the roster well before Chipper's case was resolved.

"Soon as I save some money, I'm getting me a Virago 250 to run with the big dogs," Ashley said. As for her residence, she was living in a jacked-up truck camper with tarps parked in a friend's yard off Anderson Road, where zoning was casual. She had to go inside to a trailer to use the bathroom, and the heating was minimal. Holly gave her points for enduring that discomfort. With some of the highest rents and house prices in the nation, choices for constables, even corporals, were few. She tried to remember the hardships she endured as a rookie on the bottom of the salary grid. A basement apartment with a leaky oil heater in Port McNeil. The flea-ridden back bedroom of an old rooming house in La Pas.

Ann watched her leave, the door slamming. She put her palms on each side of her head and made the la-la-la sound. "That one makes me feel twenty years older. Why didn't she stick to video games instead of joining the police? It's like seeing your delinquent kid rush out and knowing he's going to be arrested by nightfall and maybe get his girlfriend pregnant in the process."

"Maybe two girlfriends. Let's hope she doesn't wreck the car, Mom. With the cutbacks, we'll be on used bicycles." Holly took a seat in Chipper's chair and shook her head at the new landfill. A package of Cheetos had spilled, and a pool of milky pink liquid had formed beside a bottle of Lizard Fuel. Perfect for Ms. Forked Tongue. Three Red Bull cans had made it by accident into the wastebasket. A small handheld game Ashley called Patapon was in one corner, and on her coffee break she had been punching its button with maniacal delight. A pack of DuMauriers was open. At the high cost these days, Ashley kept the half-finished butts. Holly put the smokes into a drawer in case anyone came in. She'd told the woman three times to conceal her habit back of the detachment out of sight of kids.

"It's more than time to call Chipper, even though I don't want him to know how worried we are," Holly said. "What did your contact at West Shore say?" Ann had dated a sergeant a few years ago and still kept in touch. Neither was the marrying kind.

Ann gave a shrug. "They're not allowed to give out any information. He says that the all the cards are being kept close to the vest. I'm not surprised. Our buddy's being railroaded and no mistake. It's damn insulting that they didn't let you do the first stage of the investigation. Protocol goes out the window when management pulls the strings."

Holly swept her hand in disgust. "Look at this. What a pig. Wish we could move her desk into the lunchroom out of sight."

Ann shook her soft brown curls. Her haircuts were getting shorter. "She reminds me of a young guy we had in a single-man detachment forty miles outside Wawa. Unlike the rest of us, he seemed okay with being alone way up in the bush. Then we found out that he had a Facebook page where he was trolling for women, calling himself 'Hot Cop.' He was bragging about using the patrol car for his dates. They were driving up from all over the province. Some ladies have a real thing for lawmen."

Holly let a slow smile wind over her face. "The back seat, I take it. Manoeuvring around the computer and shotgun would be painful."

Ann nodded. "He was turfed. One good reason those single-officer posts are history. Pros and cons to that because now it takes much longer to answer calls in isolated areas. Look at the murder last year on one of the Gulf Islands. It's lucky that the killer was so obvious."

Holly reached for a copy of the *Times Colonist* on Ann's desk. "Speaking of our own isolated area, I've been afraid to look in the paper."

"Front page," Ann said, the corners of her mouth turning down.

"UVic Student Claims Sexual Assault" went the story, not the lead but next best. Under eighteen, the girl wasn't named. Holly turned to the continuation on page three, flapping with a vengeance. With this kind of exposure, Chipper was being condemned before even a perfunctory investigation. How would his parents feel with his name in the paper? Mentions were made of the scandals of the last four years, including an officer's answering a 911 call about gunshots being fired. He was laughing on the tape. When he arrived at the location, he never entered the house. Inside were victims of gunshot wounds. By the time they were found, one person was dead, the other dying. Worst of all, he had even been promoted.

"Bastards," Holly said. "What the hell's wrong with the screening process, letting these guys through?" Complaints about women seemed to be rare, but maybe it was a question of numbers. In the RCMP, B.C. led the nation with only 21.4 percent women. For the rest of the country, it was 18 percent. Parity would be out of reach for decades.

Holly hit the bathroom to freshen up as Ann's phone rang. When she returned, Ann motioned her over. "Interesting news about Reid." She punched speakerphone.

CHAPTER FOURTEEN

WITH ALL THE RECENT chaos, the name didn't register and Holly gave Ann a questioning look. "You're too young to be losing your memory."

"Right. Paul Reid." Holly tapped her forehead. "French Beach."

Reg's gravelly voice could grate hard cheese. Even under the new paint, the wall still held traces of the noxious Cuban cigar he had been puffing when he took his final leave of his Fort Zinderneuf. "Everything ship shape down there in my old stomping grounds?" he asked. For the first few months, he'd dropped in on a regular basis. His new apartment was a couple of hours away, so his excuse that he had friends in the neighbourhood seemed like a stretch.

"The building is still standing, both vehicles are rolling, and we're all on the right side of the grass," Holly said. "What's the story on Paul?"

"I ran into him every now and then when I cruised the park around four each day in the summer to show the colours. When they got rid of the full-time ranger in a cost-cutting move, his presence was welcomed."

In turning over the post to Holly, Reg had been friendly and helpful, but the fact that he had remained a corporal after thirty years on the force spoke volumes. Had he tried for the sergeant's exam and failed? Or did he prefer his comfortable sinecure? Ann had implied that he had been on the easygoing side and never missed a half-hour afternoon nap. But with nothing more to deal with than speeders or the occasional and unsolvable minor theft in park lots, he knew he had it good.

"Ann said that you had some information on his background. I guess she told you about our assault at French. Paul seemed on the nervous side." Shy and reclusive could mean suspicious. Had she misjudged the man?

Reg cleared his throat. "I'm not saying anything that's a secret. Paul went through AA about five years ago. He was a real hell raiser before that. Had him in more than once for fighting with his wife. They had a little hobby farm in Shirley. Couple of acres and a few alpacas. It had belonged to his father. Gone back to grass by the seventies. I guess the wife wasn't real keen on living so far from town, and the old tumbledown house didn't please her. She liked to get into the sauce, too. Double trouble."

Ann gave a slight cough, and Holly said, "I see."

"Paul got the worst of it sometimes. They traded restraining orders."

Women could be guilty of spousal abuse, too, though it was a rare man who wouldn't hit back. "I didn't see or smell any alcohol at his place." Hadn't he rescued Maddie? Or had he gotten more than he bargained for in an attack and then turned around the situation to play hero? Stranger things had happened. How many times had a murderer called 911, confident that in reporting a body, he would avoid suspicion? "How did he end up out on Seaside?"

"They didn't seem to need an excuse to go at each other like a couple of starving Rottweilers. He purely went off women after that. They got divorced and sold the acreage.

He bought that little cabin. She went back to the mainland. No kids, and he got the dog."

"Boy, has he changed. Seems like a pussycat to me. What's his means of support? He doesn't get anything from the park authority."

"Small navy pension. He doesn't need much."

"Do you think there's any chance that he could have attacked the girl?" He'd seemed so harmless, and here was this aggressive background filling in the blanks. She almost mentioned the Bible verses, but that seemed to say more about her than him.

Reg paused for a moment. "For his own good, he tends to stay away from women. Being a hermit suits him. Drives around and makes sure the paths are clear after storms. He's alerted us about small boats in trouble in the bay. Go ask the park authority if you want."

"What about when Ann caught him urinating in public?" She drew back from the guffaw over the speaker.

"Hell, I told her to forget it. If he wanted to go expose himself, there'd be places he could get more bang for the buck, if you get my meaning. Ann was a little too eager as a rookie. One of these days, I'll tell you about her first week on the job."

Ann gave the speakerphone a dirty look and spoke up loudly. "I'll remember that, Reg, next time you want a favour."

Holly gave the evening a fast re-roll. Other than being eccentric … "He *was* very kind and considerate of the girl."

"That's what I'm trying to say. I don't peg him for this. I'm assuming you made the rounds for witnesses."

"Hardly anyone was there. I've cleared the two parties camping nearby and a car that was seen the night before. Paul is the only witness. Everything happened in total darkness. How the guy got away without bumping into something or falling into a fire pit baffles me. It's like he vanished into thin air."

"You're already making an assumption that you're dealing with a man." Wouldn't that be the assumption of the century? What about that female serial killer in Florida? Overall, women killing women was unusual. And there was the size. Not that many women were so tall and strong. Aside from Ashley. "That's why you're in the job, little girl, and I'm a lazy retired old fart. See what the park honchos say about his volunteering. Go talk to him again as a follow up. It would demonstrate that our antennas are up."

"There's another possibility." She told him about the Langford attacker.

"That's a long way from here. A different kind of situation, wouldn't you say? Moving from the city out to a provincial park."

"People don't change their M.O.s unless they have a good reason."

"Doesn't mean that it never happens," Ann said.

"Where's the young lad?" Reg asked with a chuckle. "I want to remind him to keep his man pants on around you two."

Holly left Ann to fill in Reg on Chipper's situation. She couldn't bring herself to repeat it, nor did she want to hear the details again. She went back to her office.

A few minutes later, Ann came in, her arms folded.

"What's Reg's take?" Holly asked. The old man must have heard about many incidents in his long tenure.

Ann pursed her lips in an unconvinced pose. "Reg thinks that this will blow over. Said he was picking up the phone and calling an old pal at Island Division." She shook her head. "He sounded mad as hell. I told him to calm down before riling any of the higher ups."

"Chipper needs all the friends he can get. Even if he is retired, maybe Reg can call in a few markers. He must know all the silverbacks."

As he had suggested, Holly dialed the provincial park headquarters, the agency in charge of French Beach and other venues clear up to the Yukon border. It took about half an hour to wind through the departments and get put on hold for Ollie Smith. Why had it taken Reg to give her the suggestion? Her multi-tasking needed a big-time tweak. In every new post, you had to learn the information channels. Then just as you mastered the system, they moved you to another post. It seemed an ineffective way to grow an organization.

"I read about that attack. Damn shame. Our parks don't need that kind of publicity. So what do you want to know about Reid? He's only a volunteer. Has there been a problem? Nothing I've heard about," Ollie said.

Holly swallowed and gave a non-committal "I see" in an effort to draw out the man.

"On the contrary. We've had several calls and emails about people he's helped. Battery jumps, using the phone, relaying calls from anxious relatives when something happens at home. With the budget in the toilet, we're depending on the public more and more. There's only fourteen full-time rangers in the whole damn province." His tone revealed a combination of pride and frustration.

"I don't think his drinking in the past is a secret. I just wanted to ..." She started to trip over her tongue. "When I heard that, I wanted to double check my impressions."

"Since he got religion, he's been on the straight and narrow. He's a member of my Baptist church in Sooke. Even led an adult Bible group. He got the Song of Solomon that week, poor guy. It's hot stuff."

Holly felt herself rolling to the other end of the spectrum. Maybe too perfect. John Wayne Gacey and his clown shows for kids. Ted Bundy and his volunteering at a crisis centre in Florida. Even the astute true-crime author Ann Rule hadn't suspected the double life of her colleague.

"But you know, it isn't a good idea for women to camp alone. Some people might think she was asking for trouble. Those short shorts and tops these days. Tattoos up the wazoo."

"Mr. Smith, with all due respect, what a woman wears and where she chooses to go are no excuse for an attack." Was he going to suggest that single women carry protection? Handguns were illegal in Canada. In the U.S., they could be brought to public parks.

A screech of tires made her sit up. Holly made a note for the records and quickly brought the conversation to a close. A car door slammed, and the sound of a loud voice came from outside. More trouble in paradise?

Ann stood at the open door. A cloud of dust surrounded the Impala. Ashley had a First Nations teenager handcuffed and was escorting him toward the stairs. Less than five feet, he barely weighed a hundred and ten pounds. He wore jeans and a T-shirt from the Aboriginal World Games.

Holly shot a sharp look at the rookie, holding her voice in check. Appearances had to be maintained. "What's going on here, officer?"

Two bright spots of excitement pinked Ashley's cheeks. "Nothing that a few hours in the cells in Sooke wouldn't cool. Can you believe this little guy had the nerve to give me the finger when I drove by? That's disrespecting an officer. And he was hitchhiking. Also against the law. I checked him for drugs. Probably threw them in the bushes when I stopped the car to back up."

Holly recognized Trey Elliott from the Port Renfrew Pacheedaht Band, a close-knit group of a few hundred people. Not only was he a good kid, but he was legally blind, though he wore no dark glasses and carried no white cane. "Low vision" was the official definition. He had enough sight to walk from one place to another, but for his schoolwork used a special computer that enlarged print. His parents had put long, hard years into their sport-fishing business to keep him and his sister heading for college. Since he couldn't drive and couldn't ride a bike safely, often he hitchhiked home from the Kemp Lake corner west of Sooke where the bus stopped. A very proud young man and a skilled guitar player, he'd never plead his handicap. Trey thrived on his independence.

Holly's heart thumped when he looked directly at her, using his honed echolocation skills as a vision aid. "Trey, tell me what happened." She laid a friendly hand on his thin shoulder.

He was fourteen with a Nike cap, his black hair braided down the back. She doubted if he'd started to shave.

Trey stood tall as he could, his lower lip stiffening as he tried to master his feelings. Too old to cry, too young to laugh. "She's wrong, Corporal Martin. I don't know what she thought she saw. I was heading home from playing a gig. We'll all raising money for our class trip to Whistler. Some kids are holding a car wash. Dave Evans at the Stick heard me play at school and paid me twenty dollars for an hour. Then he got me a ride, but the guy could only take me as far as Jordan River."

"Oh, right. Hitching is hitching." Ashley looked as if she was going to continue up the stairs.

Holly blocked the path. "Ann, please take Trey inside for a minute. Get him a pop. I have a few things to clear up." Ashley needed a blast she'd never forget.

"Aye, aye." Ann shepherded the boy inside, casting a glance of scorn backward at Ashley, who was toeing the ground with her boot like a restive horse. When the door had closed, Holly took a deep, restorative breath. "This might be only your first week, but you've already flunked out. Trey is legally blind. He could barely see you much less show the kind of disrespect you're talking about. If he catches a lift once in a blue moon, what does it hurt? Everyone knows him. He never takes rides from strangers. We're a long way from Victoria. Learn to bend the rules."

Ashley reached into a pocket and pulled out a small, pearl-handled penknife. "I patted him down for carrying and came up with this. I saw what I saw."

"You're lucky you *can* see. Imagine what it's like for him. In my eyes, he's a hero to carry on with a normal life. He wants to be a music teacher. And despite people like you, he will be."

"So what about the knife? This is all crap."

"He has every right to carry this. He's not at school now. And I don't like your language."

Ashley clamped her jaw shut and looked at the road. At least she knew enough to shut up while she was losing. A small pulse beat in her temple, and her arms were folded in a passive-aggressive pose. As for eye contact, she stared past Holly, refusing to engage.

"We worked hard here, Ann, Chipper, and I, to earn the trust of these kids. To show them that the force is their friend, not a bunch of bullies. Stunts like this can set us back to ground zero. How the hell am I going to explain this to him without looking like a total jerk myself? You'll be lucky not to have his parents down here charging child abuse. Taking him to the cells. Are you crazy to even suggest that? Have you been watching too much reality scare shows? Grow up!"

This was the longest lecture she'd ever delivered. Holly could feel the surge of energy and clasped her hands behind her to stop from shaking. What next? Arresting a senior for waving a cane? Then she stopped to think. Her mentor's words echoed in her ears. "Everyone can make a mistake, Holly. Have your say and back off. Too much humiliation never helped a situation. Learn to pick your battles."

"So I didn't know your rules around here. Hitchhiking is illegal." Ashley tried to assume a tone of moral authority, but her deflated posture told the truth. Words could lie, voices could lie, but the body rarely did.

"You already said that. This is a very small community, and normally a very law-abiding one, where we bend the occasional rule when common sense directs. Get with the program."

Ashley looked at the sky to where two seabirds were flying, shrieking at each another. "Yeah, yeah. I hear you."

"*Yeah* is not cutting it. I want an apology, and I want it now." She cocked a thumb at the door. "Give him back the knife. Tell Trey you're new, you didn't understand how things worked here, and that you apologize. And make it sincere as hell. Ann will drive him home."

Ashley took off her cap and ran fingers through her hair. Her chin wasn't jutting out anymore. "He's a kid. I'm not gonna crawl to him."

"And you're an adult. Start with I'm sorry. You'll find the words." She exhaled. Tempted though she was to bring up Ashley's questionable career, this was not the time. "My first year, I nearly mistook a diabetic for a drunk and threw him in the tank. That would have had fatal consequences. This is part of the learning process. The lesson is now over."

With a grunt, Ashley went back inside, a marginally honest smile pasted on her face. Attitude 101. The sooner she was out of here, the better. On the other hand, she was crying out for mentoring.

When Trey came out with Ann, he was smiling. From the back seat of the cruiser, Ann retrieved his guitar. "Sit up front. You can serenade me all the way to Rennie," she said. "Do you know any country songs?"

"Corporal Ann, no way. But my mother does." His face wore such mock horror that Holly resisted a laugh.

In her office, door shut, Holly made a call to Island District Headquarters in Nanaimo and found the personnel officer who had signed the secondment to Fossil Bay. Sergeant Barr confirmed that Ashley was on probation for the third and last time. "I'll be honest with you. She would have washed out long ago if it hadn't been for her father pulling in I.O.U.s. He's retired as chief of detectives in Kirkland Lake and has a lot of powerful friends in the RCMP. He won a medal for bravery a few years ago, breaking up a gang of drug runners establishing a base in the north. Got himself shot in the process. Big shoes to fill."

"Thanks for your information. She's not stupid. But boneheaded might describe her. What did she do that got her in trouble? I'm guessing it was serious, but not enough to get her tossed out."

"Where do I start? Have you got a few hours? She hauled in a hooker near Regina. Claimed that the woman had a knife, which turned out to be a cell phone. She shoved her to the ground. Bruised her knees and broke one of the woman's high heels."

Holly whistled. "I see what you mean. That kind of thing usually merits a suspension at least."

"There weren't any witnesses other than the girl. Constable Packke got the benefit of the doubt. We thought a smaller post might give her the time she needed to settle down. Less stress and a safer routine."

"You mean Golden, if I recall correctly. So what happened there?"

"That was different. She requested the first available transfer. Claimed that one of the sergeants was putting the moves on her. That made no sense. He's been married twenty years and has five adopted kids from Korea. Father of the year. Instead of making trouble, he said to let it go. He felt sorry for her. Go figure."

"Moving on to Cowichan," she said. Her mother Bonnie had grown up there, raised by Great Aunt Stella, when her own mother died of TB and her father perished in a timbering accident. Holly had many cousins and distant relatives in the area. Before Barr even answered, she suspected that if the problems had been with tribal people, mouths were closed. They were very proud and bore their grudges with dignity. "Do you think she has a problem with First Nations people?"

"That didn't seem to be a factor in the incidents. Racism in Canada is a slippery animal, though. Sometimes it lies under the surface. As for Cowichan, we didn't hear anything either way," Barr admitted.

Holly looked at her watch. She'd taken enough of his time. One question remained. "Why pick Fossil Bay? Did we win some reverse lottery?"

Barr offered up a friendly laugh. "All her other posts had men only. Call us sexist. We hoped that you and Ann could be role models."

For a minute, Holly was almost flattered. Then she wondered if God himself was up to the task. "I don't know if she's redeemable. A percentage of officers wash out every year. Frankly, she's an accident waiting to happen. I hope you won't get to read about her in the news."

"Calm down. I've seen a couple of bad apples change with a few years of maturity. Any real harm done at your post?"

Holly had second thoughts. Trey seemed to bear no grudges, but Ashley needed a major attitude adjustment. What inside her caused this disconnect? High expectations from her father? She hadn't mentioned her family at all. Forget it, she told herself. Your job is not to be the detachment psychologist. That's why they have professionals. But she remembered what her mother always said: "People are not always reasonable, but they act for a reason. Find out why and you can change their mind."

"Kids are pretty resilient, and if we're lucky and young masculinity asserts itself, he'll brag to his friends. Let's hope he regards her as the exception rather than the rule. It's taken us a long time to build up goodwill in our community. And it gets me smokin' for some newcomer to start dismantling it with a crowbar."

After hanging up, Holly went back to the foyer and found Ashley sitting at her desk, reading a *Blue Line* magazine. "He seemed like a punk. How would I know that he was blind as a bat?" she asked Holly.

Holly looked at the clock on the wall. "If that's an apology, it's pathetic. If it's a joke, it's stupid. Get out of here even if it is early. I've had enough of you for the day. Come back tomorrow and be ready to start over. And read up on hurtful language. Making fun of people will bring you bad karma. If I were riding a toy like that scooter, I'd be very careful to keep on Fate's good side. One tire blows, and you're road kill."

Ashley shrugged and went to the closet for her street clothes, disappearing into the lunchroom to dress. A minute later the stutters of the bike disappeared down the road.

Ann returned bearing a large foil-wrapped plate and a smile to match. "Damned if his mom didn't give me a fresh pie. Last of the blackberries. Want a piece?"

"And insult my dad? He's making brownies tonight. Anyway, did you fix things with Trey?" Holly asked, massaging the bridge of her nose. She never got headaches. Then again, that was B.A.: Before Ashley.

"I think so. He's a good kid. Naturally I couldn't really badmouth our rookie, but I told him that we have to learn on the job. Professional courtesy even if she doesn't deserve it."

"I hear that she comes from a law enforcement family. Dad's a hero." She capsuled what Barr had told her.

Ann shrugged, raising an eyebrow. "Trying to live up to his record. It's tough to follow a parent into a profession. That's why I didn't go into business like my father."

"Amen. Teaching or legal advocacy are the last things I'd want to do. If I didn't like coming to work, I'd leave the profession."

"So you say now. When you get a little older, you won't be so casual about changing careers. Anyway, sounds like this is her last chance," Ann said. "And still she's coming on like gangbusters. None are so dumb as those who will not learn."

They both looked at Chipper's desk. "I sure miss ..." they both said. Holly used to link pinkies with her mom and make a wish when that happened.

She went on to relate her father's opinion of Vice President Buckstaff. "Academia isn't the polite and civilized world in people's imaginations. Especially the administration throat-cutting en route to the top. He's going to make some inquiries."

"Sounds like we could be catching a break. So she has a history of bribery and threats. But as for your dad, a civilian messing around in a sensitive matter could be tricky, not to mention the collusion idea with your job. Does he know what he's doing? Is he as impulsive as you are?" Ann gave a teasing smile as she put on her coat.

Holly shook her head as she picked up one of Ashley's empty drink cans. "He's not a people person, if that's what you mean. But I don't think he'll overstep himself. With all the years he's been at UVic, he has a lot of connections. If anyone can shine a light on this girl, he can."

Ann turned for the door. "Then we'll have to figure out what to do with the information. Like going out of bounds to get to the goalpost."

"Then the run better be picture perfect." Mixing her metaphors, she scored a two-pointer in the wastebasket.

CHAPTER FIFTEEN

"**SOMBRIO BEACH. WE NEED** an ambulance and the police."

Seven-thirty. On a cloudy grey morning with dawn tardy, Holly hadn't even taken off her hat. On the phone, Harold Richards said he was a retired logger living on West Coast Road, the only house for a mile in each direction at the entrance to Sombrio. To complicate communications, he spoke quickly, apparently working around his dentures. It sounded like he had a mouthful of marbles. Two young men had come to his house just after sunrise.

"Take your time, sir. Is anyone injured?" She took a fleeting moment to visualize the area and where a Helivac might land. Once past Fossil Bay, it was more expedient to use that method of transporting people in urgent distress. Remote parts of the island were evil places to have an accident.

He gave a slight moan. "It's all over from what the boys say. I saw some fatalities when we cut down the big trees in the old days. Eyes open. Nobody home. I don't mean any disrespect."

"There's no landing place, as I recall. Even the parking area has overhanging branches. We'll have to go with the ambulance."

"Sorry, I'm upset, jabbering like a monkey. No heartbeat, not breathing. That's what they tell me. Already cold. Must have happened hours ago."

Holly swallowed back a lump and scribbled a few notes to tell Ann where she was going. Her cohort was due any minute. "Where exactly did this happen? Where is she now? And who found her?" He hadn't said a drowning. This was far too late for anyone to be swimming. Few challenged the cold Pacific surf anyway unless they were surfing and wearing wetsuits. Neither had anyone been reported missing.

It flashed through her mind that it might have been a fall. On the Juan de Fuca and West Coast trails, with slippery logs over creeks and steep inclines, at least once a week someone was taken out. All the warning signs in the world couldn't controvert the possibility of a broken ankle, much less a broken neck. Only last month a pregnant woman had set out with her family for a three-day hike over brutal terrain with ladders and swinging bridges. Then labour had set in. Luckily the EMTs had delivered a healthy baby.

"Down by the beach. The kids hiked back to the parking lot and were driving down the road to Rennie when they passed my house. There ought to be a payphone like at French." Even Port Renfew, with only a volunteer fire department, lost its connections at least once a year. Telus had recently installed a local loop system where at least people could call each other if the system went down. The communications failures were going to cost a life one day. Anyone over fifty needed to keep their cardiac care current, their aspirin topped up, and a defibrillator handy.

"Did she drown?" Every few years, along the string of beaches in the crown jewels of the island, someone fell, drank too much, and was pulled under by a rogue wave at high tide. Darwin's losers. Sometimes in exiting the gene pool, they took others trying to rescue them.

"Let me put the boy on. Mike, come here."

A younger, less confident voice took over. "No, ma'am. She didn't drown. Not unless someone pulled her out of the ocean and moved her a couple hundred feet. We found her not far from her tent near a path in the bush."

A girl. Normally that ruled out heart attacks or strokes except for very unusual cases. She started wondering about alcohol or a seizure.

She had forgotten to jot down Harold's last name. The ability to think clearly and not panic came with experience. The best thing to do would be to take a few minutes to ask questions before all hell broke loose. Small facts and nuances could get lost in the shuffle.

"I'm alone here, but I'll be out as soon as I can. Let me get things started with the ambulance." She heard a car pull up outside. "There's my backup. Do one thing for me, Mike. Make sure everyone stays in a group. No one is to leave. And no one is to walk around anymore than absolutely necessary."

As she hung up, Ann came in, and Holly briefed her about the emergency. The woman's soft grey eyes grew wide with surprise, but waved Holly off. "You get going. It doesn't sound good."

"Call West Shore for a team. They'll want the integrated unit. We're not talking about a drowning here, nor an apparent accident. I'm not driving all the way to hell out there with no communications to find out I need them."

"My thoughts exactly. Err on the side of caution. But how did she die?"

It was a half hour to Sombrio, adding the hike from the parking lot. Long-distance policing had rotten logistics. Until the team arrived, she'd secure the scene at the beach. As for the parking lot, another officer would be needed there, too. Harold had said that he worked part time two days a week as a security guard at Sears. He could help at the lot. Cars would be coming and going.

She'd provide the squad with preliminary notes, drawings, and observations. Chances were that the ambulance might take as long as an hour, depending on where they had last been dispatched. No rush now. A chill made its seismic way through her body. Another girl, another beach. Was there a connection? She'd miss Chipper's skills. Putting up crime scene tape was his speciality, along with interviewing younger people. He knew how to talk their language and not patronize them. That's why his run-in with Samantha was so puzzling.

She came out of her office ready to roll. "Where is our favourite constable?" she asked Ann. "Time's running out. I can't handle it very well by myself."

Ann looked up from the phone. "Fifty minutes for the officers. More for the ambulance. And that's if there aren't any road delays between Sooke and Victoria. Hydro crews have been trimming in preparation for the winter."

Holly grabbed a duffle with supplies and checked her watch. Crowd control would be a nightmare. The beach was several hundred yards long. People could be marching though like a parade. A warren of paths ran along the shoreline.

"I can't wait any longer, Ann, so when little miss Ashley ..."

The signature putt-putt sound reached them. One minute early to be precise. Ashley came through the door with her helmet under her arm. "Sorry I'm late. There was a break in the water line to the creek last night, and we had no ..."

"About time you reported. Dress fast. We have a body at Sombrio." A year ago she might have worried about hurting Ann's feelings in leaving her, but the corporal had acclimated to her limitations and was the heart of the detachment. She also had one of the coolest heads in a crisis. Chipper's case proved that.

"A body?" Ashley's seriously plucked eyebrows marched to attention, and she pumped her arm. "No kidding. And I said nothing ever happened here."

"Don't sound so cheery. A woman is dead." Then she noticed a worried look on Ashley's face. After her bad day, did she tie one on last night? "What's the matter? Did you come to work sick? Of all the ..."

"No, it's ... I have to go to the bathroom." Ashley gripped her stomach and left.

"Now?" Did the woman have IBS or something worse? What a disaster for a police officer. Holly remembered her public speaking courses in training where the guys rushed out just before their presentations. "Make it fast! I am *not* waiting!" she called.

Hurrying outside, she started the car as Ann came out with a couple of bottles of water and two muffins for them. Who knew how long they'd be gone? "I don't know what's wrong with her, but the water's running and the toilet's flushed twice."

Holly checked the trunk for traffic cones. She ran a hand through her short, layered hair in a distractive motion. "Do you think this is connected to French Beach? I wanted a chance to catch this guy, but not at this price."

Ann said, "Come on. You don't even know how she died yet. It doesn't sound like an accident, but ..." Her voice trailed off with a sombre tone. Ann had been on hand for more than one multiple fatality due to ice and snow on northern Ontario roads. In one case, a moose had crashed through the windshield and across the passenger seat. The driver survived.

Holly drummed her fingers on the steering wheel. "Ashley!" she yelled. "Any time you're ready, your chauffeur is waiting!"

Ann passed her a file. "I hauled out the report from French Beach and made copies. They'll want that for comparisons."

"Good thing one of us is operating on eight cylinders." Holly tucked the file beside the seat.

The door slammed. Ashley gripped the railings and vaulted the last few feet, steadying her hat when she landed. Something glittered in her emerald eyes. "Ready. Let's go."

Hitting the siren and lights to nudge gawking tourists out of their way, they took off. Once beyond French Beach, the road grew narrow and winding, traversing clear cuts and the occasional reforested timberland. "Replanted 1975," one sign bragged. In the old days, thirty-five to fifty years was respectable husbandry. Now they were taking trees which had sprouted the year Holly's mother disappeared.

"We'll be there in fifteen minutes. Are you familiar with the layout of Sombrio Beach? Have you ridden out on your bike?" Holly asked Ashley, setting up in her own mind an arrival strategy. Every couple of minutes, another creek went by.

"I just got the bike a week before I got posted here. I was planning on making the Circle Route this weekend. Maybe see Avatar Grove in Rennie. These beaches are too cold for me. I prefer Malibu, Hawaii, long stretches of sand."

"Sombrio is mainly cobble. Hard to walk on, even if it has its own charm. Let me draw a picture for you. Just be glad that we're not at Mystic or Bear. The only access at Sombrio, aside from the coastal trail, is by overgrown logging roads. Coming in by boat would be faster. As it is, we still have a bit of a hike. The beach isn't right off the parking area like at French. It's half a mile through the woods."

Sombrio had a Spanish connection from the explorer who gave the strait its name. Manuel Quimper had arrived in Sooke Harbour in 1790, sailing in on the billandra *Princesa Real* to claim the land. Five years and a threat of war later, the Brits took possession. Quadra Street in Victoria, Galiano and Valdez Islands, and the city of Tofino reflected the same heritage. Mysterious rumours said that a hunter lost in the bush back behind the Potholes Park in Sooke had found a cave loaded with old-fashioned armour and gold from an ancient expedition. When he made his way back to civilization, he could never retrace his steps.

Soon they were travelling through Jordan River, where a huge hydro dam had provided Victoria's first power near a log landing place. Now surfers came here year round. As they exited the skeletal town where once a thousand people lived, they passed a new housing development. With ocean-front and ocean views at a premium, even fifty kilometres from Victoria wouldn't seem so far.

The entrance to China Beach whizzed by. On foggy days the perception was that the Pacific lay beyond instead of Washington State. After months of single-lane traffic, the washout from last year had been repaired.

When they skirted the water, the waves were sparkling and brave, without any sense of the tragedy that awaited them. Blue water, sky full of puffy galleons, and conifers. If death ever took a holiday, this could be the place.

They passed creeks with names from history or imagination: Uglow, Maidenhair, Fatt, Ivanhoe, Rosamund. After Loss Creek, just before the river, they turned down at the Sombrio Beach Trailhead, along a sad excuse for a road.

Ashley lurched at the rough run, grabbing for the dashboard. "Maybe we should have brought the Suburban."

"This is nothing. There's twenty feet of snow along the San Juan Ridge. We'd need a snowmobile to get up there in an emergency."

Two kilometres later they parked in the lot, amid the minivans and cars of overnight campers who used a steel pay station still prone to theft. A large bulletin board gave instructions about the park and issued warnings about cougars and black bears. Make yourself as big as you can and yell. Don't travel alone. Avoid earphones. Be alert to your surroundings. Never turn your back on the animal. Good advice, but did it work for human killers?

CHAPTER SIXTEEN

HOLLY RUMMAGED UNDER HER seat to where a pen had rolled. Her hand struck something blocky and she pulled it out, looking at it like an object from outer space. She turned to Ashley. "You had the car last. What the hell is this gizmo?"

"Um, I'll tell you later. We'd better hustle, right?" Ashley said.

Mike and Harold hailed them where the trail started, and introductions were made. "The rest of the group is still at the tents," Mike said. "You said to keep them together, not have people wandering all around. Everyone just wants to get the hell out of here."

"Thanks for following directions. It makes my job easier." She looked at him. "West Shore shouldn't be long." She addressed herself to Harold, a potbellied man with a balding head. His workpants were well-used and stained with paint from past jobs. "I'm going to put you in charge, Harold. Can you stay for a few hours? Someone with your security experience will be valuable." It never hurt to pile on the praise for civilians willing to lend a hand.

"No problemo." He pointed to a thermos. "I even brought my own coffee. It could be a long morning."

Mike's face looked red, and not from sunburn. He took off his Mariners cap and raked a hand through his hair. "I still can't believe it. We were all having such a good time last night. Lindsay was ... and now ..." His voice weakened.

"Hold on for a sec, Mike. I want to hear what you have to tell me, but I need to get things organized here first." More tourists might be arriving, even on an off-season Monday. Holly shook her head at the logistics, then sent Ashley to the cruiser for a roll of Chipper's crime scene tape. Mike's eyes widened as if the scope of the situation was hitting home. And yet in routines there was enforced order. In order not to compromise the case, every detail had to be perfect.

Mike was a wiry young guy with a bright Hawaiian shirt and board shorts. His haircut had buzzed sides but a long top gelled every which direction. "Sure, we'll do what we can to help."

"And as you can see, I have only one officer." She called over to Ashley, who was ferreting around in the truck amid clunks and clanks.

"Constable, set up cones to block the roadway. If anyone tries to come through, tell them that the beach is closed. Red tide or something sinister. Make it up. Send them on their way."

She turned back to the young man. "Mike, do all these cars belong to your group?"

He walked to the middle of the lot and considered the eight vehicles, a broad spectrum of cars, trucks, and SUVs. As he looked, he nodded as if remembering. "Uh, six are ours. The old Datsun isn't, and neither is the Pinto with a flat tire. There was at least one campsite down from us. All the way at the end of the beach. I couldn't tell you anything about them."

And for all she knew, the old junkers could have been abandoned or even stolen from another place and dumped. It wouldn't be the first time. She looked around with some dismay. It wasn't merely a case of blocking one exit. Trails snaked their way all through the bush, some leading to record-holding trees, others to waterfalls spilling into the ocean or berry patches. Mike's group was together, but suppose the others farther down the beach hadn't heard what happened and took another route this morning? Maybe they were hiking west to Botanical Bay or east back to China Beach. She told Ashley to make a note of the plates and descriptions of all vehicles as well as a diagram of the lot.

Ashley managed a twisted smile. "It may get ugly. People don't like driving all this way and having to turn around."

"Death has stubborn inconveniences. I told you what to say. Don't explain or get distracted by questions. You're going to have to learn the language of the profession. That's why I'm leaving you here for now, constable. You can handle it." Holly's final shred of patience was heading for a dim corner.

"Sure. No worries. We'll be fine. Right, pal?" She looked almost flirtatious with the old man, who was wriggling a finger into his enormous hairy ear with satisfaction.

"Keep alert for the ambulance. They usually run the siren to move aside stragglers. The trail we're taking goes right to the beach."

Holly headed down the path, noticing that Ashley was exchanging smiles with Mike. Holly called back, "Constable, put up the tape and block access to the beach. Now, not tomorrow." Usually she said please, but some people took politeness for weakness.

Ashley stared down the lot to a small wooden building. "Got to hit the bathroom, boss. I'll be right back." She left them with a nervous smile.

Mike was looking at Ashley's disappearing back. Wasn't he a tad young for her? Holly tapped on his shoulder, and he started.

"Lead the way, Mike. Where's ... Lindsay?" She'd been drilled many times on using discreet words for a corpse. This was a human being, someone loving and loved. Now heading for a cooling tray at the morgue, followed by an autopsy. This death raised many questions.

Mike shook himself like a wet dog, an apologetic set to his face. "Sorry, ma'am. Follow me." He took off down the peaty path, and she had to hustle to keep up. His runners made the tortuous trip look easy. Her sturdy leather boots would never win a marathon.

"Not that fast, Mike. I don't want a sprained ankle." She dodged a cedar root angling for a trip.

Speaking as they walked, Mike told her that he and a half dozen friends from the UBC theatre group putting on *Cats* later this fall were camping at Sombrio Beach in a get-to-know-each-other bonding. Saturday night they set up camp and ate a vat of chili that his mom had packed. After a beach fire and a party Sunday night (he admitted that they had brought beer and the hard stuff) they all went to bed. Lindsay Cameron had started with beer, then moved to a bottle of peppermint schnapps and gone to bed at nine after vomiting. The girl sharing her tent decided to bunk with others. Everyone assumed that Lindsay was asleep. As the evening went on by the campfire, some guy way down the beach had bitched at them for noise, yelling obscenities. Everyone else turned in by midnight.

Most of the gang were up by seven with the sun to catch the noon ferry back to Vancouver. When Lindsay didn't emerge by eight when breakfast was nearly over, someone peeked into her tent. She was gone, her sleeping bag and gear still in place as well as a full plastic barf bag. Her shoes were missing. Nobody went barefoot because of the stones. "I mean she was here, and then she was gone. We never heard a thing."

Everyone divided up in teams and took a turn around the campground. Jungle-thick in places, the temperate rainforest was nearly impassable off the paths. Where some giants had fallen, huge rootballs groped into the air. Past the bathrooms, someone spotted a red flash in the green bush and went to look. It was Lindsay, her body hidden by a heavy growth of skunk cabbage with leaves the size of platters.

"You didn't touch anything, then?" Holly asked, with a gulp.

"We know better than that," Mike said, taking deep breaths to walk and talk. "But we turned her over. Two of us have CPR. It was too late."

"I understand. That's a natural reaction."

How many people had any experience finding a body? It wasn't a life skill taught in high school or college. Many of her younger colleagues had managed to go through their first year or two without confronting a lifeless form. It was a rite of passage. Far worse if the body had begun to decompose or had been disturbed by animals in Canada's wilderness. That was an experience to give bad dreams for years.

Mike shook his head like a lumbering bear. "The girls are hysterical. Who could blame them? Her neck doesn't look right either."

"And there was no sign of a fall? Passing out. Hitting her head?" Chances were that the girl choked on her vomit. A stupid and unnecessary way to die. What had he said about the neck? Her heart knocked and answered back.

"Nothing to fall from. It's pretty level."

"People slip on the ice all the time. One blow in a key spot can do it."

They made good time down to the beach on the wide but irregular dirt path. Logistics occupied her mind. The gurney would have to be carried, not rolled. Once in Port McNeil in the middle of a rainstorm, they'd taken a motorboat to a small island to rescue an overturned kayaker, wading into the surf up to their waists. Hypothermia had set in, and the young man could barely walk. Without the RCMP, he would have been dead, leaving his parents devastated. She'd been proud of being a part of the rescue.

Starting at China Beach, the Juan de Fuca Trail had only been opened about fifteen years ago and was still in its formative stages. There were four trailheads with parking: China, Sombrio, Parkinson, and Botanical. The last time she'd come here had been in high school, on the edge of her adulthood, before their family life headed for the abyss.

Breathing deeply and trying to make time, she had no moments to savour the scenery. Holding dominion were deer ferns and sword ferns along with the more delicate ladies ferns. The occasional bracken spread its leafy fists into fronds, begging to be turned upside down to make children's hats. The padding of their feet added to the dull thuds of a five-toed woodpecker poking for grubs in a riddled, barkless tree. A tiny rough-skinned newt scuttled across the path. And Lindsay Cameron was dead in the midst of all of this ferocious life.

How was Ashley handling her job at the entrance? Writing her phone number for any handsome male who strolled by? Puffing up her importance by searching their cars? At least it wasn't high summer where fifty vehicles could be in the lot. Anyone camping on the beaches in October was a hardy soul.

Accidental choking was one possibility. An undiagnosed heart condition. A stroke, even at eighteen or nineteen. And for the third choice, it was one she would never have considered before the French Beach attack. Unless something broke at the outset, this was going to be a tough case. Any initial errors were hers to make, the oversights numberless.

To her discomfort, she was beginning to break into a sweat in the heavy vest and equipment. Finally emerging through a grove of Sitka spruce with overhanging branches as dark as a cave, she and Mike made their careful way down an eroded section of earthen steps to the end of the steep and rooted trail. After serious storms, blowdowns or mudslides could block the path. One large log had been recently cut with a chainsaw, the sawdust still orange and fresh, in chunks so fine that it was obvious the chain needed sharpening. Now there was a clue of its sort, she imagined, should there be a chainsaw massacre.

With trails branching in all directions, it was simple to get lost in the rainforest on cloudy days without the sun to provide rudimentary directions. Vegetation was dense and lush, even without summer rains. Moss dipped from trees in antebellum Mississippi style. No wonder European visitors marvelled. This was no Black Forest with a carpet of pine needles and under-brush neatly trimmed, visibility half a mile. If the rainforest had a sex, it would be female and fecund. Where the salal didn't dangle its sweet purple berries, thick groves of deadly blackberry dared the hiker to enter at his peril. The thumb-thick canes with ruthless spines shredded skin in seconds in payment for its rich sweets. Wind and waves and centuries had left weird and sinister root forms in the red, banyonlike cedar. Douglas firs stood tall and stately. Sedges with edges, swamp grasses, and leafy salal six feet high. As they progressed, peeka-boo shots of the water flashed like strobe lights.

Then past a concealing corner, the mighty strait spread out beyond them like a grey tablecloth. A bright orange metal buoy marked the mouth of the trail. At high tide, travel along the beaches was impossible. The huge bright balls signified escape points.

Holly and Mike turned right along the soft path, passing wooden tent platforms. Neither the picturesque cobble nor the dense bush allowed gentle camping. Without the platforms, people might use machetes or hatchets to make the beach "pretty," destroying the experience for others.

Holly estimated the tide at a moderate three to four feet, still loud enough to limit conversation. Driven by a west wind, foam-crested breakers were rolling in fast and furious, smashing against the beach, sucking on the pebbled shore with winking bubbles at the brim. The effect was hypnotic, especially when the fog rolled back and forth across the strait. In his legendary journal, Quimper had named the river Sombrio for its dark and shady appearance.

Soon they came to the campsite, spread out in narrow pri-vacy along the edge of the path. At least thirty feet separated each tent on the coveted plank bases. She turned to Mike "How many in your group? How many tents?"

"Six. Three tents. Friday night two per tent. Do you want to check the tent now?"

"Lindsay comes first." There still lodged in her heart's wish the idea that the girl might still be alive. Deep comas masqueraded as death. But they had said that the body was cold, so that theory was a long shot.

She slowed to take in the scene. "And who was sleeping where?"

He pointed to one tent as they walked. "That's mine and Britt's. The next Justin and Josh and Megan. The last one is … was Lindsay's. Megan was supposed to be with her, but …"

"And you found her…?"

"Past her tent a couple hundred yards. That's why it took us awhile."

She thought of the family that would be getting the news. So preoccupied had she been at getting here that she hadn't covered all the angles. "Did someone notify her parents? From Harold's house?"

Mike nodded. "Right after the call to you. Jesus. I didn't know what to say. Just that there had been an accident. She was hurt. They didn't ask more, and I didn't add anything. They were coming right out. But from Nanaimo, who knows when they'll get here? I hope they had someone to drive them." As he turned away, his large hand brushed his eyes. The back of his neck was strong and tanned, one of the most attractive parts on young men before age's thickening and creases.

"Contacting relatives is the worst part of our jobs. You never get used to it, and you never want to." Was it better to receive a child's body or never know her fate, imagining torture and abuse? Children of all ages disappeared, often forever. Taken from a hospital nursery or home bedroom. Last seen standing at a bus stop. Heading to Vancouver for the Olympics. Even coming home from school, less than a block away. Don't forget victims of domestic violence, her mother might add, usually men deciding that their family should die, but failing to finish the job with themselves. Every detachment had its wall of sorrow. Flyers put up by loved ones gave her the sharpest aches. "Have you seen this young man? He disappeared from a hiking trip in ___." Sometimes decades later a skeletal fragment told their tale. Was that what they would find of her mother? Even without flesh, DNA would tell the truth, for the bones would speak. Better that than a life of unknowing. After ten years, it had come down to that for Holly.

Mike led her along a path to the restrooms, two rough shacks shingled on top, male and female symbols on the doors in a quaint, civilized touch. He said, "She wasn't used to the booze like some of us. You can't mix, my dad says. Beer and vodka. Even wine. We left her alone. And I, uh, I feel …"

He cleared his throat awkwardly and stared at the ground.

"What is it, Mike? Did you remember something?"

"I gave the bottle to her. I thought that, well, you know. And she got too far too fast. I'm not that kind of guy."

"Of course not."

Why did young people have to binge, and if they did, why not learn from the experience? Perhaps it had been Lindsay's first time. Recently a man in custody had been taken to the drunk tank. He'd died hours later with triple the blood alcohol limit for survival. Yet officers swore that he had been walking on his own when they left him in his truck for a minute and tended to his friend. Apparently he'd chugged the rest of a hidden bottle. Her father had told her Dylan Thomas's last words before collapsing: "I've had eighteen whiskies in a row. I believe that's the record."

"So she was headed to the bathroom. Makes sense. But she would have been still very drunk."

"Why else would you get up in the middle of the night except to hit the can? She was sick as a dog, not off gazing at the moon. Course she needn't have gone all that way to barf when the whole jungle is around." He bit into a cuticle as if to tell himself that he was still alive through the pain.

"I'm surprised she got that far. Was there a moon last night?" She hadn't noticed. Holly thought of her first hangover, when she and her friend Val had gotten an older cousin to buy them a bottle of Bailey's. They had been puke sick all night. Luckily her parents had been in bed when she wobbled home on her bike and crawled up the stairs. The next morning she could barely spoon her cereal, her hand was shaking so much. She'd told her mother that she had the flu. Bonnie had flared her nostrils, but let her keep the lie. Her ebony, accusing eyes told her daughter that once was enough.

"It was cloudy, I think. And out here it's like totally dark. You can't see your hand in front of your face. I see where they got that old saying."

The path widened and a few downed trees made for impromptu benches for two young people, Josh and Britt. They both stood, nearly at attention, when Holly approached. Their eyes were red-rimmed and their hair uncombed. The boy had an iPod in his pocket, but the ear buds dangled over a shoulder.

"Thanks for watching over … everything. Sorry to have taken so long." She spread her hands in the universal gesture as she introduced herself as they walked on.

Holly got their names and a brief summary of what they had done that morning. It matched Mike's story.

"And the other two, Megan and …"

"Justin. They're with her. Megan was her best friend. We didn't want anyone else coming around. Or like …" Britt shivered and pulled her hooded sweatshirt closer over her ears. Broomstick thin, she wore a pair of jeans. "Animals. Even little ones."

"Was there anyone else at the other campsites?"

They looked at each other and gave a mutual shrug. "I wasn't really paying attention. A few others, maybe. We saw their fire way down the beach last night. I don't even know if they're still here," Mike said. Beach fires were legal below the tide line. In the draining effect of the strait, the next day everything would be washed out to sea.

Not good so far, Holly thought. If anything was suspicious, as Leonard Cohen said in "The Future," things were going to "fly in all directions." She looked at Britt and Josh, who had his arm around her as they walked. "How far are we now?"

"Just up the way. Officer," Britt asked, "she couldn't have just died, could she? She was sick, but ..." Her angular face was old and young at once. Each ear had a row of studs.

"I'm not going to lie to you. We'll know more when there's been an autopsy. A team is on its way." She checked her watch. Any minute now. What was taking them so long?

"An autopsy? Gross." Brit's face screwed up and she swiped at her pug nose with her sleeve. Big Josh, well over six feet, pulled her closer. She was an attractive redhead with a killer-whale tattoo on one arm and freckles on her nose.

This was turning into a parade. "On second thought," Holly said, "you'd better wait here and direct the other officers and the ambulance personnel."

About a hundred feet past the bathrooms, a narrow winding path zigzagged into the bush. It might have been an animal path, or sometimes people thought they saw an artistic shelf fungus and left the main trail to thrash around. It was human nature to want to discover why a trail diverged. Sometimes it led to an impromptu bathroom.

At the point where the path petered out were hummocks of grass and hand-slicing sedges. Standing to the side were Megan and Justin. She was softly crying into his shoulder. He was patting it, but looked stricken enough to join her. The death of a peer was an unusual tragedy for the young.

Lying face up with a small beach towel over her head was Lindsay, dressed in a man's shirt and shorts. Her father's maybe. Norman had given Holly a hand-me-down for her first year in university. Dads did that. Holly snapped on latex gloves, knelt, and tried for a pulse. A thick broom bush partially hid her from the students. In the torpor, its black pea-like pods snapped.

CHAPTER SEVENTEEN

HOLLY TURNED WITH A guarded frown. This was no time for accusations or hostility. "Did you find her like this? With the towel?"

Megan said with shaky tones short of a whimper, "No, it was my idea. I'm sorry. She looked so helpless. She wasn't breathing. We checked for that. I took CPR last year. If I'd stayed with her last night, maybe she'd be alive now. Some friend I was."

Holly bit back a comment. The moment was bad enough. The kids had done what they thought they should. They weren't trained nurses and doctors. "That's all right. Just as long as we know. It was your towel, then, Megan? Not hers?" Megan nodded. Holly introduced herself and took the information. "Mike, please stay. Megan and Justin can go back and wait with the other two, please. When the team comes, they'll give you more instructions." Her watch said nine-thirty already. What was keeping them? She hoped Ashley was keeping a sharp lookout, but she wouldn't put money on it.

Lindsay's gold-flaked brown eyes reflected only the sky. When Holly looked below her chin, despite her self-control in front of Mike, she gave a short gasp.

The bruised neck, its circumference reddened by the same tell-tale marks told the story more than any words. Alcohol had been only one factor. The girl had been incapacitated, but Holly would bet that she hadn't choked on her vomit. She'd finished being sick long before that. She gave a quick scan to the scene as Mike stood, hands dully at his side. He seemed like the natural leader, perhaps a year or two older. Perhaps that discretion made him turn away from the body.

Lindsay's small mouth was bruised as if a fist had connected. Gingerly Holly lifted the lip and saw that the front teeth were wobbly. What struck her as odd was that Lindsay wore only one black pearl stud in her left ear. The bare right lobe looked red and irritated.

"One earring," she said in a whisper louder than she intended.

"She had both of them last night. Megan was admiring them. Lindsay said she got them when her family took a trip to Hawaii to the Big Island. They were going again at Christmas. Now …" His shoulders rose and fell as if he were taking deep breaths. Then just as quickly he composed himself.

"I asked you to stay, Mike, because I wanted you to tell me more about Lindsay." She did a ballpark assessment. About her own height, five feet six, average weight, say one hundred and twenty five pounds, eighteen or nineteen years old if she were a freshman. Her rich chestnut hair fell in light waves to the top of her shoulders, spread out like a halo. Megan had said that they had turned her over. If someone had killed her and left her in a certain position, that information was gone. But wouldn't it have been obvious to Megan?

Who is she? Who was she? Who did she hope to be? The answers were moot. Setting aside the possibility that one of the students did this, something that the team would not dismiss out of hand, how long would it have taken? A minute or two? Three to pass out? Five to die and begin the inevitable processes as the spark left the cells one by one? Boone had told her about determining the time of death from stomach contents. This far from the tents, no sounds would have carried. The wind had been up last night. Even from her window, she had heard waves crashing on the beach half a mile away down the natural amphitheatre at Otter Point.

Lindsay wore an unlaced pair of runners and no socks. Easy to slip on and off while leaving the tent. So she had come out here herself, with enough wits to put on her shoes. By her still hand was a mini flashlight, its glass head cracked. Used as a defensive weapon, or dropped on the rocks, or both? Too much to hope that it belonged to the person who had killed her? Another one for the detectives.

"Is that her light, Mike?" she asked.

"I gave it to her to use our first night. She'd forgot to bring one."

Holly took out her notebook and jotted a quick summary of the last few minutes. "You and your friends will be asked to stay around until things get organized. Then you'll probably have to go to West Shore to make a more complete statement."

"But you've been taking notes, so why …"

"Get ready to do it again, Mike. It's necessary."

"God, I can't believe this is happening." He looked at Lindsay. His voice, cracking with emotion, trickled off and all was still except for the call of the varied thrush, which her father called the telephone bird. It always unnerved her.

"Officer?" She looked at his fresh face, grown older in the last hour. He sounded totally serious, even though his words were out of a drama. "My great grandparents had closed caskets. I've never seen a dead person before. She's not coming back to life. She's gone."

When you were young, you thought you were invincible. "And that's why life is so precious. Because it can be over in minutes. Sometimes a bad decision, sometimes just fate."

"Lindsay was going to be a nurse. We talked about that. And I'm in pre-med." He spoke so low that she could barely hear. "Some doctor I'm going to make. Jesus. Maybe I'd better stay in research. Not sure I can hack it."

"You'll be fine. The next time it will be a little easier. Good doctors never quite get used to it. But that's okay. Empathy means you have human feelings." That brought a nod from him as he sat on a log, hands on his knees. Memories of what Boone had told her about his experience as a coroner returned to her. Every call involved a death. Why was she complaining about police work, which often involved a happy ending and smiles all around?

Each one returned to his own thoughts. Part of Holly wanted to start putting together the case right now, to collect all the testimony and evidence. But that wasn't her bailiwick. Half an hour passed with only the distant sound of the waves and muted birdsong meeting their ears. The sun sliced through the clouds and began to warm their backs, protected from the wind. Nature was going about its amoral business, bees collecting nectar, snakes swallowing frogs, and one-lunged banana slugs scouring the detritus of the forest floor. There were two types of people: those who avoided banana slugs and those who targeted them. Sociopaths in the making. To their fractured thinking, everything moving and helpless needed to be killed. Was that what had happened to Lindsay?

At last, she started at a noise down the path. Mike caught her eye and stood. Bushes moved, and voices rose. It was the Integrated Major Crimes Unit, led by two detectives with three other constables. West Shore had put this together with the last attack and brought in the big guns after Ann had filled them in.

"Over here," she called. Chubby Ed Smith she knew from an orientation seminar her first week on the island. He had warned her that policing the long strings of parks was like confining a toothless snake in a cotton sack, but a hell of a lot less exciting. They shook hands. He was a spark plug of a man, who barely met the height requirement, but he made up in gumption what he lacked in stature. His face bore a scar down one cheek, testimony of a clash with a biker gang, where he stepped in front of a barmaid facing a punk with a broken bottle. In plain clothes like all inspectors, he wore a light jacket over a tan shirt with chinos and the same short boots she wore. He was breathing hard. Running wasn't in his job description.

He took one look at Lindsay's neck and shook his head. "You did good to call us in right away. This is no bloody accident," he said. "What the hell is happening around here?"

"I took a long shot myself, but didn't want to postpone things. What you see is what you get. She'd been doing some drinking, though. Whatever error in judgement she made, she paid the final price."

"Hell, yes, I've got a sixteen-year-old myself. First time she stayed out past midnight, I nearly lost my mind," he said, letting out a long breath. "Think we have a follow up from that French Beach attack? From the throat marks, it's a no-brainer. What about the other people in the party?"

"They're a close-knit group, and I suspect that their alibis will hold up. This guy is escalating." *And in my territory.* "You'll notice that an earring is gone. At French, the girl was missing a bracelet."

"That should help. Good catch on the coincidence." He gave her a thumbs up. She liked Ed. He'd make up in shoe leather what he lacked in genius.

Ed introduced his new partner, a gum-chewing, fresh-faced man a few years older than Holly. "This is Chris's first case. And it's going to be a tough one. He just transferred over from Port Coquitlam. Thought he was going to enjoy a permanent vacation." He gave the man a light punch on the arm in the force's camaraderie.

"Ma'am," Chris Braddock said. He ran his hand through his clipped blond hair, as if for want of something to do. The more he looked at Lindsay, the paler he got. A small piece of tissue stuck to his sideburns area, indicating a fresh but hasty shave.

"Took us long enough to get here," Ed said, kneeling by the girl. "Where's Boone? Thought I heard that junker Jeep of his pull in just as we took the path. Should have dropped him

in by 'copter, the way he walks these days, poor old geezer."
He glanced at Mike and shot a questioning look at Holly.

"This is Mike," she said. "I've already talked to him. As for
the towel, one of the girls put it there."

"Yeah, that kind of thing happens. Son, can you go back
to the tent area and sit tight until we need you? It's getting a
bit crowded." Ed pointed in the direction of the path.

"Sure. No problem, sir." Mike pushed himself up off the
log and trotted off.

"If I know Boone's knee, he'll take another few minutes,"
Holly said. "There's a copy of our French Beach file in the car.
Might save you time."

"Ann told me all about it in twenty-five words or less. If
these events are connected, that's one lucky girl. I wonder if
she'll ever know how close she came to being a fatal statistic?"

She nodded. With luck, Maddie was resuming her life with
no more than a sore jaw. Holly confirmed to herself the wisdom of releasing that information to Pirjo. And yet, if the word
had gotten out in louder fashion, more women might have
been warned. But Lindsay had come with a group.

Now that the big boys had arrived, she felt every inch a
minor player. "There's no I in team," Ben Rogers repeated from
a distant corner of her head. Like a persistent imp, he went everywhere with her. Briefly, she sketched the last few hours for Ed.

"If I were a killer, I wouldn't use the same M.O. each time.
Good thing for us that sociopaths are faithful to their methods,"
Ed said, angling the head for a better look at the damaged skin.
Had Maddie been less agile and strong or Paul not come along,
this might have been the result. "Wire for sure. Very smooth
and large. Notice how it didn't actually cut the skin. Bruising in
a narrow area. Too thick for fishing line. Not a rope."

Holly jumped in. "My constable thought maybe trimmer
line."

Ed pursed his thick lips in approval. "Good guess. You
can find it anywhere, even in my garage, not that I have time
for much yardwork. What are the other similarities?"

"Girl. Beach. Caught alone. One on the weekend. One during the week. Maybe the guy sets his own hours, has no job, or maybe he just prowls at night. No use in speculating until Boone fills in the blanks."

"And the M.E. for the toxicology," Ed said. "There's no serious rigour yet. How long do you think she's been lying here?"

"Mike said she turned in early. The rest went to bed by midnight. It's ten now. A bit cool, but the estimate should be fairly accurate. One or two in the morning? She was pretty drunk when she turned in, so the body needed time to metabolise the booze and put her back on her feet, shaky or not."

Snapping on gloves and kneeling, he moved one of Lindsay's shapely but well-muscled legs. She took good care of herself … until last night. "Died here is my guess. The blood has started to pool even though she's been turned over."

"If she was heading for the bathrooms, given that she had been sick that would be natural. Going there or coming back, who can say? But look at her heels. Perfectly clean."

"That would rule out dragging her. But she could have been carried. Maybe knocked out if she got clipped on the jaw. That flashlight's too small to have done any damage." He took a quick look at her mouth.

"Mike said it was hers anyway. Do you think the guy had his own light? Why advertise your attack with a beam?" A crime under cover of darkness again would give such an advantage. Could he see like an owl? Navigate like a bat? She shuffled her feet waiting for Boone.

The Coroners Service in British Columbia was a quirky historical tradition that would not die. A respectable person with a law or medical background could apply, but candidates often came in after retirement from the civil-service pipeline. In unnatural, sudden, unexplained, or unattended deaths, the coroner would arrive. He would establish the identity if possible, and the how, when, where, and by what means the person died. He would recommend an autopsy if necessary, sometimes against the family's wishes, and perhaps suggest ways in which a similar death could be avoided. The different causes were natural, accidental, suicide, homicide, or undetermined. Problems resulted when one cause masqueraded as another. Some cases had been filed away as accidents for decades until someone with a secret stepped forward or there was reason to exhume the body for tests. Undetectable poisons were often involved, or sometimes a spouse was convicted of murder when their other mates died in seemingly natural circumstances like passing out in a bathtub.

"Do you want me to go back to the campsite and see what's keeping Boone?" she asked, stripping off the hot gloves and mopping her brow in the rising temperatures. She and Ashley were needed back at Fossil Bay. More than one speeder or drunk driver had gotten a pass this morning.

"Hell no. I left a couple officers there. Five in the group of kids, it'll be like Saturday night in a bar. One guy says this. One guy says that. One guy was loaded. They all see things different ways." He made a grand gesture with his arms. "Some crime scene. If it were in the middle of the ocean, it would hardly be worse. Look at this place. You could lose a bloody herd of elephants."

"Makes you kind of wish for a nice locked-room mystery once in a while," she said. "An orangutan crawling in an upper-floor window."

Stooping again, Ed paid close attention to the bruised neck. *Mmm hmm* was all he said. Chris watched and took a few notes. Quiet as paint on a wall. Ed caught Holly's gaze and smiled at her about the rookie's discomfort. "Can you believe this is my partner's first homicide? Never believe it, would you? He's a cool one."

Chris looked like he was used to the teasing, but his face flushed under its fashionable stubble. "Knock it off, Ed."

"Holy crow. Do I have to walk clear to Washington State, or are you gonna call me a ferry? No jokes, please. This is Canada," yelled a gruff voice from the underbrush.

Into the grove stumped Boone Mason. He was used in cases west of the city because he lived nearby in a trailer park on the ocean. A bum knee led to his early retirement from a successful career as a private eye. Though he operated on-call with sporadic pay, the job filled lonely hours since his beloved wife had died years ago. It also limited his dates with a rye bottle. A battered doctor's bag bumped next to him, and he was wearing washed-out work pants with a knee brace and a Toronto Blue Jays sweatshirt. On his head was a straw Panama hat which had seen better days. Stuck in the brim were two fishing flies.

"I see I'm the last one at the party," he said.

Ed gave a wry smile. "It never starts without you."

"Let's see what we have here. That young, we can cross off heart attack or stroke," Boone said. "I suppose you two have already made up your minds before the real brains got here. All bets are officially off, starting now." His gruff exterior hid the fact that he had more compassion than almost anyone she knew.

Chris raised a polite eyebrow. Ed folded his arms and locked eyes with Holly as if to say *Here he goes again*.

"Remember that *assume* always makes an ass of you and me."

How many times had she heard that? But she wouldn't have traded him for Hollywood's most famous coroner.

With a creaky protest from his joints, Boone knelt with a grunt and got to work, chatting in his usual self-distracting way. Dispatch tempered by humanitarianism. Victims were not case files. They had names and significance, even though they had died of an overdose in an alley, mourned by none. You'd never hear him referring to crispy critters or floaters. His goal was to do whatever was in his purveyance to find justice for the victim.

"The marks on her neck," Holly said, stating the obvious. Not long ago she'd attended her first autopsy. One was enough. That was one career she'd never pursue. The open air was her territory.

"No kidding. You're not supposed to be mucking about before I get here, you know. And how about this beach towel, fer Chrissake? Is it hers?" The corner of his mouth rose a fraction. Hair uncombed, clothes rumpled, he never failed to get to a scene as fast as he could and then take all the time he needed. "The clock's already stopped for them," he'd say. In his presence, even Ed stood wordless.

Holly cleared her throat in discomfort. "It belongs to another girl. I moved it to check for a pulse. There was the outside chance that she was just unconscious. No such luck."

While they waited, Ed sent Chris on a reconnaissance, setting up a grid to prepare before the rest of the group arrived. A large team helped scope a scene, but they also crowded it. Once away from this very public place, there would be no coming back. Nature would reassume its leafy business. This was very rough territory, unlike in a home where even a vacuum could be deployed. In the rainforest were a million places for evidence to hide. And suppose they found something. Like at French Beach, who knew how long it had been there? On the other hand, there were the lucky times. The murderer of a woman in the Maritimes had left a new jacket at the scene, with no evidence of him but hair from his cat.

Minutes passed while Boone entered notes in a mini-recorder. Body temperature, rigour, condition of her clothes, discernible wounds or bruises, broken bones. His back was to them, and knowing that he didn't like to be watched, they had turned away but couldn't help sneaking the occasional look. "No supervising! You're not my apprentices on a cooking show. Let me breathe, goddammit," she'd heard him tell a few people with their necks craned too close.

Finally he turned. "I suppose you want to know all the secrets."

CHAPTER EIGHTEEN

"**DAMN STRAIGHT. SO SPILL** it." Ed had worked with Boone over the years. He took the older man's sharp tones with aplomb, and from the half smile on his rugged face, they were good friends.

Boone had reached philosophical mode. He popped an unlit corncob pipe into his mouth, clamped down his teeth, then drew on it for inspiration, his no-fail quit smoking method. "It's ugly, poor kid. She's been raped. I can tell you that. Before or after death is hard to tell at the moment."

Holly felt as if she'd been dunked in icy water. Talk about taking it to the next step. Rape. But she should have thought of that. It was so logical. "But she's dressed."

Boone shrugged his bullish shoulders. "Some of those bastards can be downright fastidious. Do the dirty deed and then tidy up. Play set director. Or maybe feel remorse about what they've done and want to make it right again. You see it with children who've been killed by their mothers. They tuck their little bodies into bed and pull up the covers, as if we wouldn't notice." He coughed to cover up a halt in his voice. Ed took out a huge handkerchief to blow his nose.

Swallowing a lump in her throat, Holly imagined the makeup of such a twisted mind. And the white-knuckling nerve. Taking his time when he might have been discovered by five other people. And all in the dark. "I just noticed those scratches on her arms. Was she fighting for her life?"

"Look closer. Trailing blackberry canes. Still all over the ground at this time of year. There are traces in the wounds." Boone looked around, then pointed. "He might have pulled her over where they wouldn't be seen as easily. Not dragged, though. Heels are clean."

Coming back in time to hear this, Chris mumbled something and lurched off. "Sensitive type. Had the jitters myself the first time. Not so many murders out here that it becomes a habit," Ed said, shaking his head. "Bar room brawls for the most part. Drugs more recently. Don't feel so sorry about those lowlifes. They knew the risks. But this...."

Holly felt colder although the sun was brilliant and they were sheltered from the shore breeze. "Like French Beach. I've been telling Ed."

Boone asked, "I never heard about that. You had a rape there?"

"A sexual assault, or so it seemed." She gave Boone the basics. "Two weeks ago. If someone hadn't come along, it might have had this ending."

"He ran out of luck the first time. Maybe that made him madder." Ed looked at Boone. "But you gotta admit, this is a strange place for an attack. Damn sight far from everything."

"The scene at French was impossible. The inspectors couldn't find a thing. But ..." Holly paused for effect, watching a new spark of interest in their eyes.

"But what? Don't keep us in suspenders," Boone said.

"In the yurt where the girl was pushed, I found a small fragment of paper. At the time, it didn't seem important. We had no reason to believe ... that's why no one ..."

Ed had a minor coughing fit. When it subsided, he made another note, and slapped his book shut, tucking it in his overcoat pocket. "Where the hell is it now? We have a murder on our hands. Nothing should be overlooked. I'm going to have to read the report Crew turned in on the assault. Guess he didn't think anything special of it, or he would have mentioned it. Lucky bastard's off in Calgary for a week of seminars."

"He thought the attack was a one-off." Holly felt attacked by both sides. Call it an instinct from being first on the scene before procedures started clicking, something had felt very wrong at French Beach.

"When I tried to have it tested, I couldn't get authorization from Inspector Crew. He said that thousands weren't going to be spent on a simple groping. Not with budget cuts and backlog. Maybe if ..." As she reined in her opinions, her voice trailed off.

Ed put his hands in his pockets. "They're not lying. It's a real logjam, especially in times of cutbacks. One death took a year to be labelled a homicide. Several cases have been tossed out of court because of the unreasonable delay. But I want that paper. I'll send a man to your detachment to get it as soon as you're back."

Boone held up a hand like a traffic cop. "Wait, wait, wait, my friends. Remember what I said about assumptions. Eliminate all the long shots. What about someone in the group doing this? You got to them first. What's your gut say, Holly?" That Boone used those words without a patronizing smile made her an equal, which pleased her.

Holly told him about what Mike had admitted about giving Lindsay too much to drink. "With all the time that passed before I got here, there could be alibis all around. But these kids are part of a drama cast. It's hardly a scene for wild sex." Though she wouldn't have discounted what happened in the privacy of the tents.

"I'm convinced by the strangulation. This is the same person," Ed said. "With the rape, there may be conclusive evidence, unless our guy's as smart as he seems to be."

"We'll get the word from the M.E. on whether there was an ejaculation. Left here like a piece of garbage. It bloody well makes me sick. Anything else about the scene, corporal?" Boone asked. He tucked the pipe in his hip pocket, its amber stem scored with bite marks.

Holly ran over the last few hours like a mental Mobius strip. Boone had come to hear the most important witness. A silent scream, he called it. Tell her story so that others might live safely. Holly related what she had learned from Mike and the others.

"One more thing. I took a nail scraping," Boone said, and eyebrows went up. "Unless I'm crazy, we got something under there. Course it could be her own tissue from clawing at that line. We'll get samples from the rest of the group for elimination."

"The women too?" Holly asked.

"Death is an equal-opportunity employer," Boone said with his usual wryness. "And just to make things interesting, someone still drunk could be easily overtaken with a wire like that. She was on the small side. For all we know, she was poaching on another girl's boyfriend and paid the price. Stranger things, and all that."

Boone began packing up. Ed moved off to the side to converse with Chris. Holly pictured Megan and Britt. As killers? Impossible. "Even with our advances, criminals are getting smarter." Holly adjusted her cap. "Next *they'll* be wearing protective suits and latex gloves."

"Too much television. Didn't used to be that way before DNA. Secretors, non-secretors. Blood type didn't narrow it down that much." Boone rubbed his knee as he hobbled by. "Damn. I've got to start the ball rolling on getting a replacement. Just don't want to be out of commish for six months. Anyway, one thing's certain. Traffic's going to be way down on the trail once this hits the papers."

"The attack at French is easier to understand. The sites were clean around the road." Holly said to Ed with a sweep of her arm. "Here the terrain is wicked. I'm still wondering about the other groups down the beach. Good luck checking them out if they've already hiked west."

"It's opportunistic, all right. Like someone waited to get her as far away from the tents as possible." Chris seemed to have come to himself and offered an opinion.

Ed set his jaw with a slight narrowing of the eyes. "Bare-hand strangling is one of the coldest ways to kill and one of the hardest to prosecute. Imagine looking at a face that close. Hearing the gasps for air. Squeezing the neck, tighter, tighter."

As he talked, Holly's imagination was working. It was becoming harder to breathe. To snap herself out of it, she spoke. "There's something I don't get, Boone."

"Don't feel bad. Admitting that you don't know can move you forward."

"The wire. Is the assailant wearing gloves? Wouldn't this hurt his hands or fingers?"

Ed spoke up. "A garrotte. Wooden pegs or something to turn on the ends. Make them take the pressure."

"Could be." Boone adjusted one suspender that had twisted his belly. "I'd vote for thick gloves. Gardening ones."

Holly's heart sank. "You can get those anywhere. But wouldn't they be too clumsy? The fine motor movements would be impeded."

He met her gaze with his wise old oyster eyes, pouches below from years in the trenches. "Maybe one will turn up in the site search. The wire, the gloves, what we find at the autopsy. With just two out of three, we'll be halfway to an arrest."

"Only halfway? That's depressing." In dramas, cases passed from beginning to end within an hour on screen. But she knew that weeks or months could go by. Normally the accused headed to another state on day one. And when he or she was brought in, the interrogations were almost comical. Holly loved the way the detectives told the killers to "man up," using the stereotype against them. Women seemed to do better at this kind of soft persuasion. Tears would flow down the faces of young criminals in Miami, Nashville, or Dallas.

"Cases like this where the victim probably doesn't know the killer are a bitch to solve. If you want justice every time, stick to crime novels." Ed had gone back to his notes and been finishing up a page as he stood nearby. He looked at his watch with a world-weary expression. "You're free and clear to go back to business as usual, corporal. A late lunch is better than none. Sometimes I miss those good old days when I went home and waved goodbye to work at five on the dot," said Ed.

Holly walked out behind Boone. He hadn't been this incapacitated since they'd met. He'd be in a lot of pain tonight, but he needed the money. Regular cheques from his small cocktail of pensions went to his late wife's extended family in India. When he turned sixty-five soon he'd be eligible for another five hundred a month for the Old Age Security. "A girl had to die. That's a sad way to force action on that paper fragment," she said as they walked back down the path slowly at a slug's pace.

"It's a real long shot. And you know something else, too, don't you?" His voice left little doubt in the possibilities.

"You mean that it might happen again? And soon?"

"Exactly. You're starting to think like me. The first time was a quirky assault. This time, it's goodnight, nurse. The papers will be full of it. It's going to be a rare woman who goes out on her own until there's an arrest." He put a hand on her shoulder in a fatherly way. That he'd never mentioned having kids didn't mean he had none. Many men were like that. Women couldn't wait to tell you about their brood.

"I don't want to think that we'll meet again over this ... or worse."

"Small thin piece of paper, you say? How big?"

She picked up a piece of debris from the path. A fragment of peat or shard of wood about the size of a quarter of her small fingernail. "Like this."

Boone gave her a cautious smile and winced as he navigated a rock in the path. "Cases have been solved with less."

As they passed Lindsay's tent, she stopped, something she hadn't been able to do on arriving. It was a weighty old canvas model. The boys had probably helped Lindsay lug it to the beach, showing off their muscles. Had it had been for decades in the Nanaimo family, part of happy outings? They'd probably process it on the long-shot notion that Lindsay might have been initially assaulted there. She knelt on the rough boards of the platform like a suppliant, opened the flap and peered in. As Mike had said, it looked like someone had merely stepped out for a moment. Laid out were a sleeping bag, pillow, pile of clothes, jacket, a candy bar and chips, bottle of water, presumed barf bag clumsily folded, and a lop-eared stuffed pink rabbit. A peppermint smell from an empty bottle of schnapps made her nauseous. The reek of vomit was strong. She gave a slight cough.

"It's pretty foul," Mike said, coming up behind her.

"The team will do what it needs to do."

"That rabbit," he said. "It plays 'Easter Parade.' Andy, she calls it. Her good luck charm. She always brought it to class and left it on the desk during tests."

Luck ran out, Holly thought with a tug on her heart. Funny how college students were little kids inside. To her horror, he reached for it and pushed a lever. "In your Easter bonnet," a fluty voice sang.

"Put that down, please," she asked as heads turned their way.

CHAPTER NINETEEN

AS THEY FINALLY PULLED out of the parking lot, Holly turned to Ashley. "I almost forgot. What is that thing under the seat?" She'd placed it in the passenger wheel well.

A cat-in-the-cream look sneaked across Ashley's face, and her tones were matter of fact. "Don't you have one of these? It's a sound-wave lie detector."

"Don't be ridiculous. There's no such thing." Was the woman completely mad or merely immature? The Rube Goldberg device was made of metal, oblong, and had an opening with a flap and a small antenna. Homemade? Or an old eight-track player duded up?

"That's what you think. We used them all the time in the interior. It's activated by this cool buzzer." From her pocket she pulled a small electronic device. "When we're questioning someone and think he's lying, we press this button and ..." A *BRRRRTTTT* sound filled the car. Ashley laughed. "When he asks what the noise is, we tell him about our little pal. You can't imagine how many fools fold and 'fess up. Do you want to borrow it?"

"Oh my god," Holly said. "I'm going to pretend I never heard this. And don't let me see it again."

Back at the office, Holly made sure that Ed's constable got the scrap of paper. He promised to feed it into the crime machine as quickly as possible. At least Ashley hadn't embarrassed them, as far as she knew. She promised to fax her notes on the vehicles in the lot to Ed as well. She'd also turned back a dozen cars, according to Harold. "That little girl's a keeper," he'd told Holly. "She's gonna make a damn fine officer." Ashley had seemed almost subdued at the rare praise. But she'd taken in every word Holly had told her on the way back to the detachment and even asked a few intelligent questions.

In hours Sombrio Beach would return to its quiet peace. Everyone would have to be interviewed, perhaps more than once in Mike's case since he'd admitted a fondness for Lindsay. She's been so surprised years ago to learn the mind-blowing fact that witnesses could lie. Even in the innocent, the instinct for self-protection was powerful. And what of the other sets of campers down the beach? That was Ed's problem now. Problem was, there were just too few people around. The miracle witness was not going to save the day.

Her father wasn't home yet due to Shogun's first agility lesson in Saanich. He was joining a group of twelve rookies, probably nearly all women. At least the dog had distracted him from his consuming passion for popular culture. A living interest was healthy. She never wanted to see him as downcast as he had been after her mother had vanished. Once or twice coming home for a weekend, she checked his medicine cabinet in case it contained anything that might tempt him to end to his pain. He'd confessed that he had tried a round of anti-depressants, but they'd made him sleepy. Even a year or two later, the bottle of little blue amitriptyline pills had the same three-quarter level as before.

Just before her father was due to arrive, she followed the instructions he had left for hamburger steak, mashed potatoes, and canned peas. He had the meat nicely mixed with chopped onion, parsley, and the miracle ingredient, ketchup. She almost turned to an easy package of gravy mix but knew he would have suspected the travesty, so she grabbed a couple of cubes of bouillon. Surely they had that in the thirties.

From downstairs in the crawlspace wine cellar, she selected a bottle of tank-car red and poured herself a healthy glass after setting out Shogun's chow. To stave off her own pangs, she peeled a banana but left it half-finished. The idea of eating was more attractive than the reality, and the banana reminded her of Maddie. How was she doing?

Then she heard her father crunch up the drive in his toy car. He'd survived another harrowing trip on that highway to hell or Victoria, whichever came first.

His attaché case hit the floor by the closet as Shogun followed at his heels and rushed to his food bowl. Hanging up his overcoat and coming into the kitchen, Norman wore a more casual outfit more for golfing. Plus fours, knickers, and a shirt and sweater vest with a bow tie. Much of his wardrobe came from Value Village downtown, which appealed to his frugal nature as much as his demand for period clothes. How many other men ironed white handkerchiefs once a week and put on garters for their socks?

"Smells great. I taught you well. Pardon me while I change. Shogun was the star of his class, but that teeter looks like it will be tough. And I have more good news."

About Chipper? She realized that she hadn't thought of him once since she'd left Sombrio Beach. Mulling over the murder had taken all her attention. "Dad, wait, I ..."

But he was already up the circular staircase and the squealing plumbing announced his entrance into the shower. Ever the food hound, Shogun was polishing his bowl with his tongue and pushing it around the kitchen.

After lighting the wall fireplace, Holly sat with the wine in the solarium, a glass for her dad on the coffee table. She had hit the CD, one compromise for him. Vinyl 78s were not only in short supply, they skipped and had to be changed every three minutes. Needles were difficult to source, too. Irving Berlin's "Say it Isn't So" seemed an emblematic title for the day.

She sipped slowly. Either he was getting better at wine-making or she was losing her taste buds. Then, as "What a Diff'rence a Day Made" came on, Norman strutted down the stairs. "Little girl of mine, Leo Buckstaff and his daughter Samantha aren't going to be causing *any* trouble *anymore* for *anyone*." He struck a dramatic pose. His elocution style brought spectators to his classes for key events like the evacuation of Dunkirk or Kennedy's assassination.

He patted her head and cupped her chin in his hand, looking for a reaction. Her eyes were pooling with tears, and she turned away, but a sniff gave her up.

"What's the matter? Didn't you hear me? Are those tears of joy, I hope? I haven't even given you the lovely specifics. It's very juicy."

She'd been waiting for this moment, when Chipper would be exonerated. Why not let the man tell her the good news? "It's not Chipper, but something else. You go first."

He drank deeply of the grapey purple wine, in another life a fine dye, and smacked his lips. Then he brushed a dust mote from his smoking jacket with velvet lapels. "Your old man has come to your rescue. I can get a signed affidavit from another faculty member of little Sam lying through her teeth to secure As in his English course. He knows someone in drama who says the same thing. With luck and a quick hearing, she will be out before Christmas for academic misconduct, perhaps even attempted blackmail, and have to continue her education in a third-world country. As for her scoundrel of a father, we are stuck with him. With that bloated administrator's salary and the hide of a buffalo, he'll probably never retire."

She nodded, firming up a smile. A grim tableaux of Lindsay and her Easter bunny kept forcing its way across her mental screen. "I'm proud of you, Dad. This looks like the break we've been waiting for. When will you know for sure?"

"The assistant professor is in Edmonton, but he'll be back next week. His office mate told me all about Samantha. Is that fast work on my part or is it not?" He beamed at her and smoothed back his hair. Did he take a picture of Leslie Howard with him to Barb's Barber Shop every month?

The glass doors of the fireplace were reflecting a cosy blaze. He wasn't even complaining that she had lit the propane earlier than January. Maybe he was mellowing. "I wish my news were good. I had a very bad day."

She told him about the murder, and a palpable gloom came over the room.

Norman was not an overly demonstrative man, but he shook his head and a furrow appeared between his patrician eyebrows. "I see why you're upset, then. Very tragic and unexpected. Completely senseless. I couldn't do your job in a thousand years. But as you say, someone has to."

She exhaled long and low. "I'm not staging a pity party for myself. I realized when I signed on that there would be times like this. Memories I wouldn't want to take home. But aside from a child dying, I can't imagine anything worse. And if the two park incidents are connected, you know what that means for this area."

"But you're not on the case, as it were. You told me that as a …"

"As a corporal, yes. Small potatoes in a big stew. Do you see that my limitations make me all the more frustrated? I'm not an inspector. So no matter what happens, I have to stand by and…. At least I got them to look at a scrap I picked up from that attack at French." She gave him the details.

"No kidding! You have your mother's eagle eye, all right." He drained the glass and reached for the bottle. "Then we must hope that the upper echelon does its duty as quickly as possible. Meanwhile, let's drown our sorrows in a beaker or two. What do you think of this colour, then? Rubiate, I'd say. Is that a word?"

Hangovers were bad enough, she thought, but this was a wine that warned you to stop at one. "Sure, pops. Tell me one of your Joe Miller jokes. The one about the parrots and the rosary."

He began, and was getting to the part where one parrot said, "Throw away your beads, Harry."

The phone rang, and Holly got up to answer it. A robotic notification to her father from the Vancouver Island Regional Library that the one copy of *How to Win Friends and Influence People* had arrived. Dale Carnegie's Depression bestseller was still in print. As she hung up, she noticed that the answering machine was blinking. With all that was going on, she hadn't even checked. She hit the play button, which sent the message across the kitchen into the solarium.

A man's voice said, "We're trying to reach Bonnie Martin. This is Rob Dales from the Black Ball Ferry Office. We have something she left on board. Maybe quite some time ago. Can you please call us at ..."

Holly gasped and sat down heavily on the breakfast bar stool, her feet dangling like a kid's. "What the hell?" she said. When she tried to call the number, the hours of operation were over.

"'Some time ago?' Is this a horrible joke?" Norman stood rigidly, his face draining of colour and his hand shaking.

Holly went down the stairs and put her arms around his tall, lean frame. Just a hint of a stoop beginning to remind her that he was beginning his sixties. As a rule, they weren't very demonstrative. Sometimes she missed her mother's hugs.

"Too late for tonight. I'll go down first thing in the morning. It must have her ID. She never carried a purse, just that tote bag."

CHAPTER TWENTY

UNWILLING TO WAIT UNTIL after work, Holly broke personal speed records, arriving in Victoria the next morning the moment the Black Ball Ferry office opened at eight. The Inner Harbour was the crown jewel of the city, with the dowager Empress Hotel on one side, the parliament buildings on the other along with the pink granite Hotel Grand Pacific. A horse carriage clopped its lazy way down the streets to pick up breakfast fares. She was lucky to find a parking spot in front of the newly refurbished CPR coliseum next door. Cars had already started to pull into line for the nine o'clock sailing. The old M.V. Coho had been commissioned before Holly was born, unlike the splashy new B.C. fleet, and she remembered bygone days when her parents took her to the States for the weekend on the same boat. If only she could turn back time.

Inside the office, she was directed to the lost and found, where a middle-aged woman greeted her, plopping onto the counter something she thought never to see again. A sturdy open canvas bag embroidered with a German shepherd. Seventeen-year-old Holly had ordered it from the L.L.Bean catalogue for her mother's birthday. Their old shep had passed on the year before to tears from everyone, but with Holly off to college soon, her mother's travelling, and her father's job, it was no time to get another dog.

Too informal for a brief case or an attaché, Bonnie loved the tote because she could toss everything into it, including the jerky and apples she preferred for an on-the-run lunch. She kept papers in it along with her wallet, comb and brush, tissues, and the "kitchen sink," as Norman joked.

Holly ran her fingers over it in reverence. But it had no secrets to whisper. It was empty. She looked in question at the woman, a pleasant faced grandmother with her family in a picture on the desk nearby. "I don't understand. How did you know where to call? How long has this been here? It's my mother's, you see, and she's been missing for a very long time."

Em, as her nametag read, blinked at the news as her reading glasses bobbed on a chain around her neck. "Oh my dear. I'm so sorry," she said, as she reached under a fold in the bottom of the bag. "The bag was found fallen behind a shelf when we did a major renovation here last week. It could have been there for years. We don't keep records. People usually claim their belongings soon after they figure out that it was left on the ferry. We've mailed things all over the country. Even to Europe and Asia."

"Yes, but …"

Em gave a proud smile. "I just started working here last month. I'm guessing that it *seemed* empty at first. But when I lifted this fold on the bottom, I found an address." She showed Holly the small paper label for envelopes. It had her mother's name along with her address. They had tried four Martins in Sooke before leaving the message.

Holly showed her RCMP ID to claim the bag and signed off on a waiver. "And there's no one here who could say when it came in? No log or anything?"

Em seemed embarrassed. "Oh my. Let's see. You could try old Bob Filman. He retired last year after forty years on the job. He lives over in Port Angeles." The Black Ball was an American company, so that stood to reason. The line had been started when clipper ships crossed the oceans.

Holly left a message on her father's answering machine at the office. He had told her to call immediately upon collecting the bag. She pulled into traffic and began the long haul west. At least she was travelling against the rush-hour flow. She took Government Street and veered up at Hillside to Douglas. The bag sat beside her, mute and faithful. Holly reached over and touched it as if it were a live thing. Bonnie was never without it. If she'd lost it before she'd disappeared, they would have heard. But what the hell was it doing en route to Washington State? Did the ferry keep records of cars? If she'd boarded on foot, Bonnie had vanished just before passports became mandatory to enter the U.S.

Assuming again. It made no sense at all that her mother had left it two hundred miles south of her last known call from Campbell River way up island. And yet the bag asserted a palpability impossible to ignore.

A canvas witness to her past had driven the thoughts of Lindsay out of her mind. A gravel truck gave her the horn when a light turned green and she didn't move. Holly snapped back to the present. With communication so instant, soon the murder would hit the headlines from Victoria to Vancouver to Toronto, and the public pressure would be in full force. This was no drug deal gone wrong, a fatal beating outside a night-club, the fringes of a minor gang war. Not since the beating and drowning death of a Victoria teenager by a vicious mob from her high school had the climate been so incendiary. Years later, the unrepentant female ringleader remained in jail.

At the office by nine, Holly read some online editorials on the *Times Colonist* website: "Paradise Lost for Island Women?" Angry citizens attacked the police for their lack of quick results. Had they no idea what rainforest meant at a crime scene? "Not even one person of interest?" a mother asked. One suggested that the RCMP was losing its effectiveness as a policing unit, that it belonged to a frontier era long gone and buried. The magical island was in deep trouble, despite the smug satisfaction that separated it from the rest of the country. From a national treasure to a national disgrace.

"Listen to this," she said to Ann, feeling the heat across her face as she read. "How long must we wait for justice? All over the world we are known for our natural beauties and our peaceful and progressive lifestyle. Every possible resource should be marshalled and no expense spared until women can feel safe outdoors again."

"Radio, TV, all the sources have picked up the story. The panic is spreading beyond the parks now that the scenes are linked. At UVic and Camosun, campus safewalk programs are being pushed to their limits. Other groups plan to picket at the legislature. The outdoor stores are stocking pepper spray." Ann pulled out a tissue and polished her reading glasses as the errant sun peeked through the window.

"That's a mess waiting to happen. It's almost impossible to control where that stuff goes. Remember that photographer airlifted to bear country who started spraying himself while he was in a helicopter?" A can of OC, pepper spray, rode on her belt, but she'd never had occasion to use it. Studies showed that a "velcro effect" operated with OC in that the mere threat was enough to dissuade a subject, at least a rational one.

"One bright spot. They've made an arrest in Langford for those assaults," Ann said. "The radio said that they took a confession from an eighteen-year-old yesterday. Two of the women have ID'd him."

"Can't be the same guy at all. Not the same targets. Not the same method. Plus one was a robbery."

"My neighbour down the hall said that he was thinking of nipping over the border to buy his daughter a 'lady-gun' special for when she works the night shift at the Village Market. I told him he would be in big trouble if he got caught at customs. *Lady gun*. Can you imagine?" She took a two-handed stance with the imaginary weapon turned at ninety degrees, a preposterous pose that usually made them smile. Like most Canadians, Ann and Holly didn't believe that carrying a fire-arm made anyone safer; it just upped the odds of an innocent getting shot in the crossfire. Canada had a very controversial registry too tight for conservatives and too loose for liberals. Though varmint guns, hunting rifles, and shotguns were sold, hand guns and automatic weapons were off the menu.

"What nonsense. Many rapes and attacks are committed in daylight. There's another false sense of security. And watch for the gun nuts to claim that everyone should be armed, even grade schoolers," Holly added.

"What frosts me is that it's the young, educated white women who make the news. Others are considered collateral damage as if they wanted to live in dangerous areas. What have you heard from Ed? My contacts downtown won't even take my calls."

"There's a media blackout. Ed sent that paper scrap to forensics, but I'm not holding my breath. Another of those too-good-to-be true moments. It isn't called a scrap for no reason."

Holly looked at the calendar. It had been over a week since they'd seen or heard from their colleague. "I'm going to call Chipper," she said to Ann, and picked up the office phone, on speaker function. "It's a bad sign that he hasn't contacted us. I'm thinking that he's been told not to, but you'd think …"

A subdued but musical voice answered. Holly had met his parents only once, when Chipper had been hospitalized with minor burns from a brush fire. As an only child, he had a lot of pressure to succeed. "I am sorry, Corporal Holly, but he is working at West Shore."

"When does he usually get off?"

"He used to be home right on time … before all this. Now it's as if he doesn't want to talk to anyone. At the table he is like a ghost. And he is out walking at all hours. Thinking he may see one of those men who have been preying on our women." She choked back a sob.

"We hope'd he might call us." She watched Ann's face slump in the letdown.

"My apologies for my son. I know Chirakumar likes you and Corporal Ann so very much. He calls you his ladies. But he is not at all himself, my lovely boy. I think he has lost many pounds. I can hardly spoon a bite into him. Dessert he doesn't even care to taste. And Diwali is coming. Our happiest time of the year. How can we celebrate when my son is in such trouble?"

Given her pride in her table, that must hurt. "I'm sorry to hear that. We think the world of … Chirakumar. He's a friend as well as a colleague, and we're sick about this."

A sigh came over the speaker phone. "To be very honest, I think he is showing signs of depression. Not eating, not sleeping. A mother knows."

"Did he say when he might get his official hearing?"

"The very formal part, you mean? He has already given testimony twice. I am thinking that this is killing him. Waiting, waiting, waiting. I have been making offerings to Ganesh ever since his happened. It may well take months, he tells me." There was a pause and a sniff. "I am sorry. I must ring off now. Speaking about this distresses me so much, and my husband will be needing his tea. I have worries about him as well. He is not a young man anymore."

Hanging up with her own sigh, Holly traded looks with Ann. The older woman had more faith in the force than Holly did.

A double line parted Ann's eyebrows. "We need to give him a pep talk. Even if he's not supposed to discuss the case. This doesn't sound good. He's way more sensitive than I thought. Men sometimes are, the poor babies."

Minutes later, to their surprise, Boone checked in. "They've completed the autopsy," he said, disappointment in his voice. "No semen, but lots of bruising. Poor kid had a rough time. She might have died during the rape because some of the tissue injuries are ante-mortem."

"Jesus. No good news for us so far."

"There is something. The fingernail scraping might provide some skin cells. That will take a bit longer even if they are rushing it. And of course they could be hers. When someone's cutting off your air supply, your main concern is your own neck."

Chipper would want to hear this. Maybe they should see what happened if they called West Shore. Trying his home in the evening might be the only choice, intrusive or not. A paranoid part of her wondered if his line was tapped. Surely not in Canada. She turned to Ann. "This day is dragging on forever. Ashley should be back from investigating that accident."

A car screeched to a halt outside. Was there any other kind of entrance for the woman? Ashley hadn't learned like Chipper to duck her head when entering the former cottage. Her hat came off, and she turned to grab it.

Ashley had done well at Sombrio. Were they back to square one? Ann folded her hands on her desk. Holly waited for the buzz bomb to land. Now she knew how Londoners felt during the Blitz. "What now?" asked Holly, aware that she was sounding like her own mother.

"I was coming back from investigating a fender bender the other side of Juan de Fuca Road. Went into the bushes for a pee, which was good that I did because ..." Ashley was breathing hard, as if she'd run the last mile. More from excitement than exertion.

"We're not interested in your bathroom habits. Are you saying someone saw you and reported you or something absurd like that?" Holly drummed her fingers on the desk.

"A woman at Sandcut Beach came out of the forest to the road and hailed me. Said she'd been raped. Choked with a wire. I took a brief statement, but it made more sense to ..."

Both women stood up. "A wire?" they said in unison.

French, Sombrio, now Sandcut. All spots on the coast. Two was a coincidence. Three was a pattern. Holly's spine felt cut off at the neck. But a rape, not a murder. Her mind did cartwheels for a long fraction of a second before she snapped back into the moment.

"Where is she? How badly was she injured?" Despite her concern for the girl, the double-edged thought hit her that they might at last have a witness. They hadn't let out the information about the wire, only that the women had been strangled. Maddie Mattoon didn't seem the type to talk about her attack. Inspector Crew would have warned her. But the five students with Lindsay.... Odds were good that they had mentioned it, even if cautioned. There was also the crazy possibility that it was a copycat crime. Some of the cleverest killers, if that was the right word, sandwiched their personal victim between or after two other hapless victims to misdirect the police.

"She's not beaten up. I'm not that stupid. It seemed better to bring her here. I took the initiative. She begged for a few minutes to pull herself together, so I came in here first." She shot them a defiant look. "I rolled with the flow. Sometimes you have to. That's part of ..."

Ann broke in. "We don't need a protocol lesson. Get to the point."

Ashley gulped back a breath and cast a look behind her through the window to where the Impala sat, dust motes still roiling in the air. She had probably driven like a demon. "She seems okay, considering what she's been through. You know what it's like down there, and I couldn't get a connection. Stupid fucking radio system. One of these days, someone's gonna really suffer."

Holly traded glances with Ann. It was as if the criminal had found the weak underbelly of the force distribution. But something was a bit different. "The timing is getting closer. First it's two weeks. Now it's two days."

Sandcut Beach, unlike the more established spots, was merely a slice in the forest where a person could walk to the ocean in minutes. It was part of the JDF Trail, but also a popular place for picnics. To the untutored eye of a driver, the unmarked entrance looked like a pull-off. But locals knew parking meant an attraction and kept information to themselves. A record-breaking Douglas fir, a fishing spot, a waterfall. Someone could be in and out in less than ten minutes. Any camping would be purely off the cuff. No sites. No registration. No drinking water. No toilets. Nature in the raw, like purists preferred.

"EMTs." Ann picked up the phone. At least it wasn't a matter of life and death.

Ashley gulped back a breath. "Um, I did crease the fender a little bit as I was leaving. A stump came out of nowhere and …"

"Never mind about the car. What did she say?" If Ashley had blown this one, conducted an impromptu interview that had upset the girl, she would be finding yet another secondment if not a new uniform as a security guard at Wal-Mart.

Ashley had her hands on her hips. Then she shifted and rubbed her neck with one hand. "She was pretty hysterical, but I calmed her down. Gave her some water. Told her to breathe. There are some marks on her neck. A sore shoulder. Nothing too serious."

"What did the marks on the neck look like?" Holly asked, but remembered that Ashley had seen neither victim. They needed to get back out to the girl, but at this stage, any tiny detail might be critical.

"I didn't look real carefully, but I didn't see them at Sombrio, remember? It's just so similar, though, don't you think?" She scratched behind her ear absentmindedly. "Still …" Her voice trailed off.

Ann gave the contact information, hung up, and made a note. "If you think rape isn't serious, try it sometime. I'm going to put on a fresh pot of tea. If she's close to shock, she might take some honey in it. Have a little empathy for a change. We're going to start thinking that *you're* a sociopath." She went into the lunchroom for the kettle. The sound of running water reached the room.

Ashley had opened her mouth, but closed it as Ann left. Then she flicked at a finger. Her purple designer nails had fresh stars and glitter, an indulgence hard to understand in an active profession. "But listen. You won't believe it. She claims that she can give us identification. She saw the guy. It was daylight."

Holly nearly gave her a hug, despite her patent dislike of the constable. "Saw him? All right! Maybe we have a break." The fact that the attack was carried out in daylight didn't mesh, but maybe the rapist had gotten careless. Cases like the Zodiac Killer rapist came to mind. The BTK murderer. Why was Ashley being so blasé? A posturing?

Ashley reached onto her desk for an energy drink, popped the top and slugged it back, stifling a burp.

"But what's this about her 'claiming' that she saw the guy? Why would you use language like that? To her? That's insulting."

Ashley shrugged. "I know better. Give me some credit, even if you don't like me."

Holly refused to rise to the passive-aggressive bait. "Did you make her nervous? Feed her any information? You should have called in for an inspector who knows the procedures." Interviewing was a skill which took years to learn.

Ashley shoved her large hands into her pockets. "I told you. The damn radio wasn't working. It was just as far to come here than to go to Rennie."

There was no detachment in Port Renfrew, only a fire station with limited first-aid care. Maybe the woman had a point. "Okay. She's had the time she requested. Let's get her into my office," Holly said.

What was the matter with Ashley? This was what they had been waiting for. This was no time to sound so casual and skeptical, as if she was putting the girl on trial. Was Ashley still pouting about the reprimand about Trey? Talk about thin skin. A paranoid type they didn't need in the force, nor a diva who made everything about her.

As they left the office, Holly rapped herself upside the head. "What's her name?" Being friendly and understanding would be important. The girl needed support and affirmation from a team ready to roll. They had already left her alone for an unconscionable time. Holly felt adrenaline charge her veins. *Calm down. Do it by the book. Cases have been lost by poor timing. The girl is probably a basket case waiting for you to get your butt in gear.*

"Ellen something. I didn't write it down." Ashley gave herself a rap upside the head. "Damn. I wasn't thinking straight. Just wanted to get back here."

Ellen Hughes was huddled in the back of the patrol car with a clean pillow and a soft blue blanket they kept in a tote in the trunk along with stuffed animals to comfort children. Points to Ashley for making her comfortable. Holly opened the door and bent to her level. The girl's Madonna-like oval face was streaked with dirt and tears. Holly groaned inwardly. No tissue in the cruiser? Chipper took care of those details.

"Hello, Ellen. Please call me Holly. I'm glad you're safe. Can you come in and talk to us now? You can stay in my office until the EMTs arrive. How about some coffee or tea, or maybe a cold drink?" Ann would be useful with her experience as a mother. An only child who never babysat, Holly didn't feel she had a rapport with children. Then she chided herself. *You are in charge. Act like it. And this isn't a child, it's a woman, despite her doll-like size.*

"Thanks, I don't think I feel very well. I'm kind of sore. You know? Down there?" She squirmed apologetically, her voice rising at the end of each phrase as if seeking validation. "But maybe a diet Coke?"

Holly leaned forward and put out an arm. "Here, let me ..."

"Thanks. I can walk okay." With a wince, Ellen got out and moved slowly toward the cottage, as if even breathing hurt.

Holly remembered what Boone had told her about the tears on Lindsay's vagina. She gave the tiny woman credit for courage in the face of horror. That she wasn't a puddle of sobs was amazing.

Ellen leaned into Holly's guiding arm with a look in her soft caramel eyes which would melt steel. "It was so beautiful

at the beach. It didn't … I've been there so many times.…"
Then she swallowed and squeezed her eyes together. Obviously
she was holding herself together with mental duct tape.

As they went up the steps, Ashley held the door. Holly
motioned to her, using her head. Catching the drift, Ashley
took the girl's other arm, and they lifted her up the last two
steps. Beside the taller woman, Ellen looked like a broken
grade-schooler.

Ann came forward with a tissue box and gave it to Holly.
"Shouldn't be long now. The Major Crimes unit just left. Is
there anyone else I can notify for you, Ellen? Someone who
could come right out, or meet you at the General later? Your
parents or a relative or friend?" Holly swallowed back her
own reproof. Why hadn't she thought of that? Of course the
young woman would need support ASAP. Ann's instincts
were golden.

Ellen put a hand on the wall for support, then pulled the
blanket closer and shivered although the room was close to
baking in the late morning sun. "My parents live in Abbotsford.
They'll be at work. My boyfriend Rudy, he has a townhouse
on Kaltasin Road." She gave them his cell number, and Ann
quickly wrote it down. "He was supposed to come with me on
a picnic this morning. I had it all packed and everything, but he
had to take care of his aunt. She's not really with it." She gave a
whirly gesture with her finger and her temple. "Poor old lady."
Her nose was still running. Holly offered her a tissue, and she
took a wad.

As they all stood there in the crowded foyer, Holly revised
her plans. The lunchroom had a small, duct-taped leather
couch. More spacious than her office and just as private. "In
here, please, Ellen," she said. "There's more room."

The girl followed. Barely five feet tall and one hundred
pounds soaking wet, she sat on the couch and trembled. Her
complexion was light tan, eyes slightly almond-shaped, hint-
ing an Oriental connection. British Columbia had a high percentage of Asians, railroad workers in the nineteenth century

up to post-Hong Kong refugees. Her throat had the same red ligature marks, darker than Maddie's but less serious than the broken skin and bruises on Lindsay. "Is regular Coke okay? Or we can make tea."

"The pop's fine. My throat is sore where he … his hands … he was so strong." She touched it gently and swallowed again, then took the can Holly gave her from the mini-fridge. Chipper was the only one who drank pop, and he hated artificial sweeteners. What was he doing now? He must be worried half out of his mind and bored the rest of the time. But here was an eye witness. As soon as Ellen was gone, Holly was going to contact him if she had to play phone tag all day.

Ellen took a few sips, grimacing. Her nose twitched at the bubbles and she wiped her upper lip. "Thanks. I'm a bit shaky."

"No wonder, with the shock. You're doing great. I'm proud of you." Those last four one-syllable words were what everyone wanted to hear, from babyhood to the grave. Simple, but they hit home.

A nod from Ellen. She slipped off her sandals and eased her legs up onto the couch. "Ouch. Gosh, my back hurts, too. He was pressing me against those rocks on the beach." Holly moved forward to tuck the blanket around her feet. At least Ellen wasn't crying. Getting information out of someone distracted and hysterical was a nightmare.

Holly said, "While we're waiting, I'm going to ask you a few questions. Not many, I promise. It's important that you tell your story as soon as possible, while it's fresh in your mind, even though it's hard. And you might remember more details later." She opened her notebook, timed and dated the page. With the third incident, she was getting her language letter perfect. But the fates that had inflicted this much pain on three women were teaching her hard lessons.

"Do you think that this is the same crazy man everyone's been talking about? It was on the news again last night. They haven't found him, have they?" Ellen asked. She blew her nose and balled up the tissue.

"I'm afraid that he's still out there." Holly tried to think ahead for the victim. A whirlwind was about to break loose. When they heard about this attack, Ed and his crew would be all over the poor girl. Did they have a female inspector in the area? She went to the door, and before closing it, heard Ann say on the phone, "Mr. Gemmell, we'd like you to come out to give Ellen your support. Family and friends are important now." How had she opened? Your girlfriend has been raped? It wouldn't be the first time that a rape had broken up a relationship. Sometimes it was the fault of the insensitive man, and other times the woman couldn't return to normal, even after years.

Mouthing "just a sec" to Ellen, Holly slipped out of the lunchroom for a moment and made eye contact with Ann, raising a brow as a question.

"He'll be right here. Thank God. He was taking his aunt to the library in Sooke," she whispered to Holly, who gave her a nod. "Sounds worried as hell. How's she doing?"

"Calm enough. She's tough for her size. I'm just starting to question her." She began to turn, then said, "I hope Ed's coming. For all I know, Russell Crew is still out of town. It's important to be consistent if you want to see the patterns," she said.

Ann snapped her fingers. "I asked for him specifically. Did you know I could read minds?"

CHAPTER TWENTY-ONE

RETURNING TO HER OWN battered oak armchair, Holly floated a reassuring but concerned smile to Ellen. The girl sipped at her soda, gripping it with tiny hands, the nails bitten. It was difficult not to give her a hug and say, "There, there." Almost as an afterthought, a tear trickled down her cheek. Everyone took a crisis differently. Some fell apart immediately, some later, some bounced back and forth, and some never cracked. Ellen gave another sniff. "Sorry. This is stupid. I should be grateful to be sitting alive and talking to you. That other girl I read about...."

"I'll just keep you another minute. Then you can close your eyes and rest until the EMTs come. And Rudy's on his way," she said. "The inspector in charge will talk to you, too." She kept her voice upbeat, coaxing without prodding. The earlier the information, the better. Women might want to forget as much as possible, and small wonder. But to be alive and well, wasn't that the point? She couldn't imagine the strength of that Utah girl who had been abducted for months by religious zealots, forced to live in the desert and submit to continual assaults and brainwashing. Now back with her family, she had become a spokesperson and inspiration. One in a million. Things rarely worked like that.

Ellen's voice quivered along with her pointed chin. Her long auburn hair pulled into a ponytail stuck out awkwardly. "Honestly, I just want to forget this. It's like a nightmare." She touched her neck again and her eyes radiated despair. "My necklace. My sister gave it to me. It was pink coral. We got it in Disneyland on the last trip she could make."

"The last trip?" It helped to let Ellen know that someone who cared was listening.

"She died of cystic fibrosis when she was only sixteen." Her eyes rimmed over again and moaned. "Sometimes I wish it could have been me. Mom tells me not to say that. We really miss her."

Holly nodded in sympathy. The wire method. Those two other trophies taken from Maddie and Lindsay. Everything was coming together. "Possibly it will turn up at the scene. The important point is that you're okay."

Ellen said, "Sorry. I'm being stupid. You're right. It just meant so much."

"I felt that way about a raven pendant my mother wore. She's ... not with us anymore, so I understand." Holly levelled eyes at her. She wanted to get right to the crime, but maybe groundwork would help the girl begin. "You're very lucky. You must concentrate on that."

Ellen's voice narrowed into a defensive whine. "Tell me about it. I was so totally dumb to go to the beach alone, but I've always seen people there. I mean it's not like it's usually deserted or anything." She finished the Coke and put the empty can on the table, twisting her fingers. "Rudy will be here soon. I must look a mess. Do you have a brush or something I could borrow? I could put on some makeup. I have my purse." Beside her was a cumbersome shoulder bag the size of a baby camel. She was clinging to it like a life raft.

Holly found the disconnect between Ellen's preoccupation with her appearance and what had happened to her strange, but she was hardly material for the catwalk herself. Holly gave her face and hair a few minutes each morning, letting her youth and health lead. "Not until the physical examination is over, Ellen. Rudy will understand. You're strong and smart and beautiful, and what you say is going to help catch this man so that no other woman will have anything to fear."

"I grew up in Vancouver and hated the big city. When I first crossed on the ferry, I fell in love with the island. And now …"

"A lot of us feel like that, Ellen. It's a special place. I love the wilderness, too." She made a point of using the girl's name to personalize the interview and establish rapport.

She figured that she had perhaps twenty minutes before the others arrived. "So tell me how the day started. One step, then another. We have plenty of time. This will make it easier when you have to go over the story again." *If not three more times. Poor kid.*

Taking this as a cue to provide her biography, Ellen said that she lived in a small downstairs flat in Esquimalt, but she had been staying with her boyfriend Rudy this week. He was a Shaw Communications manager in the city. "Rudy's great aunt lives in Sooke on Eaglecrest Road. He got his training in Manitoba and worked in Winnipeg until last year."

The girl seemed proud of her boyfriend, so Holly let her veer off topic. "I was in The Pas myself. And Eaglecrest isn't far from where I live now," Holly said.

"Her husband died last year," she continued. "I mean he was pretty old, over seventy, and she's been having a tough time alone. Rudy goes to see her once a week, helps with the groceries. He's such a sweetheart. His mom in Calgary made him promise to keep an eye on her. He does some yard work. Takes her for medical appointments. Sometimes he even makes dinner."

A man not afraid of domestic chores. Rudy sounded like a keeper. His support would be important for Ellen. "Go on. So you went to the beach?"

"He dropped me off. Only for a few hours. I took some fruit and drinks. A paperback." She opened the purse and pulled out one of the latest vampire sagas.

"Did you see any cars when he let you off?" The lot at Sandcut on West Coast Road had very little room.

"He was going to come back for me at noon and take me to Point No Point for a late lunch. I love the view, and the food's great." Holly had enjoyed a few meals there herself at the only restaurant between Sooke and Port Renfew.

"So he let you off around…?"

"Ten." She turned to Holly with a satisfied look. Then she paddled her fingers on the sofa, gathering her memory. "There was one car at the parking spot. It was a Honda. One of the little old ones. A Civic, I think. Red. Or that burgundy colour. It had a child's car seat in it, I think. But I can't be sure."

The child's seat part sounded odd, but maybe it would be a clincher.

"And the licence?"

"I wasn't paying any attention." She put her head in her hands. "I was thinking how nice the beach would be … and about our lunch coming up. How could I know…?" Her voice trailed off.

Holly's throat was tightening, and she took a deep breath. The last thing she wanted to do was make the girl feel responsible for her fate. "That's totally normal. If I weren't a police officer, I wouldn't think twice about it." TV shows often featured idiot savants who remembered entire telephone book pages. The average person had trouble registering the state or province of a licence unless it was unusual, like Yukon's polar bear shape or Florida's orange. The many varieties, even in B.C., were making things even tougher.

"I took the path to the beach. It's cute where people have made the big old stumps into little goblins by putting stones in the axe cuts. I had a towel to lie on and my book. Silly and romantic but a good fast read. I work at the library downtown as an assistant, so I get first pick."

Way too much information, even if Ellen seemed to need to talk. Holly tried a prompt. "Was the beach deserted, or did you see anyone?"

The girl's pale brown eyes took a rubbing with her small fist. The sclera was reddened from weeping. "I just lay down and started to read. It was so beautiful and sunny. We don't often have days like that after the rainy season starts. Then it gets too cold for me."

"I know. Go on." Not many knew that the island had regular monsoons starting in October, building to January, then tapering until daffodils bloomed in March.

The girl took another drink. "I missed breakfast, so I finished the fruit and juice. There was no wind. The waves were lapping at the beach. I got drowsy."

That sounded almost poetic, Holly thought, considering Ellen's ordeal. They were coming to the tricky part. The key information was here. Holly could feel her heart beating in an anticipating dance. What she was going to hear made the difference between an arrest and a case which might grow cold. Ellen gave a shudder and started to cry.

"Take a breath. I know this is hard. You're doing great. Really," Holly said. "Do you need a bathroom break?" She couldn't even let her wash her face. Trace like hairs or DNA could be anywhere. Or nowhere. Those traces from Lindsay's fingernails were all they had, and it might be her own skin. Then there was that stupid paper scrap. Probably another blind alley.

"There was a sudden coolness, like a shadow in front of the sun. I thought I heard someone move over the rocks. Then I felt hands coming around my neck, and I tried to scream."

"Steady now. Go on."

"I couldn't even breathe. He got some kind of rope or cord around my neck. Then he pushed me into the bushes ... where ... where ..."

Holly had been holding her breath. She coughed as her stress meter jumped ten points. The word had to be said. The elephant in the corner of the room woke up. "He raped you. Is that correct?" Holly said the words in an almost clinical way.

Ellen nodded, staring out their one tiny window. Her little doll eyes opened and closed. How old was she? Holly had forgotten to ask. Twenty at the most? And working already. Did she have plans for marriage, college, or both? At least she would have the chance, unlike Lindsay.

"Did you see him?" *One question at a time. Don't confuse or rush her.*

The voice turned hard, as if it were gaining strength at the idea of justice, or was it revenge? The muscles at the sides of her mouth tightened into resolve as she choked out the words. "I sure did. I'll never forget him as long as I live. That face is burned into my brain. He was right in front of me." She hugged herself for protection. "He was so heavy. God, I thought it would never end. It might have been less than a minute. I have a feeling that he didn't last long, if you know what I mean."

Her attacker was at least six feet four, Ellen said with a decisive tone. "A bit taller than my boyfriend. A lot younger. Rudy is thirty." As for other distinguishing features, he had a goatee, one of those special ones made by a razor. Holly had seen that style in a hundred *People* magazines. Ellen couldn't pinpoint the colour of his eyes, just that they were dark, either black or brown. His hair was dark brown, medium cut, kind of smushed up in the middle. His neck trimmed. A slight citrus aftershave masking body odor. "That smell made me sick. He pushed something over my face, a ball cap maybe, but I saw anyway. He wasn't very muscular, more wiry. Not fat at all. His skin looked pockmarked. Like he'd had acne." She paused for a moment. "Do you think that being ugly made him do this? I mean we're not supposed to talk like that, but …"

"Did your clothes get torn?" She couldn't see much of what the girl was wearing.

"My board shorts. They had an elastic waist. He pulled them off. Ripped my panties." She gave an ironic laugh. "I guess they're still there. On the beach."

Or perhaps taken as a grim souvenir like the necklace, though collecting clothing was not part of the original M.O. How could you secure a scene with one or two people, attend to the victim, and comb the area for clues with no staff and no communications? Evidence "gone with the wind."

"We'll be sending someone back to collect whatever they can find on the beach. How far were you from where the path meets the ocean?"

"Real close. I wasn't there to beachcomb. Just to the right as you come down."

"Do you recall what he was …"

"Wearing? I sure do. Cut-off jean shorts and a T-shirt. Both were dark green, maybe so he could hide. I got a good look from the back when he ran off. His eyebrows were bushy, and he wore a big metal watch. Are they called Rolexes? Probably a knock-off." Words were spilling from her in anger.

Holly was writing as fast as she could. The girl was a gold mine of information. How could she be so thorough after being brutally violated? Perhaps it was just a thrust or two before it aborted. But knowing that you might die in minutes? This kind of coolness under fire was to her credit. "Anything written on the shirt?" Hardly any T-shirt was without its own cause: a rock event, place, political statement.

Ellen scratched the end of her sunburned nose. "No. Sorry. I guess that would really help, wouldn't it? But I told you lots of things, right? Now can you find him?"

The man might as well be standing here. "You've given us a super description. Good for you to be able to concentrate. I don't think I could, that is, if …" She shut up while the going was good. Something else was different here. The other attacks had happened at night. This was during the day. Maybe that's why he used the hat to blind her. Getting bolder? An opportunist? It was as if the man wanted to be caught. The old cliché of a cry for help.

The girl shrugged. "I'm pretty good with details. I like to draw, see. I might go into fashion design and take some night courses once I save up. Hey, maybe I could work with the police. Do they have computer programs for that now? I know they used to use real artists. In the movies or on TV, anyway. My mom likes those psychic shows where they solve those cold cases."

Holly swept a hand over her own short hair, buying time to think for a second. "Back up a bit, if you can. You say that he ran off. How did that happen? I mean, why do you think he left you? Did he say anything?" Before what, before he killed you? She kept quiet, half wanting the girl to say that nothing happened. But if there had been an ejaculation....

Ellen gripped the sides of the couch. Her legs curled in a defence against pain. Stone bruises and a few small cuts from debris were all Holly could see. Beneath the blanket, the neck on her T-shirt was torn. A few fir needles fell from her hair as she brushed at her small, shell ear. "I don't want to think about this, but he had a stutter."

"Really? He said something?"

"Nothing that made much sense. Sort of like 'sssssshut up.' And he called me the B word. That's all."

Another thought occurred to Holly. "Was he wearing a condom?" In some ways, criminals were getting smarter. It took planning and timing, but television and movies had taught lessons. But a man couldn't put on a condom unless he was aroused. That made the logistics tricky.

The girl blew out a breath, shuddering at the end. "Not unless he put one on just before he attacked me. If you mean did I feel him come, I didn't. And afterwards, there wasn't ..." She stared in horror. "I don't want to be pregnant by *him*. Rudy and I are ... my god, do you think that could happen?" She gave a sharp intake of breath. A small blue vein was beating at the pulse of her throat. Panic entered her eyes.

Holly touched her forearm for assurance. "They'll tell you more at the hospital. It's not a concern with the morning-after preparations today. Just a simple pill can put your mind at rest."

"It just hurt like hell. And that cap over my face. I had sand in my eye, too. I didn't even realize until later." She rubbed at her reddish cheek. "The way he was strangling me, I was close to passing out. Then I heard a boat. The motor stopped. People laughing. You know the way sounds carry. They were way out in the bay. He pushed me down real hard, and ran into the bush. My head hit the stones, but I wasn't unconscious. My legs wouldn't work. I was taking big breaths and coughing my guts out."

"Then what happened?" So that was what stopped him. Made sense.

"There wasn't any hope in trying to get help from the boat. It was too far away and too big to come in close. Then they went off again as fast as they came. I waited ten minutes hoping that someone else would show up. And another ten to make sure he was gone. No way I could go back another route because the tide was up. I made my way back to the road, staying off to the side of the path when I could, looking out for him. Then I flagged a car. It was that constable. I told her what happened. She tried to use her radio, but the static was bad. So she brought me here. She's not as nice as you are."

"Was that red or burgundy car still there?"

She shook her head. "For sure no. So do you think…?"

"Sounds possible. There really isn't any other way to get to Sandcut without driving."

"Guess I'm lucky." Her voice turned to a hush. "That other tall officer said the same thing. Is she new on the job?"

"Actually …" Holly cleared her throat, hoping that Ellen would move on.

"She seemed kind of uneasy with me. Like she didn't know what to do."

"Everyone starts somewhere. When you began at the library, you had to learn the ropes, right?"

"I guess." Ellen leaned her head back and closed her eyes as if to make it all go away. "Are we done now? I told you everything."

"You bet. Just take it easy. I won't say relax, but you know what I mean."

Holly leafed back through her notebook, gratified at all the details. The inspectors would be pleased. A few minutes passed. Ellen's breathing slowed. A discreet tap came at the door. Ann stuck her head in and whispered, "Sorry to interrupt."

"I think we're finished here, Ann." She inclined her head towards Ellen, whose eyes were fluttering. At least she'd be home safe tonight, but how long would it take downtown?

"Rudy's here. He's fortunate that we're short staffed on patrol because he drove about a hundred kph," Ann said. "Guess I don't blame him."

Ellen's eyes snapped open and she sat up with a groan. "Rudy. I need to talk to him. Alone, maybe?"

Holly closed her notebook. "It's a formality, but we'd rather be here in the room. And I'm afraid I have to ask you not to touch him or make physical contact. Just for now."

Ellen looked like she needed a hug in the worst way. Her Cupid's mouth went down at the corners. Fragments of pale pink lipstick still stuck to her lips. "But … Okay. I understand. I just want to see him."

Ann went back into the reception room. "Come on, Rudy," she said.

In walked a tall blond man, bronzed like a Malibu surfer, his curly hair nestled around his strong neck. Either he'd recently been to a hot, dry climate, or like many people on the island, he frequented a tanning parlour. "El, I came as fast as I could. You poor kid. I'm …"

Ellen looked up at him and started to rise, but Holly cleared her throat. "Sorry, but please don't touch Ellen right now."

Rudy backed off, his hands in the air apologetically. "No problem, officer. They told me outside. We don't want to do anything that might help this guy." He looked at Holly for permission. "Okay if I sit?"

"Sure. Please." Holly felt discomfort being a third party, but leaving them alone was out of the question.

Rudy seemed to be fighting the instinct to embrace his girlfriend. He bit his lip as his Adam's apple bobbed with one swallow, then another. Strong, calloused hands gripped the edge of the sofa. "Hon, how are you doing? Damn it to hell, why did I let you talk me into leaving you there?" A bump in his long nose testified to an old injury, probably hockey like a huge percentage of Canadian youth.

Ellen let out a long deep breath as if he was the best tranquilizer. She looked up at him and blinked. "You told me to wait until you could come. But just an hour. I mean I thought ..."

Rudy folded his arms as if to keep them to himself. "I'm blaming myself. We knew about those other girls. But Sandcut's farther down. And this was during the day. Nobody camps there. If only I'd thought twice...."

"Don't talk like that, Rudy. I talked you into it. And I'm okay. Really." She touched her neck with one finger, skirting the bruise. "I lost Jody's necklace."

"Never mind that now, sweetie. But she must have been watching over you like the angel she was," he said. Rudy turned to Holly with a dark cloud passing over his features. "When are you going to catch this bastard? How many have to ..." He struggled for control, clenching his fists. He wore crisp chinos and a light blue linen shirt, loafers without socks. It was hard to see his eyes behind the stylish sunglasses with metallic lenses. They reminded Holly of American movies with the highway patrol and their motorcycles. She never liked looking at mirrors instead of eyes.

"You know how quiet and peaceful the island is. This is a first-time experience for all of us." Now she was an apologist for the force. Caught in the middle with no credit, only blame. A definite downside of policework. Stats meant nothing to people whose lives had been ripped apart. It mattered that *their* case was solved, not ninety-nine others. Who could blame them?

"Sorry. I didn't mean to come on like an insensitive jerk. I'm just worried. When can Ellen go home?" Rudy asked.

"I want to get some dinner into her, maybe a glass of wine, and tuck her into bed. It was our second-year anniversary this weekend."

Holly's eyes searched their hands. No rings. Rudy added, "Anniversary of our first date. We're planning to get married next year once we save up for a down payment on a little place in Langford. Even has a mortgage-helper suite in the basement. Right, baby?" Ellen gave a small cry, her lip trembling, and he reached out for her hand, then drew back, his voice warm and confident. "Then we'll grow old and grey together. Am I a romantic or not?" He turned to Holly. "So what do we do now? I take it that we're waiting for the detectives or whatever you call them in the RCMP."

"The EMTs will transport her to the General for a few tests. Maybe an x-ray of her shoulder, too. From our standpoint, anything we can do to make sure that this is the last attack is critical. We don't want to make any mistakes. Ellen has given us a lot of helpful information. Now it's up to us to put together the pieces."

Rudy took off his sunglasses and nodded. "Damn straight. When you catch him, better not let me within a mile. There won't be enough pieces to bury. And that's a promise."

Those mesmerizing ice-blue eyes. Did he have a Scandinavian background or was he wearing exotic contacts? She had a feeling that he made the most of them in his romancing. A wail of sirens came around the bend of the road. Holly looked toward the window. "There they are. Sorry for the delay. I can't see why you won't be home tonight." She looked at Rudy. "You can follow the ambulance to the hospital."

Ann spoke up. "An inspector from Major Crimes will meet you all there in the emergency room admitting. Ed Smith. He's been in charge since the Sombrio Beach … incident. Ed's one of our best. They've already posted a couple of officers to Sandcut to look around. They're stopping here first. I'll scan your report, Holly, and fill them in on any helpful details about where this happened."

Ellen turned to Holly. "Thanks for everything. You made it better. I wish you were in charge."

She looked as if she might have lost her best friend, and Holly felt a big-sisterly impulse in giving her hand a gentle shake. At least she'd kept the girl company and gotten a wingding of a preliminary interview. Out the back window, she could see Ashley leaning against a large cedar and smoking as she scowled. Why did the constable have to be such a downer? Couldn't she understand that a major break had arrived?

"Thanks for the confidence." Holly pulled a card from her pocket. "If you have any questions, you can always call me." Rudy hadn't moved. "So Rudy, if you can ..."

He checked his watch, looking a bit uncomfortable. "Um, about going to the hospital, I have my great aunt in the car. Beth Jacobs. When I heard about Ellen, I didn't have time to make other arrangements. Can someone give her a lift back to Sooke and make sure she gets home? She lives on Eaglecrest Road. I need to stay with Ellen now."

A noise of feet and doors came from the foyer, and they all looked up. From the snug atmosphere of the small cottage, now Ellen would pass to other professional hands.

"In there," Ann's voice directed.

The EMTs entered, an older woman and a younger man. Holly and Rudy stepped back into the foyer. It was getting crowded.

Holly checked the clock, thinking about Rudy's request. Her stomach rumbled. She was due for the afternoon off and could just as easily write up her notes tomorrow. "Sure. Eaglecrest isn't far from my house. I'd be glad to help. Ann, tell Ed that my report will be filed tomorrow."

Ellen waved off the stretcher. She had the blanket wrapped around her like a small queen. Her colour was returning. Holly imagined that in her place, a hot, cleansing shower would be number one on her wish list. But it didn't work like that. "No, I'd rather walk. I'm not sick or anything."

"Right you are, Miss," the veteran woman said, hands on her hips. "No sense in carrying you down those rickety steps and taking you in with a broken leg. But you're lying down in the ambulance. We'll make you comfortable. And I'll take that handbag for you." She motioned to her partner. "Let's get on with it, Roger."

"Watch your step now," the young man advised, taking Ellen's arm and supporting her down the stairs.

Ellen waved goodbye to Rudy as the EMTs helped her to a stretcher inside the vehicle. "See you soon, sweetie. I'm gonna be with you all the way," he said as the team closed the door.

Rudy clenched his jaw and turned away. "She's one amazing girl. I'm so damn proud of her. You'd never know that she'd been through something like this."

His loyalty pleased Holly. Not every man acted like this in a case of rape. So many marriages and relationships fell apart after an assault like this, even when the couple did their best to move on.

Rudy took Holly out to his vintage Datsun Z two-seater, with an old lady in her late seventies as passenger. She seemed to be dozing, her wobbly chin touching her chest. Pink scalp peeked through a head of curly snowy hair. At the crunch of their steps, she nodded awake and looked over with a smile. A faint tinge of lavender cologne or dusting powder moved into the air. Holly was reminded of many elderly aunties. These princesses were treasured in the Coastal Salish world, and the heartstrings of the community with their wisdom.

"Are we going now, dear? You know that *Jeopardy*'s on soon." Her crepe throat played like fragile violin strings.

Rudy looked into the car and spoke in a very soft voice, his hand on her thin shoulder. She wore a shapeless cotton print dress, and her rheumy eyes peered out from Coke-bottle trifocals. A small brown device curled in one ear like a delicate shell.

"Aunt Beth, Officer Holly will take you home and get you settled." He turned and looked at Holly, who nodded. "I have to go with Ellen for a little while. She's had a bit of a shock. Your supper delivery will be there. We showed you how to put it into the microwave. I'll give you a call as soon as I can. Don't turn off your hearing aid until you go to bed."

The aunt answered in a musical tone as she levered herself out of the car with his gentle help. Clearly they had their routines. "That's fine, then, Rudy. I'll see you next week." One blocky black orthopaedic shoe caught on the sill, and he slowly moved it. She wore opaque support stockings over her swollen legs and carried a large-print book from the library.

Rudy leaned in confidence toward Holly. "She's on a few meds, but she can handle herself at home. A care worker comes in every morning to set her up. We've talked about an assisted living centre like the one in Sooke, but she's kind of stubborn. Runs in the family." He gave Holly the address.

Holly introduced herself and took Beth Jacobs to her Prelude. Rudy was lighting up a cigarette as Ellen got settled in the ambulance. "That's a beauty," he said to Holly. "I'm a classic car fiend myself. Sometimes we tour parts of the island on Sundays. If you ever want to promenade with us, check the web at *www.flivvers.com* for our schedule."

Holly smiled. Thanks to her father, she was one of the only people under one hundred who knew what a flivver was. She wasn't looking forward to seeing him at dinner to confirm the disappointing news about Bonnie's tote bag. Each time he got his hopes up about her mother, everything melted down.

CHAPTER TWENTY-TWO

"**THIS CUTE LITTLE CAR** reminds me of Rudy's," said Beth. "Do all the police drive sports cars now?"

Rudy had been right. Perhaps she had hidden resources, but it was amazing that Mrs. Jacobs managed to live alone. Who knew for how long? Holly reached over and helped the old woman fasten her seatbelt. "It's my own car, ma'am. We're a small detachment and our official vehicle stays here."

They drove along West Coast Road, Beth humming to herself. It sounded like "In the Shade of the Old Apple Tree." Perhaps it was her grandmother's favourite because it was decades before her generation.

"People have such teeny weeny cars today. I remember our green Packard Clipper. Les said that you could whack the fender with a hammer and do more harm to the hammer. Then he said if you scratched a modern car's paint, the words *Coca Cola* showed through. What a joker. That man did make me laugh."

Holly found herself smiling. "My father might agree. He knows all the old models." At least he bowed to realities and didn't change his car to match his periods. His bank account appreciated the Smart's 61 mpg.

"Rudy is better than a son. He comes by once a week. Tops up my groceries, too. It's hard to get by on a pension these days, and I only have the old age and the supplement. I didn't work after we got married. Ladies didn't then."

Leaving that statement to speak for itself, still she looked at Holly, who angled her eyes over for a second before an empty logging truck passed them en route to collecting the last toothpick. "Will Ellen be all right? Rudy said that she had a nasty shock. What happened? Did she take a fall? She wasn't swimming, was she? The ocean is very dangerous. A friend of mine nearly drowned when she got swept off a ledge in Tofino. Storm watching. Why go asking for trouble? And then there's the jellyfish."

Holly didn't know how much to explain. Perhaps in her somewhat confused condition, it was best not to alarm the old woman. Rudy could deal with that.

"A man was … .very rude to her. She seems to be recovered from her experience. She's a strong girl. I'm sure Rudy will tell you all about it later."

"He did say so. I do like Ellen ever so much. His last girl-friend was very snooty. Butter wouldn't melt, as they used to say." Beth made a finger-under-nose gesture. "Ellen's friendly. Rudy and she bring me pizza and we play rummy. I live so far from town that I don't get to enjoy those special treats very much. The seniors bus still can't find a driver."

"Have you lived here long?" Holly asked Beth. The old woman seemed to be humming again. On close inspection, she seemed to be in her late seventies from the way the flesh was beginning to recede from her bones.

"All my born days, dear. Lester was a logger. Today they make them out to be so evil. In those days it wasn't a dirty word, just an honest living. Timber built the island. Not far from my house they put up a pretty plaque to the old Emerson School. It was named after one of the early Icelandic settlers. Bush has got it all now. Everything grows so fast around here. Even the clear cuts spring up again with life."

She paused and her parchment cheeks fluttered. "I wouldn't live anywhere else."

At last Holly made a left onto Otter Point Road and drove a few miles, past the Dodo Farm and Forest Green Llamas and Alpacas to where Eaglecrest joined. "It's the little blue bungalow on the right," Beth said. "My husband and I built it in 1960. All electric. The best of everything. I told him that I wasn't heating with the dratted wood anymore, no matter how cheap it was. He used to say that wood warms you three times, when you cut it, when you pile it, and when you bring it into the house. Filthy stuff. Enough fir splinters in my fingers for a Christmas tree."

Holly found herself missing her grandparents in Sudbury, who had passed a few years ago. Her mother's people had died well before their time. Great Aunt Stella Rice had raised Bonnie herself.

They pulled into a small yard. Once it had been well-landscaped. But now, only a husk of a garden with deer fence, an overgrown lilac, and a spindly rose bush remained. Someone had been keeping the wilderness at bay, but only on the margins. A ramshackle single garage had a sinking roof so thickly covered with moss that it maintained its own ecosystem. In the temperate rainforest, growth was fast. What was strange was a very large, fairly new boat trailer attached to an old Dodge Ram one-ton dually pickup at the rear. Perhaps Beth allowed someone to park it there. A neighbour or maybe Rudy. As a telecommunications manager he would have a reliable income. Their own bundled Shaw bill for cable TV, Internet, and phone of $180 a month indicated the company's sizable profits.

"I'll see you inside and make sure you have everything you need," Holly said, helping her out of the low-slung vehicle. As they went to the porch, Holly was pleased to see that the house was in good shape. At least Beth hadn't become a hoarder. What looked like a scratching post sat by the door. "So you have a cat?" she asked as she took Beth's elbow to help her up the steps. The woman had a bad hip, and from the gnarled hands, some arthritis. She rocked like a ship as she walked. Was she on a list for a replacement or toughing it out like so many old people?

A sad voice answered, "I had three, but a mountain lion got Taffy and Buster last summer. Those cougars are dangerous. Bears I don't fear. They go the other way if you make a fuss." As she opened the door, a large tortoise shell ambled out. "Yertle," she said. "That kid's book I used to read to Rudy when he was a little guy."

As Holly knelt to pet it, she noticed that it was chewing with great difficulty, lips pulled back from the teeth. Conditioned to disciplining Shogun, who picked up every rotting fishbone on the beach, she said to Beth, "He's eating something. What have you got, buddy? Something bad for you?" Grabbing the cat on the back of the neck like a good mother, she bent to take what he had spit up. It consisted of mashed up white fibres.

Beth tsked and shook her head. "Another cigarette filter. He loves chewing them. I told Rudy to take his nasty butts to the garbage. Yertle gets up on counters and picks apart everything."

"Nicotine can be poisonous, and the filters, who knows what they're made of? You wouldn't want your cat to get sick." Unrepentant, Yertle was pouncing after a small quail no bigger than half a golf ball. A final round of hatchlings. The quail flapped off the ground and headed for a low bush, leaving the cat switching its tail in frustration.

"I think he's immune by now. I've had Yertle for ten years. I'm just going to tell that boy that he can't smoke in the house. Do you think he will get mad at me?"

"Rudy seems very nice. I'm sure he'll understand."

Holly wasn't trying to intrude, but sometimes a home visit had a larger calling. Underweight animals, those with hair mats and no grooming, often belonged to owners who needed help themselves. More than once, she'd seen a child who wasn't being nurtured or a woman with a black eye. With discretion, she'd made sure that the right authorities were contacted. Her mother would have approved. The young, the weak, and the old needed advocates, if they didn't realize it. The door wasn't locked either, common in her neighbourhood, too.

On a table inside the door was a package. "It's my supper," Beth explained, putting an appreciative hand on the foil. "Still warm. All I have to do is put it into the microwave. The cabbage rolls are especially tasty."

Holly looked around. "Is there anything else I can help you with?" The small living room had an old bulky twenty-one-inch television, a patched leather recliner, a sofa, and a curio cabinet with Beth's treasures. A picture of an older man in waders with a rod in hand looked down from the mantel. The place was a time capsule for the fifties, but it was spotless, the oilcloth on the table shiny and free of crumbs. An army of pill and supplement bottles sat on a ledge above. An antique toaster, the kind that flipped the bread, was still in use, next to a jar of homemade jam.

Beth said, "I'm fine now, dear. Thank you for the ride. May I offer you a coffee or tea?" Her careworn face begged for companionship. How lonely it would be living alone out here, even with a cat and visits from Rudy.

"My father is expecting me, but thanks."

"Do you live with your father? How lovely. I never had any children of my own. That's why Rudy is so important to me. What a blessing."

As Holly left, Beth grabbed a jar from a shelf and pressed it into her hand. "Take this, dear. It's my new batch. Fresh off the blackberry bushes last month. Nature's bounty."

At home in minutes, Holly grabbed a glass of buttermilk and a cheddar rice cake. By now the task force had been out to Sandcut Beach. Would they find Ellen's precious coral necklace? Tire tracks from that mysterious red car? Surely with the girl's description of her assailant, something would gel. Once this rape got into the papers, the pressure would be formidable to bring in resources from other detachments and set up a real task force. Closing the parks wouldn't be an option. The island couldn't be turned into an armed camp.

Filling the hummingbird feeder as a few dive bombers came her way, she stood on the front deck in the waning light to collect her thoughts and watch the sun's last apricot surrender. It looked so peaceful out there. And yet women weren't safe.

Out on the mighty strait, small fishing boats still trolled for halibut. A hundred-sixty-two pounder had had its picture in the paper this week. Choppy waves bounced the boats about, yet they were sturdy little things with high cabins like cockpits. Her neighbours Jackie and Bryan were hooking up their boat trailer to their vintage Ford 350 Diesel, which sounded like a combination of a tank and a backhoe. Coming down to the property line, she stopped to chat.

"Is that it for the season?" she asked. They kept their boat at Jock's Dock, the closest marina.

"You bet. I start my work at the hatchery making babies." Bryan belonged to the Salmon Enhancement Society, which sounded kindly and progressive but basically gutted female fish, scooped the roe, and put it in beds for fertilization. Brutal for the female, but no worse than spawning upstream until she dropped of exhaustion and became food for bears and eagles. "No fry left behind" was their motto.

Holly returned inside to find supper in the fridge thanks to her father, who had a late seminar. She took the glass plates from the fridge and popped them into the oven for his return. Sockeye salmon, scalloped potatoes, and carrots. Most women would have treasured him, but these domestic qualities never impressed her mother. Doing good for people was her mantra, and teaching useless courses did not make the grade. But she never used the "those who can't do, teach" observation. "Norman may live in the clouds, but he's a damned good father. I'll give him that," Bonnie admitted.

When he got home later with the dog, Holly was in the solarium reading and highlighting a chapter from *Blood Spatter Pattern Analysis*, a textbook best consumed well outside of mealtime.

He went to the kitchen table where she had placed the canvas tote bag. Reverently he touched it and looked down the stairs at her. "It's your mother's all right. I thought I'd never ..." Nikon's name was printed on the side along with an embroidered German shepherd image. This wasn't the same as the raven pendant, where a kernel of doubt waited. There were thousands like it, maybe a few with that same scratch, skeptical police had told her. The tote was unique.

She filled him in on more than the basics which she had left on his answering machine at the office. "I've tried calling this Port Angeles man, but no one answers. He may be out of town."

He cracked the knuckles on one hand, a nervous habit. "It's been a bad day all around. Seems like it comes in bunches. I have the last word on Samantha Buckstaff. Might as well spit it out."

What did he mean by the last word? "Spit it out" didn't sound promising. She looked up from her book with some concern. Would Chipper never come back? Sexual assault was a felony, after all.

In clear defeat, not like the cocky attitude he often assumed to make her laugh, his shoulders sagged on his lean body with the tiniest hint of a pot. He wore gabardine pants, a white shirt, and a diamond patterned sweater like Mickey Rooney as Andy Hardy. "Vice President Buckstaff has upped the ante, I'm afraid. With the financial situation so tenuous, that poor anthro bugger who reported Samantha's efforts to blackmail him is in dangerous territory."

Holly's heart sank. "How so? I thought you were sure you could get him to talk."

He shook his head. "Not with his tenure coming up this year. Nor the other person in the drama department who had the same experience. Buckstaff has threatened to cut the annual play as a budget control method. They lose money every year. University theatres don't turn a profit. It's a question of tradition. The infant phenomenon is going to prevail. Damn shame. You know what they say about academia."

"Right, it's so vicious because the stakes are so small." But were they? Her father made over $110,000 and had premium benefits.

"I was so hopeful," she said, heading for the kitchen with him.

"So was I. I guess I led you on with my ego. That's what I get for boasting. Pride goeth before a fall," he said, tossing back his head in a leonine gesture.

"Hey, you tried. Chipper will have to fight this on his own. It was a long shot anyway."

"How did that salmon look? Jackie caught a thirty pounder today and brought it over. I used Bryan's recipe, spreading mayo and mint on top."

Everything went well with salmon. It was even sold candied. The sockeye run up the Fraser had been the best since 1910. At least something was thriving along with the banana slugs. He dished out the food onto their plates, and she took them to the table. The ever-present bottle of homemade wine appeared. White. The greater of two evils.

"I have some good news of my own. We could use it." She told him about the possible break in the case thanks to Ellen Hughes.

"That's what I needed to hear. What a price for that young lady, though." He raised a glass to her. "I knew my little girl would make the island safe again."

Holly couldn't help smiling. "I had nothing to do with it, Dad. And anyway, even if we have a description, there's no guarantee that the guy will be caught. I've told you the ratio of solved murders to unsolved."

He forked into the salmon and chewed thoughtfully. Shogun got the skin as a special treat, smacking his black lips over his bowl. Holly gently took a bone from the salmon and placed it at the side of her plate. Her cousin Terry had once helped her make a lure using a fish bone. Once, the fish came in such numbers that they could be scooped into the canoes. Even hundreds of years ago, the First Nations knew where to put their river seines.

"After all the details that she told us, I am worried about Ellen being our star witness. I hope the police are watching her. On the other hand, if I were this guy, I would be long gone if I thought someone who had seen me was still alive and talking."

Norman put down his utensils and took a restorative drink of wine. "That sounds quite ruthless. That someone would be afraid to testify. What a shameful blot on the justice system. It reminds me of the mafia. Where's Elliot Ness when you need him?"

She savoured the last juicy morsel. If there was anything this side of heaven, it was salmon. "You have to think like he does. He's a killer, and it might not be the first time."

"You mean a serial killer? I wasn't thinking of those ramifications."

She felt a bit ashamed of leading him on. There had been only one death ... that they knew of. Yet had that M.O. been checked across the country? Ed would be onto that. It wouldn't be the first time that a rapist or killer struck several times, stopped for a couple of years, then started again. Usually it wasn't a case of mere self-control. Often they moved or were even in jail on other charges. "Maybe I'm overstating things. One is enough for now. There aren't that many missing women on the island that ..." Her voice drifted off and she saw him swallow.

"What can it mean, your mother's bag being on the ferry? Turning up after all these years. There's providence at work here," he said.

When her mother first disappeared, Holly never had believed that more than a decade would pass. "Logistically, it makes no sense at all. Like the pendant turning up in some-one's car." The young man at a car wash who had sucked it up in a vacuum had given it to a thrift shop, where it had stayed unsold for months. He didn't remember anything about the car, so that had been a dead end.

Her cousin Terry had worked for the small island air-line whose flights her mother had used to relocate abused women. If he had in his possession even the smallest piece of information that could lead to the truth, she wanted to know. She'd been trying to reach him to fill in the blanks on her mother's last known days. He was still in the Yukon, out of reach.

Then the phone rang. "Pardon me," she said. Her father moved off to the solarium with his coffee.

"Guv, it's me!"

Her knees nearly failed her. "Chipper! Ann and I have been trying to reach you. How the hell are you doing?" Was this a good sign or was another blow on the way?

He cleared his throat. "It's no picnic. They have me down in the basement at West Shore going through cold cases." He sneezed. "I think I'm allergic to the dust."

"Is there any word on your hearing? How long is this going to take?"

There was a long pause. "Weeks. Months. I don't know. I had a thought. Did you ask your dad about Mr. Buckstaff? The university's big, but I ..."

How could she tell him that her plan hadn't worked? The realities of finance over justice prevailed. Best not to even mention it and look like they'd failed. "Not very well. Buckstaff's a VP. They don't travel in the same circles. He has a lot of power, I'll tell you that much. We thought we had something on the girl, but it fell through."

"She's sticking to her story. I'm trying to keep busy and not think about it. Meanwhile Mom is praying every waking moment and goes to pieces if I don't eat enough at dinner. Dad, well, he's just Dad. My rock."

She tried to keep him talking. "So what about these cold cases you're working?"

"Something has turned up. I also have access to national databases, so I can trace crimes with the same elements. Guess what?"

That sounded promising. What was the most distinctive feature in their current crime wave? "The garrotte?"

"Manitoba had two cold cases using wire. Or rather what they suspect was trimmer line. Was I right or was I right? Both girls were in their twenties. Caught alone walking at night."

"What's the description of the guy?" At least he sounded upbeat. With his usual sunny disposition, it would take the burden of Atlas to keep him down for long.

"That's the problem. One girl suffered brain damage and still is in a coma. It's less than fifty-fifty that she'll come out of it. The other was found dead. She was raped, too, like the first one. No semen. No trace. A total strikeout."

"He must be one cool and careful character." The images chilled her. Holly felt a quickening at her pulse. "Where was this? And when?"

"Just outside Winnipeg. Selkirk and Portage La Prairie."

She tossed her geography dice. "Smallish towns but not villages. Driving distance from the big city. Perfect trolling spots."

"One was about five years ago, the other four. Nothing since then, as far as we know, but sometimes killers find a hiding place in the bush for their victims that is never discovered. Remember Clifford Olsen."

Canada's most notorious child killer and a B.C. resident. He had blackmailed the government into giving his family $100,000 in return for divulging the location of several victims' remains. A devil's bargain. He'd died in prison, but that was little consolation for the grieving families.

"Holly?"

"I wish I could do something to help you, Chipper, but …" She felt so helpless. How could she keep up his spirits? Ann was much better at this.

"How's everything at the detachment?"

"So far all we're doing is mop up after the rookie. She's a total disaster. I can't wait for you to get back." Recently Ashley had improved, but no need to tell him that.

She thought she heard a swallow over the line.

"Me too."

CHAPTER TWENTY-THREE

FIRST AT THE OFFICE that morning, Holly found a message to call Ed. What a super guy he was to keep her posted. Was it the paper analysis? She double-pumped her arm. "Yessss."

"Results are in. It's a puzzler," he said.

"I know it was small. What kind of paper was it? Could they tell that much?" What she found in that yurt might have nothing to do with the case. A dozen people could have been in there in the weeks before the assault.

An amused laugh came over the line, and her expectations sank. Was Ed making fun of her? He'd seemed like a regular guy. Certainly not one of the mossbacks who patronized women.

She let silence be her ally. No use sounding like an eager teenager. When still he said nothing, she gave in. "I'm still here, Ed."

"They ID'd it all right. It's a tiny piece of cigarette filter paper, type unknown. Might be found anywhere. Floats on the breeze if you get my drift." He didn't laugh.

"Okay. Sure. At least we know *what* it is. But now ..." Had she expected a miraculous breakthrough?

"Come on, corporal. You don't think we're going to be able to go anywhere with this, do you? In a public park? I went along because the two cases seemed to connect, and of course because we had a murder."

Protesting would only make her look foolish. "Guess not. I owe you one for trying, though."

"At the risk of my reputation, I took you seriously enough to do DNA on it, just in case. After all, a cigarette comes in contact with saliva," he said. "The fragment was pretty degraded. No telling how long it had been out there. That part of the test will take longer."

"What, like months?" Surely advances had been made, the rapid-fire television tests aside. A pop can had provided evidence when a criminal tossed it where his observers could find it. Similar busts had been made by cops waiting patiently for someone on a street corner to butt out a cigarette and leave.

"A few more days. Boone pulled a few strings for you."

"What about Ellen's case? She gave us everything but the kitchen sink." She hoped the girl was moving on with her life.

He gave a frustrated sigh. "She did, and your report was very helpful. Points to you on that score. By the time she got to the next interview, she was pretty tired and disinclined to go into more detail. We ran the description every which way but loose. VICAP in the States and CPIC here. Nothing. Either he's never been in trouble or that he's never been caught. If we had a vehicle we could match him to, we'd have a better lead. There are too many reddish Hondas around. She didn't know the exact year either. The morning it all went down we told the ferries and the airport to be on the lookout, but we can't keep that up. We'd need a hundred men on each ferry from seven a.m. to nine p.m. Vancouver, Seattle, Port Angeles, or Anacortes. He might be creative and take the boat from Nanaimo to Vancouver."

"I don't know. If it's the same person in all three cases, he seems to want to stick around. That might indicate that he has a job or a family. It's not impossible that he's married.

Even with children," she said. "Were there any forensics from the rape itself? Ellen went through hell. I can find out through Boone's channels, but I'd rather hear it from the lead detective."

"Flatterer. We figure he used a condom. Any trace on her went back to her boyfriend and contact they had the night before. He was very cooperative. Seemed like a solid guy. Stayed at the hospital the whole time until we cut them loose around midnight."

"Damn. Poor kid. After all she went through. It's discouraging."

He chuckled. "Are you sure you want to run with the big dogs? Because you're going to have to have a tougher skin than this. Face it. Cases don't always get solved. Not in month, years, or decades. Some bodies are never found. That would be far worse, don't you think?"

"I know all about that. But listen. My constable ..." She told him about what Chipper had found out in Manitoba.

After a few days of phone tag, Holly called Terry again. When on the tenth time his answering machine didn't pick up, she yelped for success.

"Welcome home, Island Girl. Aunt Stella told me you were living with your dad now just before I left for my holidays. I couldn't believe it. You never came down when you were in Port McNeil, but Fossil Bay? That's hardly an hour. I won a derby with a monster hali there a few years ago."

"Still the same shy and modest guy I remember." Everyone knew that, contrary to the strong and silent aboriginal stereotype, Terry never shut up, and he loved to talk with his hands. Some of the family teased him about having an Italian merchant hidden in the genetic woodpile.

"So when are we getting together? And don't tell me that you married some lucky guy because you're much too choosy. How's your dad, anyway? I only met him once, but he seemed like a nice guy. Too bad the family ..." He trailed off rather than remind them of the fact that Bonnie's disappearance had strained relations with the family. They had broken contact a few months after it became apparent that Bonnie was not going to be found. Some were suspicious of Norman's status as an outsider. That rift made Holly's overtures to the Salish side of her past slightly tricky. She felt a greater loyalty to her father.

Talking to Terry made her nostalgic for those old times when her mother had taken her up to Cowichan to meet her relatives, historically known as "The People Who Fell From the Sky." The mythic stories fascinated her, and she even learned a few words in the language, a minefield of glottal consonants.

When they'd finally settled on a time and place, she said, "I'll be there Saturday morning. About noon?"

While she was in relative mode, she called Great Aunt Stella Rice up island. She'd tried to reach her several times to see if the wise elder had any information on Ashley's brief time at the Cowichan detachment. For all she knew, Ashley might become a permanent fixture at Fossil Bay. This time, the elderly Coastal Salish princess picked up the phone

"You are coming up here again soon," she said, almost as a demand. "And you have more information about your mother? You made me a promise."

Holly chafed under the strict vow she'd made. There was no sense in giving her false hope, but she told her about the tote.

The old lady was a long time in responding. Knitting needles were clicking, a habit that indicated that she was thinking. Stella's art had provided sweaters, hats, scarves, and mittens over the decades. Now she had Puq, a little wool dog to provide some of the material.

"That makes no sense at all. She was at my house the day before she disappeared. Her destination was Tahsis, not the States."

"I may be able to pinpoint when it was left on the ferry. Maybe someone else found it up island and then went back over the border." She paused.

"Raven the trickster, I suppose. This does not make sense to me."

Stella's usual enigmatic expression. Did she mean misdirection?

"I called you for another reason." She explained about Ashley, couching the language in positive terms so as not to predispose Stella. Cowichan was a very small community with a reserve, and the RCMP officers were well-known and generally respected from what she knew.

"I remember that one. She gave a talk to our high-school students about the dangers of dropping out of school. It seems that her own sister ended up in, what do you call it, the sex-trade business?"

This was news. "Really?"

"The girl died from a drug overdose in Toronto. Constable Packke's message to the young people was to get an education. It was a harsh talk, but we understood why. She stayed for another two hours taking questions from a group of girls. I was very impressed with her. That takes courage."

Holly was beginning to put things together about Ashley. A law-enforcement father to impress, a sister to mourn, and a message. That might explain why she was rough on the hooker. Had the woman been procuring young girls? And the officer whom she accused of making advances? It wouldn't be the first time that a "pillar" of the community had something on the side. Ashley had made a mistake with Trey. Since then, things had gone smoothly. Not that Holly didn't want Chipper back yesterday.

Saturday, Holly navigated the cozy tourist and retirement town of Sidney by the Sea, located near the Swartz Bay ferry to Vancouver and the international airport, with matching real estate prices. A plane zooming over her car made her duck as she turned off the Pat Bay Highway. Was that a moustache on the pilot? How could anyone live near such noise? And the new runways that planned to accommodate more international flights would increase the traffic.

On the radio, Lady Antebellum was singing, "I Need You Now" when Holly pulled into Second Avenue and parked in front of a neat renovated cottage, circa the First World War. Its front porch had been enclosed to provide extra living space. There were no sidewalks, and on a grassy strip in front of a picket fence, a huge stump had been carved into a mask like the Easter Island statues.

Inside the fence, a perennial garden splashed rainbow colours from late-flowering yellow and purple mums. Flowers grew year-round on the temperate lower island. A lemon tree, carefully guarded, was Terry's prize. Ceramic sculptures of frogs and turtles anchored nooks of interest. Following the flagstone path, she made her way to the stained-glassed front door and pulled a bell string with a brass wolf on the end. Very artsy. Terry's wife, no doubt the gardener-cum-landscape architect, taught at Camosun College and exhibited her sculpture and carvings at local fairs. Most of them featured Coastal Salish animal images and mythic themes.

A young woman her own age dressed in a long red-print cotton skirt and white linen blouse answered the door. Silver Thunderbird earrings decorated her ears. "Holly? Terry has told me so much about his favourite cousin. Welcome to our home."

Ricki gave her a warm handshake and invited her in. Like her husband, she had the light copper complexion and sleek ebony hair of her people. She bore a resemblance to Bonnie Martin in the seventies. In the foyer was a bright moon mask in the style of another relative from Holly's childhood, Silas Seaweed. She tried to remember Terry's totem. A bear? Certainly not a deer like hers. Try though she may, she couldn't shake the idea that the diminutive ungulate was wimpy. But as her mother said, it had chosen her and she needed to work with it. No do-overs. All animals had their strengths and weaknesses.

"Chef Terry's in the back getting charcoal ready. Please share our meal. And you must meet Piper. You will be her auntie."

"I'm honoured." To refuse the hospitality would shame the family. Here was her cousin married and with a child. Was that option in her future? Too soon to say, biological clock or not. She heard no ticking, but was it a wilful deafness? By her age, her parents had been married and with a toddler. She felt childish herself still living at home, but there was not the same quest for independence in a close-knit society like this.

With an overstuffed sofa and chairs, the living room was full of books, art, and kids' toys, judging from the nature, between five and ten years. "Piper's a very cute name." Niece or a nephew? Hard to tell. She wasn't one for holiday cards other than Stella. Catching up would be important. Being an only child gave her some isolation, and she didn't regret the status, but wondered at the alternative. Suppose your siblings were an embarrassment, like her mother's sister, who'd humiliated the family by stealing from Stella? She'd left the area and never returned.

Through the tiny kitchen, crowded with modern appliances and a monster fridge covered with kids' colouring sheets, they went outside. A dozen youngsters tore around in party hats, throwing favours, blowing whistles, and generally raising an innocent hell, grass and food staining their clothes. Every now and then one fell, but silently, without fanfare, the toddler would be pulled to his feet. First Nations children didn't seem to have the same self-pity of other whiny kids. Perhaps it came from the days when they had to be quiet and hide from a marauding tribe. Bonnie told her that a baby's nose would be pinched so that he would have to breathe through his mouth and not be able to cry. Was that true, or one of her mom's rare jokes?

Terry she would have recognized from a hundred feet, thanks to that dazzling smile and soft olive eyes. He threw open his arms and grabbed her, swinging her around. Putting his hands on her shoulders to give her another onceover, he nodded in approval. Funny that she'd had a crush on him when they were teenagers. He was a few years older but treated her as an equal when they went fishing or roamed the forests. Her favourite memories were camping overnight with him, building a log, twig, and skunk-cabbage-leaf shelter and roasting a rabbit over the fire. How good it had tasted with only a touch of salt. Later he gave her the tanned skin. Yes, the rabbit was his totem. That seemed worse than a deer.

Releasing her, Terry bent down as a young boy plowed into him. Gently he set the boy free after ruffling his hair. "Take it easy, Jeremy. You don't want to start making the girls cry now. They won't like you when you're ready to date." He turned to Holly. "Gotta love 'em at this age. Later, look out, world!"

"Like us, you mean. Remember when we went camping up in the Olympics and got caught in a freak snowstorm?" Ricki came over, looped her arm through Terry's and smiled at their reminiscences.

"I thought our parents were going to send the RCMP across the strait. When we got back to the trailhead a day late, the highway patrol was waiting for us, along with other people who'd been stuck up in the mountains at the park." Terry had built them a quinsy, a rough snow lodge. He was her first hero.

With a strong jaw, he had a neat moustache and a bold hawk nose. Damn fine looking man even if he were her cousin. Her tomboy status made her closer with the boys. A knife in a case on her belt had been standard attire when she visited her relatives, even a little axe one summer. They'd chopped alder for a raft and lashed it together. The day of the big launch, it was so heavy from the green wood that it wouldn't support any weight and floated off. "Look out, Seattle," Terry had said as they both waded to shore.

Terry wore a long-sleeved rugby shirt with colourful stripes. Then from a washtub of ice, he hoisted a light beer and motioned her to a canvas chair. Holly accepted a soda. It wasn't safe anymore in B.C., even for a woman her size, to drink one beer and pass muster with the breathalyser.

Ricki shielded her eyes from the sun and scanned the yard. "I'll find that rascal Piper. I don't want you to miss meeting your niece, Holly. I'll bring you a plate, too. I bet you have a hearty appetite just like your family." Giving her husband a teasing poke in the ribs, she turned and walked toward a group of children.

With his wife gone, it was time to get serious. They spoke for a moment about the raven pendant. "I remember Aunt Bonnie's silver raven stealing the box of light, the sun in its beak. But you're sure it's the same piece of jewellery?"

"There are lots around, but this one had the same small flaw."

"I hoped someone would, well, ask questions. Never made sense to me that she just vanished, along with that Bronco." His dark eyes crinkled at the corners. "I figured you went into the law so that you might in a better position to find her someday."

"So you think something happened to her, too. It's good to talk to someone about it. Whenever Dad and I get onto that topic, it's really tough." She had long ago jettisoned the absurd idea that her mother would have left on her own. Maybe in fiction people developed amnesia and wandered off. Not in real life. "I haven't been able to do much until I got back here. The files tell me nothing, and I've made so much of a nuisance of myself that when the records people see me coming, they shut the door. Everyone says that it's a bad idea to investigate your own family."

"Sounds like they've given up, and that pisses me off. Aunt Bonnie did so much for our women and families, but she ran into a lot of very bad people. That time when she faced down Joe Blough. He'd been beating up Jeannie for years. Your mom made sure she got a restraining order and then a fair divorce settlement. She stood right in his yard in front of the neighbours, shook her fist, and dared him to lay a hand on her. What a prosecuting attorney she would have made. Just didn't like the court scene, I guess."

"She was some debater. When she finally lost her first argument with me, I was eighteen." She'd had the same thoughts herself that many men in Bonnie's dark world must have hated her. "What happened to Blough?"

Terry shrugged. "He left for a mining job in Whitehorse. That was five years ago. Not long after, he was killed in an accident in the shaft." He pounded the arm of the pink plastic Muskoka-style chair. "Bastard. The women had a big party in Cowichan that night. I wish your mother could have been there. She always said that despite the fact that Canada had no death penalty, some people had no right to walk Mother Earth. Even a life in jail was too good for them."

"She was so passionate." Holly remembered the times she'd seen her mother's face stained with tears. Once a bi-polar man had killed his family of four with a sword, then committed suicide. "Jeannie was a success story, but not all the women were so lucky. Mom said that civilization lost its way when the old matriarchal societies changed." She closed her mouth. Now she was sounding like an elder.

"Turning things around takes time. Aunt Bonnie did a lot of good in our community. To me she was a warrior."

She waved away a bee buzzing around her pop can. "She knew the risks." Like in policing, she thought. Percentages be damned, there's no place we'd rather be.

Ricki arrived with a plate for Holly with a hot dog, salad, and chips. "Thanks, Ricki. Sorry to take your husband away." She tried a hearty bite. Smoky, lean, and perfectly cooked. It might be deer sausage, one good use for her totem.

The woman waved her hand. "Family is important. I hope Terry has information that can help you. He told me about your mom when we first married. I'm so very sorry. I can't imagine what you go through. Or your dad." She looked away as she mentioned Norman. The younger generation seemed to have more understanding for him than those his age, who couldn't comprehend why he loved that Ivory Tower.

When Holly had finished, she put aside her plate and rummaged in her pocket, handing Terry the receipt from Otter Aviation she kept in her wallet. He read it slowly and nodded, stopped to admire a balloon his daughter had brought over. Little Piper gave her a shy look. She was a living doll with long black, red-ribboned braids. Her shirt said, "Daddy's Little Cub." She'd never seen Holly before, and gave her a shy hug, prompted by her father.

Holly marvelled at how delicate and fragile a child's body was. If she ran into a case of abuse, it wouldn't be easy to stay neutral, maintain a civil demeanour when you wanted to apply a slap or worse to someone who had no business replicating. "Your Auntie Holly is a policeman," Terry said, and the girl's huge bright eyes saucered. "She finds the bad guys and protects us, don't you, Holly?"

Holly nodded semi-seriously but added a wink. Piper giggled and ran away to find her friends. They were so innocent at that age. No wonder Ann liked to go to the grade school for her DARE program to educate about drug use. Ricki excused herself.

"You worked at Otter, Terry. Is there anything you remember that might help? It was a long time ago. Even the slightest and stupidest detail might make the difference." Her eyes sent a silent plea. Terry had always come through.

Ricki was calling for him, waving a large knife. It was time to cut the cake and sing. He stood and tapped his watch, holding up five fingers to his wife. "I was at Otter for three years as an apprentice. When I got my papers, I hated to leave them but the offer here in Sidney was too good."

"And the owners, the Hamilton brothers? Tell me about them."

"No way had they anything to do with the disappearance. They were straight-up guys. They thought of Aunt Bonnie like a sister. Gave her special rates and dropped everything if she needed a flight. You know that sometimes she had to go where there weren't any roads or where it was quicker to fly. Like Esperanza, Zeballos, Tahsis." He named tiny settlements on the wild west coast, a land of fjords.

"She took her Bronco to Tahsis, her destination. Past Gold River. The last we heard from her was at a motel in Campbell River. Then she vanished. The early snow storm in the hills didn't help. That country is brutal."

His eyebrows contracted in sympathy. "What about the files at Otter? Did they say more about this one-way trip?"

"Gone in a fire years ago. Bernie was killed in a crash on Denman Island. Phil went east. Nobody knows where. He was pretty depressed about his brother when he sold the business."

Terry nodded. "He had a breakdown, I heard. Bonnie knew plenty of people on the mainland. Her reputation was huge."

"And I remember the date of the receipt. She didn't go to the mainland to Williams Lake at all. She was home. So who did, and why? What the hell's there except for hunting and fishing and a road to Prince George?"

He rubbed the bridge of his nose. "Seems I asked Bernie that myself. I did all his tune ups. Normally he'd talk your ear off. This time he clammed right up. Said that if I didn't know anything, I was all the better off. Mentioned a chain. And weak links."

A chain. Of events? Of people, like the Underground Railroad? How many others were involved? "Nothing more?"

"A couple of times I saw your mother with other First Nations women. Usually from up north. I didn't know them. They used the flights to get off the island as quietly as possible."

That made sense. She remembered something her mother had said about some people being too broken to fix. And then you either left or paid with your life. "I got some initials from a notepad. LS. Probably a person. Sending a taxi to McD."

"Micky D's. It's a common meeting place."

"That much I figured out. LS mean anything to you?"

"Your mom was pretty discreet about naming names. And I was doing my mechanic's stuff, not sitting around with the clients."

"But Williams Lake. Maybe I can see why she used Otter Aviation."

"Major airlines have schedules, traceable records. I'm betting that in these cases, the Hamiltons didn't file flight plans. They were pretty loose that way even if they could forfeit their licence. And she could go door to door, not fool around flying to Vancouver first. There are plenty of fields where you can land a small plane like that."

"You're probably right. Cash only, too. My mom took several thousand from a joint bank account around the same time. She could have taken a lot more from their other accounts. You know how Dad socks it away."

"That's not much to go on, all these years. Nothing else has turned up?"

Taking a breath, she told him about the tote bag. The more she learned, the less sense it made.

"What? That's crazy. The same bag with the cool German shepherd on the side? Sure I remember it. And you don't know when it was left on the ferry?"

"I'm trying to make it fit, imagining that Mom took the ferry to the U.S., came back, and headed for Campbell River, two hundred miles in the opposite direction. The logistics are ridiculous. Did someone steal it from her? Maybe if I finally get in touch with this retired guy, I can pin it down. The bag is distinctive. He should know if it was found a year ago, or five, or ten."

"Wish I could help. There's an image, though … a word … every now and then it jumps in and out of my memory. I'm not even sure that I'm not imagining it or receiving it through another sense. My grandpa was a shaman, or what passed for it fifty years ago." He pinched the bridge of his nose until it was white. Seconds ticked by. For once Holly wished she were a hypnotist, able to re-summon lost memories. "A harp."

More word association time. Crazy varieties of the term shot through her mind. Harp seal. Harp on something. And the old-fashioned instrument in a hundred shapes and sizes. "A harp? Are you sure you heard right? What could that possibly mean? Are you seeing a picture of it, or is the memory verbal?"

Memory was an elusive animal. The faster you ran after if, the faster it ran. But if you relaxed your guard, it could come bumping into you of its own accord.

"It was something I overheard. 'Look for the harp.'" He spread his hands in frustration. "I was doing a tricky carburetor adjustment in the big Quonset hut while Aunt Bonnie and Bernie were walking through. I wasn't paying any attention. It didn't seem important at the time. I'm sorry."

He turned as Ricki called again with a little more salt in her tone. Then he put his broad hand on hers and squeezed gently. It was calloused and scarred from the dangers of his profession. "Listen, I have to go. If anything else comes to mind, if I think of anyone who worked at Otter back then, I will call you faster than an arrow." He mimed a shot at a tree.

Holly took her last bite and put down the plate. "You've given me one lead, Terry. Thanks." She glanced at her watch. "Now I really have to fly before the Pat Bay gets clogged with the 2:30 ferry arrival." Victoria had only three bottlenecks: The McKenzie–Island Highway intersection, the Colwood Crawl, and the arrivals of the ferries in Sidney. Ten minutes of traffic was a cheap price for life in paradise.

As a cheer went up from the kids, Holly closed the pretty little gate behind her, brainstorming all the way to the car. Harp. A pub name? The island, more English than the English, had its share. An advertisement for Guinness or Harp beer? Images of St. Patrick? She nearly pulled out in front of a scooter carrying a very large man, Canadian flag on a pole dangling above him.

CHAPTER TWENTY-FOUR

ALL ANN HEARD IN the office was the persistent ticking of the wall clock, louder and louder until her ears ached as much as her heart. Chipper's desk sat as a reproof. Every day it gathered more of Ashley's trash. "That's it. I have to get out of here. Even for twenty minutes." She tossed down her pen in disgust and watched it bounce on the floor.

Since Chipper had been MIA, she'd been coming in earlier and earlier, hoping that the music from his Mustang would reach her as he returned to work. He reminded her of her son. She'd been scarcely twenty when she had Nick. His bastard of a father had taken off. Back to Newfoundland and his family's lobster boat. One blind date had changed her life forever. Add a forty ouncer to a two-hundred pounder and let 'er rip. Rod had been charming with that Newfie accent and off-colour jokes. Sure she had had a few, but back then they would have called it consent. Willingly, she'd driven with him in his car to a spot overlooking the ocean on a moonlit night. In denial at first when her period was late, then fearing reprisals from her dragon mother Phyllis, she let it go too long. Then there had been no turning back.

Months in cheap rooms in Vancouver had been a nightmare, but she'd worked her ass off as a waitress, then as an administrative assistant, and when Nick was in his teens, finally took courses and got on with the force, determined to make up for lost time.

Holly wasn't due until ten, and Ashley had called in with cramps again. No one was available for traffic duty. Ann got in the cruiser, welcoming that old familiar feeling of action. She drove a few kilometres to the pull-in area near Shirley, their favourite hidey-hole for speed checks. A few cars whizzed by, then seeing her, slowed suddenly, their red lights flashing as they braked. Ann narrowed her hooded eyes. Smoky's onto you, fella. She opened her aluminum car cup and took a sip of Rooibos tea strong enough to trot a mouse. Chipper had introduced it to her when he gave her a selection for Christmas.

It felt good to be out of the office and away from that imprisoning chair. If Holly called her on it, she'd say that with Ashley away, someone had to show the colours. Getting out of the car after fifteen minutes to stretch her back, she saw something moving way up the hill behind her. Bears were no big deal, especially with the car for refuge. But suppose it crossed the road. North of Victoria, four cars had hit a bear on the Malahat and caused a ricochet collision.

She picked up a sizable stick and began beating an alder. "Go away, Bruno or Bruna! Get back into the woods!" She yelled again and kept up the thrashing.

"Are you crazy down there? I'm not an animal," came a woman's voice way thirty feet up the slope in a thick patch of bushes.

Ann gave a self-conscious chuckle and tipped her cap back to better observe. "My apologies. Are there still any berries up there? I thought they were long gone."

Down the path came a walking salal bush. When the twined bundle hit the ground, a tall thin wiry woman in heavy Carhardt overalls, rubber boots, and a toque stood before her. Collecting the evergreen leaves was one way enterprising

people made money year round. They sold the greens to
florists to highlight bouquets. How much they made, Ann
couldn't imagine, but it must have provided incentive, especially for retirees on a fixed income.

"Officer, are you setting up for one of those mean old
speed checks?" The woman had a horsey, weathered face and
sensible pigtails for her iron-grey hair. "I don't even have
a car." She pointed into the underbrush, where sat a rusty
Raleigh bicycle. The woman put down the bunches, tied them
with string quick as a wrangler, and wiped her sweaty forehead
with the back of her hand. She had a healthy, rawboned look,
the kind which might make it to a hundred.

"Busted," said Ann and extended her hand. She grinned
when the woman turned it into one of those hippy shakes,
which had about three positions. "Do you come here often?"

Elaine Robson, as she called herself, replied with a pucker to
her thinning lips, "Nearly every day. Almost ready for another
spot. Don't want to milk the horn of plenty." She smiled at her
own mixed metaphor, then took a plastic flask from her belt
and gulped down half a litre. "Hot work, though."

Ann felt a curious hunch overtake her like an opponent
in a race closing in. "Were you here two weeks ago? I mean
in this spot?" Chipper would have been in the area when he
stopped the Buckstaff girl's car.

Elaine screwed up her face in memory. A few scratches
worked down her long neck. "It's likely. I have about ten
picking spots. Next up will be at the Invermuir Road intersection. Most people don't know I'm in the underbrush. Those
blackberry brambles do a number, though, even though I
have my armour on."

"So you've seen us before on traffic checks."

Elaine tucked her bottle back into the holder. "That
gorgeous young Sikh. Another woman younger than you.
Then recently a different woman. Tall drink of water. Struts
around like she owns the place. Free entertainment, watching those poor, unsuspecting sods pulled over. Mostly they

go quietly. Some get mad, though, as if something wasn't fair about the catch."

Ann was holding her breath. Her ears were hot with a sudden burst of excitement. "What about the day the man stopped a young girl? She was driving a gold sports car. Worth a chunk of change."

Elaine leaned against the cruiser and shook with amusement. "I remember that. The girl was pounding on the car and doing all sorts of damn fool antics. I felt sorry for him."

"Think carefully because it's very important. Did you see him touch her at all? Even a hand on a shoulder?"

"Are you kidding? I'd sooner kiss a rattlesnake, not that we have them on the island. She had the foulest mouth I've ever heard. He just stood with his arms folded a good five feet away and tried to reason with her. Wasn't no use. She was having none of it. Quite the brat."

"Then you observed the whole incident? Including the taxi arriving?"

Elaine gave a hoot, and a bead of sweat dripped down her nose. "To be honest, I was embarrassed to be listening in, but I couldn't help it. I saw the whole thing. An older man, was it her father? They left together in her car. Should have taken her to jail for that cheek. That young fellow had the patience of a saint. Me, I would have slapped her six ways to Sunday. Damn, the world is going to hell. Not sorry I'm checking out in another twenty."

"You heard *everything* the officer said to her?"

"Certainly. He was the model of courtesy. He wasn't yelling, but his deep voice carried quite well."

"And the father?"

Elaine pushed her bottom lip forward to moisten it. "You can see where the daughter got her bad manners. He was yelling things like 'You'll regret this. Do you realize who I am? I'll have the best lawyer in Canada on the phone in half an hour. Blah, blah. Your badge is on the line....'" She stopped short. "'Paki.' What a bigot, and stupid, too. Anyone could tell the man was a Sikh. That's not their usual territory if I remember my geography."

"And the officer's reaction?"

"Nothing but sir this, and sir that. He was telling them that they could either pay the fines by mail or contest them at a court date." She gave Ann a tongue in cheek expression. "Of course we know how those go unless you can prove some kind of extenuating circumstances."

Ann let out the loudest whoop and stopped short of tossing her hat in the air. Her back had even stopped hurting. "Lady, I'd like to buy you a drink. In fact, I'd like to buy you a whole bottle. Some people need to talk to you, and I mean yesterday."

The friendly creases on Elaine's weathered face arranged themselves into a smile that matched her buck teeth. "Any time, any place. Make it Crown Royale Black."

CHAPTER TWENTY-FIVE

A FEW DAYS LATER, no one was happier than Holly to see Chipper's Mustang in the parking lot next to Ashley's Yamaha. The Sequim, Washington, station her father had tuned in when he borrowed the car was playing its forties to sixties classics. She waltzed up to the door with those iddy biddy fishes in their iddy biddy pool on her lips. Fossil Bay: biggest little detachment in the west! The three musketeers were on the road again.

She opened the door with a flourish, heading for a high five with Chipper. Ann was laughing, wiping her eyes. A country station was on the radio. A platter of exotics pastries sat on Chipper's desk. Ashley had a small pyramid on a paper plate and was digging in. The largest bouquet of flowers in the City of Gardens was on Ann's desk while a dozen colourful paper lanterns hung from the ceiling.

"Guv! We saved some for you! It's Diwali, our festival of lights. My mother made up for lost time. She was baking all night," he said, giving her a squeeze with one long arm as a faint hint of sandalwood met her nose.

"Perfect timing," she said. "I'm heading for sugar overload. What are these?"

"Gulab jamun are the soft balls. Jalebis have the honey. And kesar kaju burfi use cashews."

"Chipper was telling us about Diwali," said Ann with amusement. "It may be more than a coincidence that he's a free man."

"Diwali celebrates the victory of righteousness and the lifting of darkness, like in justice. In southern India, the story is that Lord Krishna even freed the prisoners that an evil king had held in jail," he told them as he struck a pose like the handsome god.

His gleaming grin and merry eyes left no doubt that he was back to normal. Had he lost a few pounds? Stress could do that. According to what he'd said on the phone last night when he related the good news, Elaine's testimony reached Island Division HQ just as they were turning the investigation over to an independent task force from the Vancouver Police. Burned too many times from internal investigations, the RCMP was determined to appear as unbiased as possible. Now the case was closed. Elaine Robson was not only a convincing witness, but a former justice of the peace. There was some question if Samantha might face public mischief charges for lying to authorities and causing a costly and unnecessary investigation. Chipper had waved it off, calling her a kid in over her head. Holly thought that he was being too kind, but perhaps he was simply glad that it was over. He was not the type of person who was ruled by an instinct for revenge.

Ashley punched him on the arm. "Is this guy for real? And he gets to wear that turban, too? Far out. I asked him about his teeny knife, but he won't show it to me. And you know what they say about teeny knives."

"Tell the truth," Chipper said, trying to keep a straight face despite his blushing. "You're going to be very sad leaving this little detachment. It's one of Canada's best-kept secrets. Somewhere else you might have to do some actual work. And I hope you change your mind about that sewing machine. I don't want to have to shovel you off the pavement one rainy day."

Holly watched them banter, surprised by how well they got along, having only met. Chipper had someone he could see eye to eye with, for a change. As for Ashley, she'd volunteered to vacuum and dust the office, even doing a few windows. Maybe there was hope.

Ashley began piling her personal belongings into a cardboard box, her lower lip pooched out in a pout. "I'm sorry to leave before anything gets done about the Beach Beast, that's what I call him. I wish you could have found that bastard."

Chipper looked at Holly. "I've been following it in the papers and catching the scuttlebutt at West Shore, but you know how those inspectors are. Never give any of the ongoing details. They were all excited about the eyewitness. Then everything went quiet. Sometimes that means they're close to making an arrest."

Half way through her own dripping jalebi, Holly wiped her sticky fingers on a serviette. "It's hard to understand. Ellen Hughes gave us a description down to the last detail. It went out to all of the media."

"No trace evidence, nothing. It's like he's an invisible man," Chipper said. "Operating in the dark for the most part. I don't know how he did that."

Holly was still thinking about that silly paper shard. Nothing was going to come out of that dead end.

"He's probably half way across the country now," Ann said. "Knowing that he was seen this last time makes a big difference."

Ashley closed her personals box over an assortment of chips, Joe Louis pies, and energy drinks. For once, she seemed serious. One light blue eye took up a corner squint of scepticism. "I still say that there was just something hinky about that Hughes girl."

Everyone looked at her, but Holly spoke up. "What do you mean? Sure she was lucky to escape, but she described the guy to a T."

"Come on, Holly. Too much of a T. I mean, if she'd had a photograph, it couldn't have been any clearer. And that detail about the stuttering. Come on." She parked her butt on the desk.

Holly took the second last sweet ball and munched. She thought of herself as a skeptic, but this was heading for new heights. "The M.O. was exactly the same. A beach park, single girl, choked, raped. The trimming line garrotte was kept out of the papers. If you're saying she was lying, how could she know all of that?"

Chipper said, "Ashley could be right about word getting out. Now that I've been at West Shore, I can see how it's different in these larger detachments. Fifty people. A hundred. Civilians working there, too. One careless moment from an officer."

"If you're talking copycat, why would anyone do that unless he was totally unhinged himself? I can't buy that."

"Surely you aren't implying that the girl's lying about a rape," Ann said. "Nobody fakes something like that."

Holly counted on her fingers. "French, Sombrio, Sandcut … all on the Juan de Fuca Trail. Just to indulge your theory, Ashley, and while we have four keen minds, who would be in these areas and why?"

"A hiker." Ann.

"A logger." Chipper.

"A fisherman or just a boater." Ashley added, pumping her arm. "Fastest way in and out is by water. What's your response to that?"

Chipper cocked his head like a wary falcon. He popped the last morsel into his mouth. "Suppose you are right, shorty. Then how would he get to the beach? There aren't any docks. Set anchor and swim in?"

"I agree with you," Holly said. "Occam's Razor. The simplest situation is usually the answer. He parked and walked in. We just didn't find the car. Maybe it was that red Honda Ellen mentioned."

"Oh sure. I'm surprised she didn't give us the exact year, the way she was spinning them."

Ann spoke up. "I remember that you thought that she was making it all up as she went along. You're a bit young to be as cynical as I usually am. So what is your theory?"

"You guys are being far too literal. Things only need to be possible, not probable. Occasionally you get a clever criminal, or maybe the better word is cunning. Remember that David Westerfield case where the neighbour came into the house at night and took that young girl to his RV, then killed her? They thought it couldn't be done, so they decided that she'd left the house on her own. The defence called witnesses that swore that the flies and larvae on the corpse had to date from a time after he'd been under surveillance. But they were wrong about the variables. I followed the case on Court TV. That's when I decided to get into law enforcement."

Impressed by the methodical review, Holly noticed that she didn't even mention about her father's career. Maybe the rumours about Ashley had another side, as she had thought. Chipper had almost gone down because of false charges.

Ann joined in. "With the entire outdoors as a staging scene for an operation, anything can happen."

Ashley's curls nodded agreement. "I gotta feeling about this. That's why I asked to read your report, Holly. What she said to you was totally identical to what she told me on the way. Same phrasing and everything. Like it was rehearsed. First this, then that. People tell stories in different ways if they're telling the truth. I learned that at the Depot."

Holly shuffled her feet, feeling defensive. "She said she wanted to be a graphic artist. Maybe she was just being thorough."

"Huh," said Ashley in dismissal.

Then the phone rang. Ann answered it. She handed it to Holly. "It's Ed. He has some information for you."

Holly listened, her eyes widening. "I see. Yes, I understand." Then finally she thanked him and hung up. "This is getting weirder and weirder."

"Not another attack," Ann said. "You look more puzzled than alarmed."

"That scrap of cigarette paper. We got DNA."

Chipper punched the air. Ann grinned. Ashley gave a low whistle.

"Don't celebrate. It wasn't human."

"Huh?" said Ann. "What was it, then? A passing seagull?"

Holly gave her lip a tentative pinch. "Even if it had been human, we had no one to match it with anyway."

Chipper asked, "So what now?"

Ann got up to go to the file cabinet and began shoving papers into their proper slots. "It's watch and wait, then. On the plus side, after this latest attack, no one will be coming out here."

"True." Holly pressed her temple with her knuckle. "This is giving me a headache, and I never get those. I need a new perspective."

"Our man's back," Ann said, "Take a day off. You're overdue."

"I've wanted to get out to Avatar Grove in Port Renfrew." It refreshed her to go to the woods to worship in her own way. Recent logging had revealed an ancient stand of cedars only minutes from the town. Named by crafty conservationists in honour of the iconic Cameron film, the spectacle was getting worldwide attention and re-galvanizing the movement to save the forests.

"The film was super. I'd like to see that place," Ashley said, "before I get transferred out of here. Maybe they'll send me to the mainland. Big time homicides."

"Don't be in too much of a hurry to get shot," Holly said. With a quick analysis, she inferred that Ashley might like an invitation to go with her to the grove, but no thanks. The girl had stepped up a notch, but she wasn't friend material.

"Ladies. No worries now. I will apply masculine logic to this case. It may be over in mere days," Chipper said with a teasing rise of one sleek eyebrow. As he carried Ashley's box outside for her, Holly heard him ask the woman if she wanted to see a show and have dinner in Langford now that he had been "pardoned."

"There's still no water at my place," Ashley was saying.

"No problem. You can shower at my apartment. And if you're hungry, tonight my mom is …"

As the door shut, Ann caught her eye and smiled. "They grow up so fast," she said with a snicker.

Holly had never seen Chipper's place. Not that she was jealous or anything, but she wondered what had happened to that Amy he was dating from the vet hospital.

CHAPTER TWENTY-SIX

THE TOURIST BOARD HAD made quick work of spreading the word on Avatar Grove. "Megahits on the Facebook page, tweets every day, and my boyfriend and I put up YouTube videos. It's a cool place. Like holy, my gran says. She weaves with cedar bark. You can to cut a line and pull upwards until the strip narrows to nothing. That way the tree isn't hurt. You take only what you need from Mother Earth," the young First Nations girl said at the visitor centre nearby a giant jumping fish statue. Tiny Port Renfrew was hoping for a large influx of sightseers for its restaurants, camping/RV spots, and new time-share cabins. In summer, Botanical Beach and the West Coast Trail got the draw, but fall and winter were lean times.

Holly felt pounds lighter without the formality and sheer weight of the uniform, duty belt, and vest. Instead she wore soft, faded jeans, a dark blue hoodie, and comfy running shoes. The spit-shined boots could have a short vacation in the closet. Her dad would probably get out his historical polishing kit and give them a rubdown.

Glad that the road dust had settled with the slight drizzle, she crossed several small bridges across the San Juan River.

Logging had picked up in the area, and a loaded truck passed her. The paragraph from the Ancient Forest Alliance site she'd run off at her computer indicated the necessary turns on the confusing web of timber-access roads. Ten minutes later, red tape on bushes drew her to the makeshift parking spot. Perhaps soon these cedars and firs would have the same draw as the iconic Cathedral Grove up island.

Using a helpful rope someone had provided, she rappelled down to the lower area, where the rock star stood, the "gnarliest tree in Canada." The western red cedar thirty-seven feet in circumference and twelve feet across had an enormous burl farther up the trunk, caused by a fungal infection. Sadly, only small parts of the grove were protected, and some larger trees had been flagged for falling before the international attention. Satellite pictures revealed that 88 percent of the old-growth forests on the southern island had already been harvested, and 95 percent on the flatter terrains. Heli-logging was pursuing the remaining old gods and making it look dramatic on television. To Holly it was a massacre. But like it or not, in her profession, she couldn't be an activist.

Monster trees over five hundred years old had many strikes against them. For maximum growth, they needed to be near a good water supply, like creeks. Next, they had to survive century storms with winds over 150 kph, including the occasional tsunami like the one which had come through in 1700, according to oral legend, or the more recent one which devastated Port Alberni. Finally, they had to escape the woodman's axe, or more lately chainsaw. The only action that would save the rest would be the government's decision that their tourist draw outweighed their board-foot value. Forestry companies that owned or leased the property would have to be shamed into concessions or recompensed as in the case of the Sooke Potholes Park. People didn't look at land in the same way they did in 1890 when trees were either an obstacle to farming or money in the bank.

Holly had halibut and chips at the Country Kitchen restaurant, two light beers, and a wedge of warm and fragrant apple pie with ice cream. The more gruelling hike to the upper grove had given her an appetite. After the thrill of the big trees had worn off, she felt sleepy and bloated. Huge lunches weren't her style. Worse yet, the case kept nagging at her. Maybe it was a good thing she wasn't an inspector. How could she ever sleep?

Grinding her mental wheel over the evidence, she thought about what Ashley had said about Ellen's story. But faking a rape for the attention? It wasn't as if she needed affirmation from her boyfriend. They were already getting married. That would have been a ridiculous risk.

Outside the restaurant window, all was serene. A tortoiseshell cat slinked toward a wild azalea bush. Down on the docks, a few remaining boats bobbed on the incoming tide. A young man took a last drag and flipped a cigarette onto the ground. Boat. Cat. Cigarette butt. Animal saliva? Swallowing the last coffee too fast, she started coughing and knocked over a full water glass. With a handful of serviettes, she mopped up, thankful to be one of the last in the restaurant. Three ten-dollar bills remained on the table for the poor waitress.

What had Ben said? "As long as a case is unsolved, you are never off duty." She walked down the dark hall to a pay phone. No prayer of finding a cell tower out here. Sometimes it was "cash only" at the businesses without credit cards or debit working. Today the wheel of fortune spun her way. Dialling the detachment, she asked, "Did any calls come for me?"

"Damn right. I nearly fell off my chair. That DNA on the saliva was cat," Ann said. "Can you fathom that? I'd ring Bump's neck if I caught her chewing a cigarette filter. But then she's an indoor cat. Shouldn't be any other kind."

So Ed had taken it another step. "Listen, I was thinking …" Before she went off half-cocked, she needed Ann's opinion on how to proceed.

"Whoa. Catch you later," Ann said. "Chipper's back from a call, and we've got a fender bender by Anderson Road.

Damn curve has no visibility with the broom grown up. Doesn't sound serious, though. Stop by on your way home. Chipper brought samosas."

As she stared at the silent receiver, thoughts were whirling in Holly's mind. Rudy's aunt's cat. The boat trailer in the yard. Coincidences went only so far. Didn't he "mention" pointedly that he'd never been to French Beach? But he'd spent years in Winnipeg, returning recently. Chipper's unsolved attacks in Selkirk and Portage la Prairie had the same strangling M.O. Was she being as loony as Ashley in even entertaining this theory? Had Rudy the hubris to think that after a few years and a move across the country that he was home free? What was Ellen's part in all of this? A victim herself or an equal partner?

But why would the happy couple concoct such a story? Easy answer. A bold move to throw suspicion on someone. To provide a totally different description to send the police in another direction. Innocent people often lacked alibis. Who knows what might stick if enough spaghetti were thrown at a wall?

Classic misdirection. Isn't that what Great Aunt Stella had said about Bonnie's tote bag? But that would keep. If that honkin' big boat trailer in Beth Jacobs's yard belonged to Rudy, where was the boat?

The local Lion's Club phone book included Sooke, Otter Point, and Shirley. She paged through until she came to Beth Jacobs. Chances were the old lady was home. She didn't drive and she didn't look like a dedicated exerciser. Holly hoped that Beth wore her hearing aid. A precarious balance was in operation. Holly didn't want to spook her or imply that she had any extraordinary interest in the woman's helpful nephew.

When Beth answered, Holly made small talk. "We wanted to see how you were doing. In our community we try to call the seniors who live alone. Just to be sure that they're all right. Are your Meals on Wheels arriving on time?" She felt a twinge of guilt lying to the old lady.

"How sweet of you, dear. And yes, they are very reliable."

"And how's Rudy? Still getting in some fishing?" she asked with a catch in her throat. Something deep inside called her dishonest. This wasn't the old lady's fault. So what? A girl was dead.

"I should say so. He brought me a lovely spring the other day. Must have been ten pounds. He even portioned it out for me for the freezer. Salmon's so easy. All you need to do is pop it into the oven with a little mustard. The grainy kind."

"I like it that way, too. Where does he keep his boat? My neighbour's is at Jock's Dock."

A merry trill of laughter. "The old *Alice May* is at a marina in Port Renfrew. The charges are less than in Sooke, he says. Rudy is careful with his money. That's a good trait for a young man, don't you agree? He'll be married soon enough. Ellen is so perfect for him. Am I going to spoil those babies. Never had any of my own."

Holly rang off with myriad feelings. Means, maybe; opportunity, surely. What motivates evil? Lack of that little empathy gene, for one thing. So Rudy's boat was here. If that scrap of paper had been clinging to his clothes at French Beach, he wasn't swimming to shore. He would need a dinghy. But how did he see at night? Granted that there were some campfires and other lights at more civilized French Beach, but not in the heavy bush at Sombrio. That one factor bothered her. Using a flashlight would have given him away. None of those present had ever mentioned one except for Lindsay's.

Oblivious to the kitchen clatter and the roars of a soccer game from the television in the bar, Holly tried to sort out her whirling thoughts. Was she stretching the possibilities so far beyond reason that they were going to snap back in her face? She needed a close look at that boat. Why hadn't she asked Beth where Rudy was now? Something like, "I suppose Rudy has to work today." It was a weekday. He had a job, but perhaps as a manager he set his own hours. If he were at the docks, that car wouldn't be hard to spot.

She made the short trip to the marina and parked in the lot. Only a dozen boats remained. Charter businesses sometimes made a buck in the winter from the occasional stubborn tourist from Chicago willing to brave the cold winds of the strait. But like her neighbours, most people had already hauled in their smaller crafts for the season. Perhaps Rudy spent weekends or holidays living on the *Alice May*. Of the dozen remaining vessels, only one looked large enough.

She moved closer, ambling down the dock to get a glimpse of the names. There was the *Alice May* itself, an old wooden dame but spiffy with a fresh dark blue paint job, rocking gently at the last space. The open door to its cockpit and a shirt hung up to dry warned her that someone must be around. In a heap on the deck was a collapsed plastic dinghy with two short oars. Presumably he could inflate it with a foot pump. Boat, strike one. Dinghy, strike two. One problem: no search warrant and little reason to try to get one. No stolen goods or illegal substances were in sight. Nor did she have reason to think anyone was in danger, so she couldn't hop aboard and toss the cabin. Where was a good fire when you needed one? As if to mirror her feelings, the sky was clouding over fast. A few drops of rain fell onto the boards.

A rake-thin man with a white Santa beard and a pair of shorts revealing spindly calves and varicose veins was cleaning his small outboard two berths away, scrubbing its side with a wooden brush and whistling. His T-shirt read "Tap Out."

"Hello," she said, tipping back her ball cap. "Looks like a bit of chop coming up."

"Sure is. I was going to go out one last time, but the marine forecast says sixty knot winds are coming. And we got ourselves a king tide, too. So she's headed for my garage and I'm taking the RV to Tucson tomorrow. Hate that winter rain."

"I would if I could," she said, smiling. Tide times were printed in the daily papers. A king tide happened only a few times each year. Some connected it with global warming as an indication of the hazards of high seas. "Have you seen the owner of the *Alice May*?"

The man scratched his chin with some suspicion, eying her up and down, and she realized the powers of a uniform. But as a woman she had the advantage of seeming innocent and sincere. "No problems, are there? Rudy's a nice young man. Gives me a fish when I come back empty, which is more often than not."

She folded her arms and leaned against a post in casual fashion. "I heard he might want to sell his boat. My dad's looking for one just like this. This time of year prices are lower."

The man checked his watch. "His car's acting up, and he left it with a friend in Rennie. Kind of amateur mechanic. I took him into town about fifteen minutes ago to get some groceries and a two-four at the liquor outlet. I'll be going for him now. Should be on board in half an hour tops if he's done."

"I'm due back in the city myself. Just playing hooky today. I'll leave him a note, telling him where to call." With that along with a reassuring smile, she pulled a notebook from her hoodie pouch, sat on a spar and pretended to write.

When he had taken his bow legs down the dock and out of sight, she walked closer to the boat. Leaning a certain way, she could see up into the pilot house and down into the cabin. What she noticed at the entrance to the lower stairs shocked her. Dark green goggles. Huge mothers, army style. But not for underwater use. Night-vision, unless she was mistaken. Stores that catered to civilian wannabe spymasters were carrying all kinds of hi-tech gear.

A chill started in her breastbone and exploded in all directions like fireworks. What might give someone the ability to sneak around dark campsites all the way down the coast? Silently. Drifting away later, far from any notice. A boat with a dinghy. The monster in the night with those huge eyes. At the time she'd thought it was a kid's imagination. Now it was all coming together. Even the approximate time. But who would have believed her?

Rudy botched the attack at French. That must have been frustrating. A bruised ego out for revenge. That accounted for the risks at Sombrio. But he had succeeded there. And with the storm of media attention, why not stage a bogus attack to divert the attention? Two crazy people are greater than the sum of their parts. Half the force was out now looking for a non-existent man. Either Ellen was the most browbeaten woman alive or she deserved an Academy Award. Did Rudy meet her recently or did her complicity date back to Manitoba? Where else had he left bodies in his wake? A trucker in the States had preyed on women across the country and dumped them like trash. Rudy was not going to add one more prize to his collection. Not on her turf.

She had a slender reason to check the boat now. With its size at about thirty-five feet, in minutes she could give it a onceover. If she was caught, could she talk her way out? The RCMP motto was *maintiens le droit*. Uphold the law. How often the rules shackled the officer at a price to the victim. Again she calculated. So many feet to the cabin. Down. A quick visual. Back and out before those ample minutes were up. Then she could reconnoitre with Ann and her superiors to arrange the logistics. Best of all, the boat's bulk blocked anyone coming down the dock from seeing her.

After giving a final scan towards land, she stepped carefully onto the deck. The boards creaked slightly, but a wave washed through the drain holes in the gunwales. While she had been oblivious, the wind was rising and it was getting rough, even in the harbour. Little white butterflies in the water were turning to angry scallops of foam. No wonder there wasn't one boat out there. What had the man said? As high as sixty knots? The tide was cresting on the beach at least a foot higher than normal. A recipe for disaster. Search and rescue might have a busy night. Anyone going into the water at this time of year had hypothermia to worry about, even with a life jacket.

A floating kelp bed bumped the boat, its bulbous stems buoying it like an island, holdfasts having surrendered with the sea's movement. Grey clouds tinged with black scudded across the sky, and more drops began to fall. Seagulls screamed and a blue heron winged to land, delivering a bomb on the dock that might have blinded her. She knew better than to look up.

If only she'd had her vest and duty belt. The stun gun she didn't carry normally, but the pepper spray and gun were at her disposal. An arsenal, and now nothing but her wits and a few half-hearted self-defence classes. Why hadn't she paid more attention when the instructor had shown them how to take down a two-hundred-pound man with a simple pinkie-finger grip? Because it looked easier than it was. Truth to tell, she probably knew just enough to hurt herself. Holly made a vow to take a weekly upgrading class.

The cockpit looked utilitarian, empty of everything but two captain's chairs and the instrumentation. Clipped to the wall was a fire extinguisher. A couple of empty beer cans rolled across the floor with the ship's motion. Maritime charts stood upright in a small bin.

She stepped slowly down into the hold. It was amazing how much designers could stow in a small space. This was the galley and dining area. Beyond the curtain would be a bedroom. On a table sat a fused glass plate with a silver charm bracelet with a trumpet, a gold brooch, a black pearl earring. Maddie's gift from her gran. Lindsay's earring. Conspicuously there was no pink coral necklace like the one Ellen claimed to have lost. It probably didn't even exist. Who owned the brooch? Did it come from the Manitoba cold cases or did some other girl sleep at the bottom of the strait?

Her heart began to race. There were disadvantages of falling into a pot of jam, delicious though it was. Her watch read only five minutes since the old man had left. Stick with the plan, but ramp up the timing. What if Rudy recognized her though the old man? A woman looking for a boat to buy was suspicious, even though she'd mentioned her father. Maybe he was planning to leave the country anyway. But not in this storm.

A flush crossed her brow, and she felt herself sweating, even in the cold wind. Get out now, she told herself, but she seemed to be moving in slow motion. Now that she knew how this crime had been committed, she was halfway to an arrest. Ellen's testimony would be central. The girl looked weak, easy to turn once away from Rudy's hypnotic influence. Another wave lashed the boat, and she reached for a table bolted to the floor. "Wheew. Get your sea legs," she whispered, turning for the stairs to the deck where the open air awaited.

"Fuck you" were the last words she heard before she dropped.

CHAPTER TWENTY-SEVEN

HOLLY HAD NO IDEA how much a headache could hurt. A pneumatic jackhammer was breaking cement in her skull. Was the pounding her own heartbeat? Opening her eyes seemed like a bad idea. She'd rather not move at all. When she tried to get up, she couldn't move her arms and legs. Where the hell was she? In the trunk of a car? The room was rising and falling, punctuated by the sound of crashing below.

The *Alice May*. Now she remembered where she had heard that name. It was the boat in Robert W. Service's "The Cremation of Sam McGee," the one "on the marge of Lake Lebarge." Her fate was looking like Sam's, but instead of burning, she would drown.

From lying on her stomach, she squirmed to her side, then let her eyes confirm the nightmare. Her hands were tied tightly in front of her with polypropylene rope. She was on a double bed. The bed behind the curtain. Where someone had been. The throb of the motors vibrated through the floorboards. She had assumed that she was alone. That might be the last assumption she ever made. How many second chances did anyone expect?

Voices came to her. Rudy. Ellen. She'd walked right into their little web. What were they saying? "No problem, babe." Then "But what if" and then "Not a chance in hell that they'll ..."

Out the small porthole, bright orange crab pots bobbed past. Tourists rented them at the Corner Store in Sooke. This time, the crabs would be doing the eating. The next time a foot floated onto a beach in the Salish Sea that encompassed Puget Sound, Victoria, and Vancouver, it might be hers. Running shoes were notorious floaters. In the last ten years, the total was ten. Only a few had ever matched. Some were faked by teenagers with a morbid sense of humour and access to animal bones.

The waves tugged at the boat as they headed out into the strait, buoyed by the monster king tide. The farther the better, and certainly out of sight of land. She'd be weighed down, perhaps with a fishing net and anchors until her body was bones, bleached like the skeleton of a dead seal.

She heard a noise on the stairs and a door opened. With only two small portholes, it was dim during the storm. The feeble light backlit a blond head.

"I had a feeling I'd find you here. Whatever you're doing in civvies, good choice. You haven't got a little surprise for me under your pantleg, do you?" Rudy said as he hauled her to her feet and gave her a rough patdown. "Good girl. I thought better of you. This is going to make things way too easy. I prefer challenges."

An officer's worst nightmare. Not merely losing his weapons, but not even bringing them to the party. She had made the kind of rookie mistakes that Ben had warned her about. First, setting out without backup. Second, thinking that Rudy was the only one around. Third, believing that she could get in and out before he returned. Three strikes. Game over. With a sociopath, she doubted that she'd get another chance.

Rudy had the biceps of a bodybuilder and the neck and shoulders of an Angus bull. He wore jeans and a cable knit sweater. On his head was a white captain's hat with gold braid and a long bill. He yanked her up the stairs and shoved her onto a bench. Water was sluicing over the decks as the boat charged ahead. The Canadian shore was a grey mass behind them. He nodded at Ellen, in a yellow slicker with her hair stuck to her face. In typical west-coast fashion, the rain was horizontal, a SWOW: solid wall of water.

"We can't stay on auto-pilot more than a few minutes, Ellen. Make yourself useful for once and go up there and steer. I want to get around the point and out of sight. Now hustle!" With not a word, the girl went up the stairs to the pilothouse, holding on to the railings and pitching from side to side. Her face was contorted from the blistering rain, but she looked determined.

The boat lurched, then headed straight west, bouncing in the roughening chop. A tarnished pewter filled the sky, lit at the edges in the false hope of sun. If it weren't late October, Holly would have sworn those were snow clouds. How long could the boat take weather like this? As far as the middle of the strait? It was about seventeen kilometres to Washington, which was fogged in. Over she'd go, and Rudy would head back to shore. The only man who had seen her on the docks was en route to Tucson and might never hear about her disappearance. She'd become one more in those cold cases Chipper had been reading. Worse yet, it would be a final blow for her father. Both of his loves gone without a trace. She swallowed a lump in her throat as her eyes burned from the salt spume lashing the deck.

"I was seen on the docks," she yelled, holding her aching head high. Things were blurry, or was it the rain running down her cheeks? You couldn't bluff a bluffer. Did she expect him to beg forgiveness and turn himself in through a sudden change of heart? That would imply that he had a conscience. Her hands were tied in front of her, one tiny advantage, she realized as her thoughts stared to focus in the cold spray.

"Hell, old Jack has a memory like a sieve these days, and he'll be on his way out of the country tomorrow. Don't think anyone's going to connect us. You weren't dressed like a cop. Probably had your hood up in this pathetic little undercover affair. No biggie." Rudy lit a cigarette and puffed. His fingers were nicotine stained. As the cigarette sizzled in the wet, he held a hand over it and took another drag, watching the smoke disappear in the wind.

"My car's still at the marina. I had lunch in Rennie. They're going to remember me." She saw a flicker cross his face. Handsome though he had seemed, he was stone cold gruesome now.

"So friggin' what? Do you know how fast I could make a car disappear on this end of the island?"

She tried another bluff. "We've suspected you for some time. One of our officers had serious doubts about your story. We knew about the dinghy."

"Who, that twit who picked up Ellen? Officer Ditz? Piss off. Don't expect me to believe that. No one's been sniffing around after Ellie Bear or after me. You're just trying to cover up the fact that you're a total fool."

Ellie Bear. She nearly laughed. The girl was about as harmless as a scorpion. Yet was there the slightest self-doubt in his tone? "We've been talking about it at the detachment. I sent in trace material from the yurt at French Beach. The cat's saliva was on a piece of cigarette paper. I'd say that it stuck to your pants when you came in with the dinghy. Little things come back to haunt you."

He roared even louder than the tempest. "Do I look freakin' stupid? That is the most dumbass thing I ever heard. Did you go to clown school to learn to make up that shit?" A curl of total contempt came over his lip. They rose and fell, shuffling their feet as the boat bounced over the waves. Holly had the strangest feeling that her mother was in the same watery grave. She wasn't traditionally religious, but wasn't there a part in the Bible about the sea giving up its dead?

"You know what, little miss lawman? I'm just going to take me a big old west-coast chance on that."

What did she have to lose now? Keeping him talking was her only weapon. "Like in Winnipeg. My constable's on those cases, too. It's all coming together, Rudy. You need another M.O. That trimmer line is very telling."

"Figured that out, did you? Two points for you, then." He stroked his soul patch thoughtfully. "Maybe it's about time that I took a little vacation. Aunt Beth is going to assisted living. I was talking to a social worker about her last week."

Something sour rose in Holly's throat. She was close to vomiting in her anxiety. Strange that he had feelings for someone. But there were all varieties of sociopaths. Hitler had loved his German shepherd, Blondi. "Make it easy on yourself and Ellen. There's no death penalty in Canada."

At their feet was a coil of rope fastened to a cleat. A wooden-handled boning knife was stuck next to it in a cork buoy. He could have been operating all over the island, picking up strays. Young women were suckers for a nice boat. Having a partner gave him an advantage of an extra pair of hands and an alibi.

Time had slowed to a slug's pace as the boat fought the rising wind. On any given day, from her house she could see three cruise ships or freighters in the shipping lanes. Not now, when she might need one.

Rudy bent his face to check his watch. Quickly she searched around the deck, weighing her deteriorating odds, then flexing her hands. The wet rope had given a half inch. Ellen was occupied at the wheel in very tricky seas. Another wave pounded them, and the old boat's timbers creaked. At least she wasn't facing a handgun. Rudy probably didn't even own a firearm.

As the boat crashed down, making little headway in the gusts, Rudy jostled to one side, scrabbling to his feet and bracing against a handrail. He wore slippery moccasins, a bad choice. A wave broke over the side and soaked his jeans. "Ellie, what the hell's happening up there? Do you want to swamp us? Do like I showed you once and keep her into the wind.

Grab a brain. The troughs are going to bury us. Once it's calm again, we'll head up to Tofino for a few days. You always wanted to stay at the Wickaninnish Inn."

Over the roar of the motors and the howl of the wind, it was hard to hear anything else, but Holly cocked her head at what she thought was the stutter of a helicopter motor. They couldn't see back into the harbour anymore, but from around the point, flying low, came an angel of mercy. The red, white, and blue colours of a search-and-rescue helicopter.

Rudy looked up, and at that moment Holly shoved him towards the rail, throwing her shoulders into the effort, then dropping to the deck. Flailing, he hit his head as his foot tangled in the rope pile. Over the side he went, roiling in the waves as his hat floated off. As the boat moved on, he dangled like a fish, barely able to keep his head above the dark water. He'd have been left behind had one end of the rope not been secured. A bullhorn sounded over the chaos as the helicopter blades kicked up chop in all directions. "Hello, the boat. Officer Martin. Are you all right down there?"

Holly crawled on her elbows to the knife, held it with her feet, and sawed her bonds, taking a nasty cut on her forearm without even feeling it. When her legs were free, she stood shakily and braced herself, still holding onto the knife.

Holly waved acknowledgement and an okay sign to the hovering craft. Ellen lurched down the stairs, off balance with the boat's heaving. "Jesus, where's Rudy?" She ran to the side, looked back and screamed.

From above, a voice boomed. "There's a police boat coming out. I'm sending a man down. Hang tight. We don't want you in the water now. If anyone has a weapon down there, drop it now. You have been warned. Our sights are on you. Someone will be down to bring the boat in."

With undisguised satisfaction, Holly looked toward the wake, where Rudy was churning in the whitecaps as he coughed and yelled. She would have preferred letting him drown, but that was outside the letter and spirit of the law.

With no capital punishment, he'd still rot in jail. He could apply for parole every five years until the next millennium. Being labelled a dangerous offender was the fail-safe answer in Canada.

"It's all over for you both. Follow my directions, Ellen," she said. "Keep the engines running at low speed and turn back to land, or we'll be swamped on the rocks." They were still hundreds of yards from shore, but the marker buoys bobbed out a warning about tricky rock shelves in the channel. The last thing they needed was to open up a hole in the hull and take on more water.

Her hands sore and aching, Holly pulled at the rope until she had him close to the boat. Rudy was spluttering, and the image of a drowned rat came to her mind. But rats were far more moral. Now he was as helpless as the women he had attacked or killed. No way was she hauling him in. He wouldn't die in five minutes, even thirty, though the water was cold. But even now, she didn't trust him.

"Get me out of here, you bitch!" he yelled.

"That will be your official name before long," she said. "Killers like you have a special place among the inmates, even in civilized Canadian prisons."

She couldn't resist a smirk. If he'd had his way, she'd have been on the wrong end of the food chain. As for Ellen, if her lawyer was smart, he'd get her to cop a plea and assure a conviction against Rudy, especially given the disappearances of the girls in Manitoba. Closure for the families would be hastened if their bodies were recovered. A bizarre sense of place for their crimes left many killers with an amazing mental map. Where else might Rudy have plied his trade?

With a smart defence lawyer in this high-profile case, Ellen would probably become the "used and abused" girlfriend, threatened so that she would help him in his ugly work. Forming a passion for her assailant. Sadly, perhaps like the infamous Karla Homolka, complicit wife of the killer Paul Bernardo, she'd be walking the streets again with a new identity in ten years ... even less. It wasn't beyond possibility that Ellen might find another man with a similar dangerous hobby. Some girls couldn't resist bad boys.

With the precision of a SWAT team, an officer was lowered toward the deck. Like a black angel, he descended, slowly twisting on his line, then dropping in front of her and detaching the harness so that another officer could follow. The boat was close to stalling and a huge seventh wave nearly swept Rudy back out to sea. Then they turned slowly and headed toward the shore. Ellen had gotten the message. She didn't want to die either.

"Al Skidmore," the officer said in a loud voice over the din, extending a meaty hand and flashing the widest grin she'd seen in years. His trim red moustache added a British touch. "That's a strange fish you've hooked. What did you use for bait?"

"Myself. I'd prefer throwing him back, but I think too much of the strait," she said as another man landed. His name was Dale. It was getting crowded on deck, just the way she liked it.

Al helped her haul Rudy on board, cuffing him hand and foot and setting him against the side of the boat. Ellen sat on the stairs, crying to herself. The boat started to wallow, and Holly didn't like the way successive waves were beginning to pound the deck. "I'd better get up there and zigzag back to shore. That's why they sent me," Dale said.

"How did you find me?" she asked Al, still amazed at the miracle of her rescue.

"Constable Packke," he said. "She was in Rennie. Saw your car and came onto the docks about the same time the boat started up. She watched Rudy hop on board and head out like the hounds of hell were on his tail. She called Fossil Bay, and they made connections with us and one of the West Coast Marine units. You're damn lucky one of ours was in the vicinity on manoeuvres with the Coast Guard. Normally they're based in Nanaimo. Any more cutbacks and we'll be paddling kayaks."

From around the peninsula, a large police boat was charging toward them like a one-man cavalry. In the lashing rain, she squinted into the distance. Turning to Al, she said, "Is that ..."

"Yes, ma'am. Not bad for a rookie, if you get my drift." He looked at the blood dripping from her arm onto her pants. "Say, do you know how bad you're hurt?"

In the prow was Ashley, waving for all she was worth. A small tear formed in Holly's eye and she swiped at it, beginning to feel the sting of her cuts. Had the constable really wanted to see Avatar Grove, or had that been merely pretence to befriend her? Whatever the case, Holly owed her a life.

She turned to Al, whose face was getting darker, like everything around her. "Down in the hold, get the jewellery...."

EPILOGUE

SORE HEAD AND SEVEN stitches in her forearm, Holly was back to normal. Knowing that the next day she'd be at the detachment with her staff gave her more of a lift than the shot of Demerol she'd been given after a concussion was ruled out.

She'd been on a razor edge climbing onto that boat without a warrant, night-vision goggles or not. The first thing that Ashley told her when they met en route to the hospital was that she was prepared to say that she had witnessed Holly being grabbed by the toxic pair and taken aboard. When Ellen fell apart in the first rounds of questioning and turned against Rudy to save herself, Ashley's little lie became a moot point. Holly was still mulling over the ethics of her constable's means-to-an-end philosophy.

Her father had outdone himself: pot roast and Yorkshire pudding with pureed parsnips flavoured with maple syrup, canned corn, and fresh sweet-potato pie with a flaky lard crust. "Don't ever put yourself into that kind of a situation again," he told her, shaking his finger for emphasis. He still wore a touch of flour on his temple. "If I lost you, I ..." His voice trailed off, and to distract them both, he poured more Canadian champagne, a rare treat.

She hadn't told him what she'd found out about the Hamilton brothers and the flights her mother arranged. The strange harp image. Sometimes she needed to digest the information before reopening his wounds. As she finished her pie and cut another piece, she chose her words carefully. Her brain was still fogged from a night at the hospital and a nap at home until an hour ago.

He looked at her without blinking, his sky-blue eyes bright with interest. "But as you say, Bonnie never took the flight. She was home that weekend with us. So who did?"

"One of the many women she helped, I guess. If we can only find her. What could that harp mean? I've free-associated as far as I can."

He looked at her down his aquiline nose. "It rings no bells with me. One of us is going to have to go to the mainland," he said. "To Williams Lake. So much time has passed. If only I'd known some of this." The private detective he had engaged in the beginning had come up empty-handed. Every year Norman put a search ad in the paper and was usually approached by con men out to make a quick buck.

"I managed to talk to Bob Filman this morning," she said. "He remembered when the tote bag appeared because it was his wife's sixtieth birthday and he thought he might take it for her if it wasn't claimed. They had sheps. The date was a year after Mom disappeared."

"And that could mean?"

He wanted her to tell him that Bonnie could still be alive. But she couldn't. "I don't know, Dad. She was never without it." It's misdirection, she thought. It has to be. Either that or it was stolen from her before that last ....

Fog was rolling its slow thighs over Otter Point to the east as dusk fell. How alive the strait was. One minute all was hidden, and the next, the bank blown to the U.S. side, the sun would come out and all would be revealed. Step by slow step, she hoped that she was approaching the answer to her mother's disappearance, but the adult in her said that sometimes, the answer did not arrive in a person's lifetime.

"I have a week's vacation coming up."

The CD player started up "My Heart Belongs to Daddy," with Mary Martin singing her heart out. Shogun snored in his dog bed. She'd come too close to dying this time. Meeting her mother in the world beyond was not the current plan. "I'm going to find her and bring her home."

OTHER HOLLY MARTIN MYSTERIES

She Felt No Pain
A Holly Martin Mystery
9781926607078
$16.95

The verdant lushness of Vancouver Island is not without its dangers.... Summer on Vancouver Island gets off to a rocky start with the discovery of the body of a homeless man. RCMP Corporal Holly Martin notices drug paraphernalia nearby, and the autopsy reveals death from a combination of heroin and a synthetic opiate. Information leads Holly to believe that he had hidden something of value at the site of his death. As Holly struggles to connect the dots, a record drought heats up the vacation paradise, and one match could send Canada's Caribbean into flames.

And on the Surface Die
A Holly Martin Mystery
9781894917742
$15.95

In this new series by the acclaimed author of the Belle Palmer mysteries, RCMP Corporal Holly Martin takes charge of her first post, a detachment in tiny Fossil Bay on the wild south coast of Vancouver Island. Drunk drivers, speeders, and the occasional theft from tourist cars lead the crime roster, but her first day starts with a distress call. A scuba diver has found the body of a girl in the surf. A tragic drowning caused by a fall? The late arrival of tox-scan results for crystal meth, the most recent plague to hit the island, raises ugly questions. Just before Holly makes an arrest, a record-setting typhoon roars in, empowered to destroy everything in its path. As the wind howls and trees crash around her, Holly struggles to survive and to bring a murderer to justice.

VISIT US AT

Dundurn.com
Definingcanada.ca
@dundurnpress
Facebook.com/dundurnpress